HIS ALPHA

CURVING STRAIGHT LINES

RACHELLE MILLS

Dedication.

To the International Wildflower Pack for holding my hand through everything. To my family for giving me the freedom to achieve my dreams. To Roxy for helping me every step of the way.

If the moon made me this way, then why does it feel like a curse?

He is the Alpha, and I am his Beta.

It's time for me to bend straight - there are some lines I must not cross. But every time I see him, the lines curve, gnawing into my soul.

This is our destiny, yet nobody can know that the Moon has both blessed and cursed us with this forbidden love.

A hidden, dark fire. It was our secret. A secret we denied - a secret too dark to share.

We don't bend that way.

I left. I had to escape the torture, the heartache. I lived among humans. I studied them. I found myself. Or, should I say, *The Professor* discovered me. They can never know that a human male seduced me, or that I loved him - it means certain death for both of us. He taught me everything I know, made me the wolf I am today. But even that love was not enough.

I return to my territory. Leaving the sophisticated freedom of the city for the stifling traditionalism of my pack - a place where my soul, my desire, my love, must be locked away and hidden.

This ache is my one true companion, never leaving my side.

Perhaps the pain never ends, but I must go on. I'm not the runt I once was. My body is lean, muscled, and powerful now. I see my transformation in their eyes.

I see it in his eyes.

He may be my Alpha, but he will come to me. The moon may have cursed us both, and our path may be full of torture, pain, and lines so curved that we get lost, but I have no choice.

He has no choice.

It is time for me to bend straight for the pack, but in my soul, I know my lines are curved and undulating, and that they all lead to him; my rightful mate. My cursed mate, one that fate demands and that our society forbids.

I don't know how to go on....

Table of Contents

Chapter 1

Tommie.

Goodbye eyes.

His sight holds his silver blades when he's brave enough to face me.

Watching him fidget with his belt buckle. How many times have I undone that belt, only to look into his eyes while taking him in my mouth? How many times has he helped me up from my kneeling position to lick himself off my lips? Saying, *Thank you, Tommie*, in-between breaths. Everything always ending in a, *Thank you*.

The professor is a smart man; doing this in a public place. I now have to maintain a certain civility. A song playing in the background has a certain heartbreak tone to it that mirrors my *feelings*.

He doesn't take my hands in his. Instead, he's sitting down holding his own together, fingertips on his knuckles, rubbing them gently.

How those hands taught me all I needed to know about pleasure. Now his words are teaching me all about pain.

His eyes are roaming everywhere that's not important. The pictures on the walls of perfect landscapes, out the window - looking at the people coming in. *He should be looking at me.* At what his words are doing to me.

"I told you this was for fun, I told you I don't get attached, Tommie. So don't look at me like I'm breaking your heart, you knew the outcome." His voice just a whispered breath that hurts my ears.

"You never told me that." My hurt words are barely able to contain the quiver of my voice.

"I did, you just chose not to listen." Another volley of whispered words so no one around will hear the little secret we share. I won't cry in front of him; I'll save that for when I get home. "It's final." His voice an octave more pronounced in depth.

This coffeehouse he asked me to meet him at is where we had our first date. Coffee and conversation, nothing more. Just a friendly hello. Getting comfortable in each others company.

We met a few more times, very casually, nothing serious. As the time went by he was able to become more to me; he weaved himself into the fabric of my life. I remember our first kiss; it was the first time I'd ever kissed another guy. I thought I was never like *that*. It was so very cautious on both our parts.

I can't believe I left my expected life for him, for this *human*. Now he's using this place for our final goodbye. I can laugh at the irony of it, except at this moment, laughing is the last thing I want to do. "What about all of your stuff?" My eyes still not leaving his face, hoping to catch a glimpse of regret of how hard this must be for him. The only thing I catch is *relief* that he's getting rid of me. I'm the dead-weight

he's throwing overboard, and I'm sinking, hardly able to keep from drowning.

"Keep it, nothing that I want anyway."

That hurts; he doesn't want anything from our life together. How can I be replaced so easily? How can he just turn me off as if I'm a light switch? Once I lit up his life, now he's cut me off, darkening me forever.

"So this is it?" I'm trying so hard to hide my trembled hurt. I had no idea he had another; he'd promised me they were just friends. Aren't lovers the last to know? Thrown away like pieces of unwanted garbage. Right at this moment, he looks as if he's the color grey, sucking up everything that was good between us, leaving nothing but a haze of lies in its place.

"I'm sorry. It's not you, it's me."

That makes me exhale the breath I was holding. Always the famous last words of parting lovers, trying to make the one getting dumped feel better.

"I should go. I'm sorry, Tommie." He's not sorry. My eyes watching as he's able to walk away so easily.

Looking at his back one last time, I have come to memorize every vertebrae, every mole, every curve of him while taking him from behind. Pulling my eyes, it takes everything within me not to explode from the inside out. It's as if I'm in a fog. He's left me sitting all by myself, with a full coffee in front of me that I can't stomach to drink.

Just think, only a few minutes ago I was so happy to see him sitting there, waiting for me, giving him a wave as I enter the shop. *I should have known*. I should have gone with my gut feeling that something was wrong when he didn't smile or wave in return.

It's not a long walk back to my place. My steps feel heavy, as if every single one I take is grabbing onto me like quicksand slowing me down. My shoulders are hunching forward and my eyes are pooling with tears that I am trying so hard not to shed.

Heavy. That's how I feel when I turn the key to the apartment. Walking in, it smells like us. Going over to the fridge, pulling out the light-amber sadness that whiskey can bring. Taking the bottle, throwing the cap away, I let the first swallow burn its way down my throat. It's better to feel this than anything else at the moment.

Grabbing a hand-rolled, sparking it up, taking the first puff into my lungs and slowly holding it in for as long as I can. Exhaling it out lazily, gradually this stick does what it's supposed to do, and my eyes start to get half closed.

Sinking into the couch, tipping the bottle to my lips again, taking several pulls quickly, the liquid settling at the bottom of my stomach, starting to warm me up. Another inhaled breath from the stick has me blowing big puffs of white smoke that hover in front of my face for just a moment, before ascending to the ceiling. *I need this.* I just need to go somewhere else, even though, in the morning it will hurt even worse than now.

Somewhere deep in whiskey thoughts, as the night continues on, I come to the realization that it's time for me to go back to my pack. There is nothing tying me here anymore.

Except what's waiting for me at home is a whole different kind of pain that I'm not sure I'm ready for.

Chapter 2

Tommie.

The early morning dew still clings to the grass as I pull away from my apartment. It was the perfect location; close to the university and within walking distance. That was the big sell to my parents when I first came here. After four years, I never thought I would leave, envisioning my entire life with him. Making my trips back to the pack less and less, and only when I knew Tate would not be there. Prepping my parents slowly for the reality of me not returning to the territory I'd been born to.

Now that's all changed. Rejection has a way of making you get back to your roots, to find comfort in the known,

even understanding I have to go back and face him. I would rather face my mate, than face my lover's new lover.

The lesser of two evils.

Hours of driving and thinking back, reminiscing about how it all started. I can't blame him; I blame myself for falling for him.

It's a conscious effort to not feel the top of my lip with my finger, the image of his mouth on mine, the way his stubble always tingled my upper lip.

Does he even know I'm leaving?

I guess I just outgrew him - his preference had always been for the younger looking.

When I first caught that glimpse of him from far away, I'd had to lean against the wall to catch myself from falling. He had someone else then, you could tell by the way they were looking at each other. New love always has such a pure look to it.

Such a promise to it.

It was startling when I realized I was attracted to my professor. That small confession to myself became the catalyst, the hidden truth, that maybe I was slightly *curious*. He'd planted the seed in my head - how *cunning* of him. The way he would lean over me in his lecture, a thigh brushing against my arm just enough for me to feel the heat of him. Nothing lingering, nothing substantial. just a quick brush of his body against mine, something that gave a different meaning to the wolf watching within.

It started out with just a touch. Innocent enough. But isn't that how all grooming starts? *Innocently.*

The Professor invited me for coffee and offered help with my assignments. I couldn't believe then how lucky I was to find a teacher taking such an interest in me. A freshman away from home for the first time, just eighteen years old. No friends yet in this new and daunting place, something I think he understood. He became my friend, slowly creeping into my life. A predator studying his prey, learning its habits. I can see this now as I look back with a clearer view of the past.

I remember our first kiss. The way his fingertip brushed the hair out of my eyes, back when I wore my hair long,

rebellious. That second of crystal foreshadowing of his intentions that had me freezing up.

Sensing this, he'd stopped just a fraction away from my lips.

"Have you ever kissed a man?"

His question had my heart racing, throat tightening. My lack of answer had him smiling like he'd just found an unopened treasure. He'd set the scene; his room, his bed, soft music playing. I'd ignored my sense of logic that said it wasn't right, not stopping, even when I'd known I should.

His breathing became deeper, eyes dilating closer to me. I told myself it was just a kiss, nothing more.

I can handle a kiss.

Hands on my waist brought me closer, I'd had just a moment to gasp before his lips found mine. So soft at first, so intimate. He'd made me feel so *special*. The space between us growing smaller and smaller while I could only focus on his lips. I'd tried to pull my face away, but he'd held it between his hands. Feeling as if he was drowning me in the sensation of him.

We made out as if he were a teenager again.

I'd tried to regain my ability to think, to reason with myself, that it was just a kiss, nothing more. I'd promised myself that it would go no further

The truth was I liked to kiss. And I like to be kissed by a man. But I'm not gay.

He'd pushed me down to the bed, laying himself on top of me. Pressing himself into me, a small moan actually coming out of my mouth. He'd been quick to capture it, moaning himself. Nothing but arms and legs entwined, hips falling in love with each other.

The bed springs squeaked in delight underneath the movement of our bodies. It was as far as I was willing to take it that night, yet I was excited, harder than I'd ever been before. He could feel it, knowing how to rub himself against me, how to build my own needs up, wanting just a little more and taking me out of my comfort zone.

An expert playing with a juvenile.

That night he stunned me in a new way of thinking. An older man. Charming, intellectual, dashing, and oh so perverted.

I was his fantasy, as he started to become mine.

We made out for what seemed like an hour, our kissing becoming more and more. A deep hunger settled into me as if I'd been starving for this my whole life. I'd felt his hand graze over the top of my jeans, feeling me up, exploring, investigating.

A light touch at first, nothing too serious. I'd thought to myself, *this is okay*, it's just a touch, nothing more will happen. For some reason, I was drawn to him. Tentatively my hand wandered to his zipper, feeling how excited he was for me.

He was proud of what he had between his legs. A moan so deep came from his chest that I almost thought he was half-wolf. But I knew better; we don't have half breeds.

When his fingers expertly went to my zipper, pulling it down, I hesitated, pulling away. Too much too soon - I'm not like that.

He could tell, sense it from years of practice. I was just too caught up in it to realize what was happening in the moment.

His lips refocused on my neck. Teeth biting softly into my flesh, it was the first time I'd ever had teeth against my neck from anyone - wolf or human - and it was the most erotic feeling I'd ever been exposed to.

When he once again met my lips with his, I opened my mouth slightly all on my own, letting his tongue slide in without prompting. That brought a smile to his mouth that I felt against my own.

I liked that smile, I wanted him to smile more.

Pulling himself away from me, looking into my eyes, he gave me that very first, *Thank you*.

Acknowledgment that I'd made him happy.

The night ended with me leaving his place in the late night hours with a smile on both our faces. Driving home, thinking it was okay as long as it didn't go further, that I was just slightly curious, nothing more.

My memory of him starts to fade as I crest the last mountain top, having me seeing a canopy of green meeting the sea of blue. Old-growth forest looking oppressive and stern the closer I get to my territory.

Turning off onto the hard packed gravel road, it twists and turns along the hillside. A warm breeze is coming in through the open window, bringing the scent of home, of cedar and pine, and the subtle taste of *him*. The wolves already know I've arrived. The call goes up into the fading day, the howls are long and welcoming. How long has it been since I'd shifted into my nature? I have repressed that side of me for so long. Not allowing my secret to burst from the seams; the first rule being never to tell a human. That would have been instant death for both him and myself.

For him, I was willing to subdue my beast.

The closet has a way of casting shadows on who you are. He turned on my light and opened my door, only for me to force my very nature back to the same closet. .

It was a give and take.

I got so caught up in his world, his friends, his life, that I comfortably forgot about mine.

It's old-world rules that I have to follow now.

Suffocating.

Oppressive.

Stifling.

The path straightens out as I approach the pack house and for a moment, the thought strikes that I'll get to have my old bedroom back across from his.

This should be interesting.

I'm not the same little juvenile that went away. I'm a full grown Beta. But, then again, he isn't the awkward youth that I left behind. He's an Alpha, almost on the brink of claiming his birthright.

Remembering it like it was yesterday, us as best friends, he was my future Alpha, me his future Beta. Our destinies were written by the moon. The day that we shifted into our fur, the both of us realizing what we were to each other.

Our world shattered.

His words coming to my ears even now, clear as if he was sitting next to me in my truck.

"I'm not like that." He'd looked so devastated. My whole body mirrored his feelings.

"I'm not like that either." Spitting words out at him, refusing to look into his eyes.

I think we both cried. Not in each other's arms, but alone in our rooms, begging the moon to reconsider our paths. Neither of us wanting what she wanted.

We weren't gay.

Our families, our pack, would crumble. An Alpha needs a female mate, an heir to carry on his bloodline.

From then on a bitter resentment started to come between us. Where once we were constantly together, sidekicks united, we rarely remained in the same room together for too long. That bond does tricky things to you; makes you have buried thoughts about the other male that you would never have considered.

Decent thoughts turning into indecent desires.

The pull to him was so great that I'd decided to go away for school. An excuse to get away from him. It was better that way for the both of us. He had an obligation to fulfill and I had an obligation to let it happen.

Stopping the truck, the front door opens, revealing a crowd of friends who have gathered for my homecoming.

Putting on my best smile, I open my truck door get out.

It's time for me to bend straight.

Chapter 3

Tommie.

Welcome home.

"Tommie!"

Smiling towards the squeals of females. Picking them up and hugging each one of them close to my body. Maybe a quick nuzzle to their necks.

It's more than what's expected of me.

"You leave those females alone and come hug your mother." Her tone playful, happy, and light with such a show of expectations. "We've missed you so much." My mother has tears in her eyes as she says this. Patting my cheek with her hand, another kiss on both sides before she lets my father pat me on the back.

"Good to have you home." Even he's emotional which in turn makes me slightly choked up.

"Good to be back." Giving everyone my half turned-up lip.

Looking around, I don't see him, *I smell him.* The air is heavily saturated in his singular scent made just for me. It's so strong, that goosebumps appear on my exposed forearms. This is how the mate bond works - how your body is just naturally drawn to the other. It's a drug that's as tempting as ecstasy. Especially since I know how good it could make me feel.

"Are you hungry?" The Luna makes her appearance after my family has had their fill of me. She has a sweet face that smiles with her eyes. *He* has her eyes. Green like a field of wild clover.

"I could eat."

That response makes her happy as it puts her to work, my mother following behind eagerly. I could never be what a Luna is, I could never think of being his Luna.

How would that even work?

Leaving the rest of my stuff in the truck, I let the tide of wolves drag me to the kitchen. Everyone wants to know how it was; going away to college. Most don't leave the pack to further their educations, ending up taking positions inside the pack authority. Telling them of my adventures, I leave out certain details that would have their faces scrunching with disgust.

"Tommie, we have to hang out." Hazel gives me her famous smile that drops males to their knees. I know this because I was one of them. *Long ago.*

Before I even knew who I really was.

"I'd like that."

She lets her eyes travel down the length of me, boldness always did suit her. Letting my own gaze travel her curves,

soft and inviting. Auburn hair that catches the partial light in through the cracks in the drapes. Streaks of cinnamon and brown sugar highlight the strands around her face. Her skin a honeyed dew that shows a love affair with the sun. Pink lips are inviting to any male who has eyes for that kind of thing. I kissed her only once. It was something that I will always remember. Awkward and sloppy - I like to think I have improved since then.

Laughter, catching up on all the comings and goings of pack life that I haven't been around to watch. Hours go by as we all talk and the beer is passed around freely. It does feel good to be home in a way. Promises are made that I will go out for drinks really soon with everyone. Going to the truck to get the rest of my belongings, this has become the longest stretch of not thinking about the man who taught me how to be *myself*.

Hazel's on my heels, following me outside. "I'll help you carry them up to your room." Hands reach out to grab the bags that I would have had to make a second trip for.

"Thanks, Hazel," I reply. She's already opening the door to the truck, looking around as if it's her space she's reaching into.

"No problem, Tommie." Pulling a bag from the front seat only to have my stash fall to the ground.

That right there is quality at its finest. I'm not sure where I will be able to get more of that top grade when I run out. A little anxiety travels around me, I *need* that to keep myself level.

"You smoke?" A little smirk curves her lips with a glint in her eyes.

"All day every day." Giving her a quick wink.

She smells the inside of the bag with her eyes closed; she seems to know *quality* when she smells it. "I think we're going to be real good friends again, Tommie." We both laugh, and that feels good because it's not fake or forced.

Making our way to my old room, I notice his door is closed. Opening my own I immediately notice it smells of him, as if he's been in here recently. Looking at my bed, the sheets look like they've been slept on. I want to put my nose in the bedding to smell it, but that would look too strange. *I'll do it after she leaves.*

"Thanks, Hazel." I try to herd her towards the door, but she sits on my bed, stretching herself out on top of the sheets.

"I like your room." She's looking around at all my juvenile pictures, my trophies that haven't been boxed up to make room for the older version of me.

Her fingers run along the stacks of books on the shelf behind my pillow. My favorite one has been dog-eared so that I can keep reading from where I last left off.

"Interesting."

That's all she says while looking at the collection that kept my mind busy on words instead of him. *I need the distractions. I'm going to need a lot more books.*

Unzipping my bags, I start to put my clothes away. The ones that only remind me of the man that turned me in for something younger, something newer. My thoughts drift to the way he would make me try on outfits for him, getting me comfortable with being naked around him. He'd watch me with eyes that coveted my young flesh. I was still a juvenile - still not filled out - concave chest, long, gangly

limbs. It's an awkward stage for males to go through, until we fill out naturally with the transition to adulthood.

In the professor's eyes, I was *perfect*.

It's all about the grooming for him. The chase. The acceptance. The goal. I can see this so clearly now, how could I have been so blind? It was a slow progression at first. I was a little embarrassed, but he made it seem so normal, so natural.

"I bought you a new shirt, Tommie. Try it on for me." His voice with an anxiousness to it as I started to undo my top button. He'd watch, eyes dilating with such keen interest. He'd be sitting on the couch sipping on his bourbon with his legs slightly spread. "Come here." Motioning me with his hand when at first I hesitated, because I was embarrassed about what I looked like then. For him, I was the perfect body type. He would hand me his glass to hold. "You can drink it if you want?"

Taking a small sip, before scrunching up my face in horror with how nasty it was. He'd chuckle in amusement when I made that face, before refocusing on me with a *glint* in his eyes. I'd stand in front of him, between his legs, while

his fingers undid the rest of the shirt buttons, slowly, while pressing a kiss to my rib, or a kiss where the skin and waistband of my jeans met. Kissing the flesh on either side of my hips.

When the last one was undone, he'd stand up, letting his hands roam around my flat chest and skinny arms. Absolutely no shape to me *yet*.

"You're so perfect."

When I'd look him in the eyes, trying to see the falsity, there was none.

For him, I was perfect.

Except then, I'd had a year to go before I'd start to transition into my nature, becoming much more physically powerful.

He kissed me then, after my compliments, bare-chested, his hands roaming all over my back. His thick lips kissing my mouth while his hand rubbed me through my jeans. He was able to get me comfortable with him touching me this way, to the point it felt so good I could explode from him just doing that. He never finished me off, his hand always

trying to creep inside towards my flesh, but I wouldn't let that happen because *I'm not that way.*

That's a line I didn't want to cross. Yet.

When that would happen, me pulling away from going any further, he would never become mad or frustrated. He told me he understood, that he didn't want me to do anything I wasn't ready for. We would resume our kissing, something I was now fully comfortable with, to the point that I craved it from him. Since I was comfortable with him touching me over the top of my pants, he would continue doing that with such vigor, that I would eventually cum from the friction a masterful hand could bring to me.

After a concert one night, he'd come to my place for the first time, looking around, stating that I need more pictures on my wall. *Where are the things that make me...me?* It was as if my plain walls were a reflection of me, and he told me that's not who I am, that I was full of color and life. We talked about things that opened my mind to bigger ideas than I'd been taught.

Eventually, our talking led to *me* kissing him; no more him needing to prompt me. I'd let my tongue seek entrance

into his mouth. Me demanding more of a kiss while he smiled the whole time at my *bravery*. His hand again on the outside of my shorts, rubbing firmer than he'd ventured before.

The feeling he'd given me had been too much to say no. Working me up and down, over top clothing that I wish would come off *now*. It wasn't long before I started doing the same to him, learning the lesson he'd been teaching me. He would moan and press himself more into my hand, Allowing me to get used to feeling what an excited man felt like. Nothing offensive about it, I'd thought. It's over top clothing. *This is okay.* No flesh exposed.

No skin on skin.

The professor stroking me up and down, sending me almost to the moon. "*Let me feel you, Tommie.*"

I hadn't protested that time, when his hand slipped inside my boxers, gripping me firmly. The power of his hand making me squirm but never articulating the word *stop*.

I was too far gone. *He had me.*

My hips bucked into him. I could feel my excitement building up, stomach pulling in, ready to explode. He'd known. Stopping so that I could only whimper out. Pulling my shorts down and off, while his eyes fell in love with what I had to offer. Taking my fingers and entwining them with his, wrapping them around my length, encouraging me to relax. He'd wanted to help me get off - and he did encourage me. I hadn't thought it was so wrong; him touching me, as he slowly, lazily, pumped me up and down. His hands were warm and oh so wonderful once he'd completely wrapped himself around me.

A master at work. And me the apprentice.

Looking in my eyes, he'd asked how it felt. Always loved asking me that same question whenever we did something new. Him whispering into my mouth how good I felt in his hand as he continued to stroke me up and down. His tongue going inside my mouth as I instantly opened my lips for him. Nipping at them, sucking the bottom into his smile. Teasing me with light and gentle pecks to more rough and aggressive kissing that would leave my body on fire. His hand keeping tempo with the kissing.

It was always his way at first. His pace. And I was hooked.

Pulling his own zipper down, he'd exposed himself for me to see; to get comfortable with seeing another man turned on. It had been impossible to stop staring at the visual of him pleasuring himself, while he'd mimic the action for me. His eyes always watching mine.

In that moment, I think he'd wanted me to touch him. *But I just couldn't touch a cock.*

The professor had taken me to the moon. I'd thought, *It's okay,* because it was just touching. Nothing more would happen. *I won't cross that line with him. I'm not like that. Just experimenting.*

Long, strong strokes all the way to the tip, down my shaft, to the base of me. He'd kept repeating this action, driving me mad. I'd had to swallow down the growl that needed to tear out of my chest. That's the only thing - while he was awakening my one side, I'd had to hide the other, and in this way, I'd never felt truly *satisfied.* Now that I look back.

He would always bring me just to the brink, only to slow his rhythm down. Making me whimper, almost begging him to continue. That was his cue to really push the limits of my comfort zone. His kissing and licking of my lips had me become an expert on how *he* liked to be kissed.

I was being taught well by him.

My body tensing up, along with his. Both our moans long and drawn out. Bringing us to completion at the same time, the both of us open-mouthed, dilated eyes, glazed over with pleasure. Our breath caught in our throats, he'd made it so our bodies pulsed out our enjoyment over his own chest.

When we'd finished, he would look at me with love. It was that emotion that I was drawn to the most. That did *satisfy* me for a time. It made me feel wanted, accepted, normal. That this was standard, and there was nothing wrong with what we were doing.

He'd lean into me, our fluids rubbing together, kissing me, pulling away from me with eyes that screamed happiness. He'd whisper his, *Thank you, Tommie.* Bringing me to his mouth, kissing me as if it were a reward from him.

I think I cried when I went home, with the realization that maybe the moon had gotten it right, that maybe I'd been born that way but was too blind to really see it. I'd needed help along the way, and she put that man in my path for my education.

"Tommie, you still with me here?"

A book hits my back. Not hard, just enough to pull my thoughts back to the present, instead of living in the past.

"Come on, let's go smoke some of that." She puts the baggy in her pocket as if it belongs to her.

Before she has time to react, I dip my hand in her pocket pulling out my weed that she has no claim on. "Stay away from my stash, Hazel." Giving her a grown-male voice, I actually see her shrink slightly. The power of Beta that I now possess.

Leading me out and down the stairs, everyone has already gone their own way for the night. Going out the back door, she pulls me along by my hand until we reach an old, half-dead tree. Sitting on the ground, she begins to

crumble up the green into tiny, fine pieces. She has a smile on her face while her tongue sticks out slightly, showing the effort of getting the first twist of paper right.

Hazel smells it before handing me her idea of the perfect roll. I think I need to give her an education in the finer things in life.

The first inhale from a joint is calming. The big, white smoke that seems to linger in front of your face. Sitting here with Hazel, getting burnt out of our minds in the now darkening night, has both of our eyes slightly at half-mast. The effect of the good stuff is felt within minutes of the first inhale. I can tell it's affecting her as she sinks herself into the ground. Her smile becomes more, eyes lighting up as she starts to giggle to herself.

"That's some quality, Tommie." A laugh in her voice.

"It is, isn't it?"

Her hand touches my upper thigh, and I look at her for a brief moment, before shifting my body slightly away from hers.

The first tingling touches my skin. Eyes watch me. It's not a familiar feeling; being watched. I know the minute his eyes land on me, I refuse to look up until the very last moment of his approach. Feet crunching the dry grass that's been burned brown in the hot summer sun.

The seams of his grey shirt stretch across the valley of his chest. The rise and fall of his shoulders as he walks towards me. The way his hips move - as if he's rhythmically perfect. The reaction of desire affects me and I have to look away at something else, anything else but him.

Face flushing, short intake of breath, nervous stomach as he makes his way towards me.

He's a vision of the finest quality I have ever seen, will ever see.

Full grown.

Full male.

My whole package.

"Tommie, how are you?"

The texture of sound that comes out, his voice reminds me of velvet; rough yet soft at the same time. It's a slow-burning seduction he's giving me without his knowledge. Stopping just in front of me. I have to look up from my sitting position on the ground. Trying to exhale softly so they don't notice.

His hands are in his pockets, his smile is sin.

I want to do the most sinful things to him.

Running my hands through my hair, because I suddenly have no idea what to do at this moment. "Tate. I'm good."

Hazel takes his hand in hers, as if it's the most natural thing to do. She pulls on his arm so that he sits on the ground with us. I'm having a hard time focusing on anything but him.

"You need to try this." She takes the joint that I just had in my mouth, touching it to his lips, and I can see his eyes closing slightly with the taste of my mouth in his. He inhales long, filling his lungs up until he can't take anymore. He holds it inside before releasing the cloud-like vapor into the warm night air.

"It's been a long time, Tommie." His eyes bore into me, scanning my features. I feel every place they hit. My mouth, neck, chest, thighs. When his gaze hits between my legs, I need to shift my position slightly.

"It has. Four years since I saw you last?" Small talk, nothing that means anything to us. Nothing of substance. Keeping it on a comfortable level.

"I guess you're right. It has been four years. How was college? Did you learn lots of things?" He's not looking at me, preferring to have his focus on Hazel.

"You could say I've had a very well-rounded education." Hazel's hand is now on his inner thigh, trying so hard not to look but failing miserably.

"My dad said that you're going to start working in the office, never pictured you as an *office boy*." He gives me another once over.

"Never pictured me as one either, Tate." When the stick makes it back to me, I put my lips to the white paper, tasting him on it for the very first time.

Moon-sent pleasure vibrates the core of me.

Why put my education to waste? *I was taught a lot of things, Tate.* I plan to put my education to very good use. It's me who looks into his eyes briefly, for just a fraction of a second too long, lingering on his face, getting him used to looking at me.

I can tell it flusters him to an uncomfortable level.

He looks away then, into the darkening tree line, before pulling Hazel up in one swift motion. "Come on, Hazel, it's time for bed." He nips at her ear, and my stomach turns on itself.

He doesn't look my way again as he chases her into the house, and I'm left sitting underneath the tree that's barely living.

Chapter 4

Tommie.

"Tommie! You look tired this morning, did you not sleep well?" The Luna regards me with her kind eyes.

"I just need to get used to being back and the noise of it all." Putting another spoonful of cereal in my mouth so I don't have to talk again.

I can't tell her that her son kept me up most of the night while he fucked Hazel until she went silent. I could tell they were at least trying to be quiet. Unfortunately, I heard every moan, every whispered gasp he made. The flex and shift of the mattress underneath their tumbling body weight. Even with the pillow over my head, I heard it all. It's when he

made that soft whimpering sound at the back of his throat that I felt like my gut was getting kicked over and over again. It was hard to hold myself still and be quiet at the same time, the pain at times had just been too much.

At one point I'd thought, *good,* now I can go to sleep. But then they'd started up again and I'd had to resort to sleeping with my headphones on. The music that was playing only managing to remind me of my past, of my professor.

Laying there in the dark, while my mate was banging someone in his bed, is a surreal feeling. Almost an out of body experience. It should have been me in there, me underneath him, *not her*. I think it was his way of giving me a crystal clear message; *he's into holes, not poles.*

The music pumping through my head, trying to drown out sounds I couldn't quite stomach, music that my ex-lover put on my phone knowing my love for small indie bands. He would always surprise me with new songs. I'd want to discuss the music for hours with him and he'd humor my obsession while I, in turn, humored him with *his*.

He'd taught me how to play the guitar, while a glass of red wine was next to his foot, always encouraging me to take

a sip of it, to get used to the taste of the mature. Except I wasn't mature yet, I was just eighteen.

His crooning voice was mesmerizing to the animal inside me.

The professor liked teaching me about the finer things in life. Art, books, wine. He was eccentric in his special way. He would ask me my opinion on worldly things that made me feel grown when I was anything but. It was a good feeling having him pay attention to the things I liked, just as I was expected to pay complete attention to all the things *he* liked.

While we'd discuss my favorite band at the time, he would have it playing on his stereo. We'd sit there listening to the way the artist strummed the guitar, blowing my mind with how talented he was. It was then that I would feel his hand on my upper thigh, his body getting closer.

My music in the background.

It wasn't too long before kissing became deeper, him on top of me, grinding on me. By then I was so accustomed to it, that I never put up any resistance. In fact, I would start to initiate some of this all on my own. Whenever this

happened, he was more than happy to oblige my desires for him.

Always he was the teacher. Wanting to take me to new levels in my learning.

Even now as I think about it, I have to adjust myself because I feel myself getting hard.

Standing up, slowly taking off my clothes for him, because I'd finally become more confident in my skin. I understood the allure of being watched as each article of clothing came off. My boldness surprising even him when I would *demand* he take off his clothes.

"I want to see you, take them off."

Words barely out of my mouth before I'd find myself staring at his upraised cock. He was more than willing to comply to my request, always that small smile lingering on his mouth before it's replaced with a guttural moan, my hand encasing his now familiar masculine length.

Trimmed smooth, just like the way he loved me to be.

He'd sink deeper into the cushions as I pleasured him, because after all, he was teaching me not only to receive pleasure, but to give it as well. Instructions that I was always too willing to learn, and I would put a lot of effort into getting it just right. The kissing would start up again with his familiar touch working me up and down into a state of unparalleled want.

He always knew the signs. *I was too far gone to stop it.*

My hips bucking into his closed hand, my excitement building up. I'd been only too ready to explode, only to whimper out as he'd stop my release.

His head bent low, taking me into his mouth for the first time. Flashing me glimpses of heaven with the way he would run his tongue over the big vein that dominated the underside of my shaft. Letting the tip of his mouth taste that first drop of fluid that would bead at the tip of me. Again I'd thought, *this is alright,* because I'm not the one doing the sucking.

That's a line I won't cross.

Intense. The way his tongue flicked over the head of me. Groaning out loud, shoving myself more and more into his

wet mouth. He'd been more than welcoming. Looking back, I can't believe some of the noises I'd made.

Shocks of pleasure would shake my inner thighs, my balls pulling up tight towards my body, my stomach starting to spasm inwards. And then he would stop. Right before I blew my load into his mouth, straining to get his body closer to mine.

"Do you like that, Tommie?"

His tongue once again finding my skin, showing me what an expert can do. The whole time inching closer to my face with his cock, getting me comfortable with his closeness and the sight of so much male dominating my gaze. Taking him in my hand, he'd let out a drawn-out moan in appreciation.

I'd realized I loved watching him take me into his mouth - the way his tongue teased along my shaft. He'd bring me almost to the point of no return, then ease off in a torturous game. Playing with my balls, licking them gently. The first time his tongue made contact with my hole I froze up. But the way he stroked me made it impossible for me say *stop*.

So he'd continued, licking and sucking, bringing me to near completion before slowing everything down again.

For a long time. Over and over again, taking me almost to the peak then easing off.

A buildup of pleasure.

The whole time he would be saying things to me - how as a lover it's important not to only to receive, but to *give*. That a relationship was a give and a take. Never once in the beginning of our relationship, did I hear him say that it was just for fun; to not get attached. Those words came much later to ears that didn't want to believe what they were hearing, because by then, I was already in love with him.

The big finale finally arrived, teeth clenched together, unleashing into his mouth wave after wave of what he had been working the entire time for. My essence hitting the back of his throat while he drank it greedily down. Swallowing, savoring it as if it was the most precious thing my body could give him.

Once done, he'd slowly crawl up my body, his mouth coming closer. I could smell me on his breath, lips that wanted to press to mine.

A little hesitance on my part because I'd never tasted my cum before but thought, *well it's mine*, not his, so it might be alright.

"Kiss me, Tommie."

Words spoken low and deep. Waiting for me to go to him. And I did. There was the first hesitance of the kiss before tasting me on his tongue. Pulling away from me after I cleaned myself off him, his smile of relief as he said...*Thank you, Tommie.*

My turn to provide him with pleasure as he angled for my mouth, my hand doing exactly what he liked me to do to him. Tight along the tip, the grip firm and controlled, up and down motion with the concentration of touch going to the head. When I leaned down with the tip of my tongue, I'd let it swim, his taste slightly saltier than mine. It would be something I got very familiar with. At the time, all I did was touch the tip of my tongue to the tip of him, nothing more, and I'd thought, *As long as I'm not deep-throating the guy - I'm alright.*

My lines becoming harder to maintain, the curves becoming more pronounced.

Feeling Tate behind me, without even having to look his way - the current of air just shifts with his presence. A shiver of desire slowly travels down my spine, settling deep within my belly. I don't look at him as he takes a seat across the table from me. His eyes fall on me - it's a long look he takes. The burn of it sets fire to my skin but I keep my head down, finishing my breakfast. Taking my time, as if he doesn't bother me, as if I don't feel the way his eyes are traveling all over me. Pretend that he doesn't affect me the way I affect him.

That will confuse him.

Still not looking at him, getting up and putting my bowl in the sink. I want him to think I'm not a threat, that our secret would be safe with me. I'm not some wolf who will tell things that no one wants to hear.

"Tommie, do you mind helping out with chores, lots of wood to be split this weekend." The Luna requesting for jobs to be done and I am only more than happy to help her out.

"I just have to go to my room for a minute and I'll start on the woodpile."

She gives my cheek a pat as I walk by. "You're such a good male, always were."

Giving her a wide smile, all I can feel are those eyes sizzling into my face. Still, I give him no acknowledgment that I can tell he's looking at me.

Closing the door to my room, I roll one up. I can do this with my eyes shut. My tight roll always holds up, even to the wettest of mouths. Opening the window, lighting a joint, inhaling and trying to hold it in for as long I can with a little cough on exhaling. A few more drags of this quality has my eyelids slowly sinking down. Putting a pair of sunglasses on, I change into something more appropriate for splitting wood all day. *No need ruining good clothes.*

The rest of the day is spent chopping wood by myself, getting high over and over again, and just losing track of time. In a way this feels okay for now - the physical labor of it making it a welcome change to what I'm used to.

Around dinner time, I decide to take my shirt off when I can feel him prowling around the area. I still don't acknowledge his presence, *why spook him?* I don't want to make him feel uncomfortable; let him get used to me, the

way my body looks half naked. Let him get used to the feeling of the bond that's wrapping around. I'm in no rush unlike my teacher - I like fully grown, adult males.

Now that my shirt's off, I have his complete attention. It's not the young juvenile that left four years ago, one that looked younger than a pre-shifted male.

Muscles engorged with the day's physical work, sweat dripping down my chest. I turn from his gaze, letting his eyes hit my back. It's a comfortable place to look - nothing deviant about a back. That's what he's probably thinking at the moment. He's also saying, *it's not like I'm checking out his chest or package.* I know all this because, I was once like him.

Let him start on the safe places of my body. The places that will creep into his mind at night. It's the other places that he'll want to see soon. I will give him those visuals in time.

The student becoming the teacher.

Chapter 5

Tate.

The firelight casts a flickering glow, Tommie's face in shadows, sparks flying high into the cloudless night sky. Trying desperately not to watch him, not to stare at this male who has captured my complete awareness. Not in a good way, not in a friendly way, but in ways that make me feel sick to my stomach because, *I'm not that way.*

The night still holds the warmth of the day while the fireflies flit across the fields haphazardly, as if they don't have a care in the world. The insect's buzz around, tickling at my ears, I try focusing on the hum of their combined wings instead of his deep, slightly raspy voice.

Sitting on the lawn chair, drinking my beer, head resting back, it gives me a perfect view of Tommie without the risk of being caught gawking. His skin holds a dark tan from being outside after he's done with work in the office. I bet his skin tastes warm. I can't help the way my eyes keep falling on him.

No one else can hold my attention.

He's made no attempt to look at me. To even talk to me since he's been home for the last month now. Instead, I think he goes out of his way to avoid me. I'm thankful for that - he's not interested in things that he can't have. Yet in another way I want to ask him - how he can do that so easily?

Do I not affect him the way he affects me?

The acoustic guitar is balanced lightly on his knee, the group of wolves gathered around singing to the chorus. It's as if he's singing to the moon herself - his musical notes drifting through the air on a current of sound.

Tommie's fully into it, playing the kind of music that's trance inducing. His voice vibrating along my backbone, making my legs feel slightly shaky. *The way they feel just after I've pleasured myself.*

Some of the wolves' hands are drumming along to the beat. Other voices join Tommie in singing, but his tone is all I can hear.

He plays the guitar well. I have always wanted to learn *how to play.*

Hazel's sitting by his feet on a blanket that's spread-out full, holding several other females on it. All of them looking up at Tommie in ways that make me jealous - because of their freedom to openly covet something they want,

Dreading the day he came back for good, I'd always make an excuse as to why I had to go away until he left again for school. He wasn't what I expected coming back. I thought for some strange reason he would be thinner, more artsy. *Flamboyant,* even. I never expected him to be the same wolf, only full grown male. He's thicker, taller, his definition of muscle peeking out every time he flexes or turns, the shirt becoming tighter on his body.

Chiseled contours - architecture in its finest form.

When I first saw his shirt off, the excitement of it hit me hard. I couldn't take my eyes off of him. The axe held easily in his hand, coming down hard against the wood, cracking it

down the middle. His back a temptation of pleasure, a draw for greedy eyes. I allowed myself this glimpse of him. *It's only his back.* it's not like I was looking between his legs. *No harm in looking at his back.* But as I started to get used to looking at his back, my eyes started to focus on other areas that made my stomach slightly nauseated. Thank the moon he always stayed with his back turned to me. I was content to just watch him chop wood, glistening with sweat that made him that much more appealing.

The temptation of him is hard on my mind because, I'm not into that kind of *temptation.*

Hazel picks up the melody easily, her voice a seduction of inflection. Eyes closed, swaying her shoulders, she only stops singing long enough to inhale the joint that's made it back around her way.

If she wasn't so lost, she would be one of those females you dreamed of spending the rest of your life with, having a family with. Instead she's just there to fill in time, the both of us using each other to fill in the gaps left by others.

She makes it easy to close your eyes to the real her - it's too difficult to really look at who she is *now*, who she's

become. Her mate's death has changed her into something that's not her; just the shell of her remains.

Without missing a beat, she taps Tommie on his thigh, motioning him to bend his head down towards her. Getting close to his lips, almost touching, she exhales out the white smoke. Heavy and thick, he sucks it up into his mouth before he rights himself again. His eyes slightly closed as if savoring the taste of it. Holding it in for as long as he can, he smiles her way and I have never wanted to be smoke so bad in my life.

I want to be in his lungs, saturating the inside of him.

Feeling sick with the things I'm thinking, disgust rolling my stomach in waves. No amount of beer or weed can make these feeling seem *right*, seem *normal*.

Conflict of thought, ebb and flow. *Disgust versus want.*

Another song rises as Tommie starts to play. It's pleasing the crowd - a known tune. Lots of voices start belting out in harmony to the chords being strummed. Still, it's Tommie's voice that stands out the clearest. Hazel is giving him her eyes as she tries to sing to seduce him. I'm the bystander gawking at the boldness of her. Fingertips caressing the back

of his leg, feeling the muscles of his calf flex with each tap of his foot on the ground keeping the rhythm of the song.

He doesn't take the bait she's putting out.

More logs thrown on the fire cast his face in a dancing soft glow of orange and red flames. Even in the darkened night, I can see his face blushing with small little dimples at the corner of his lips, while he leans into her mouth, listening to her whispered words. She's saying things that only he can hear. He's staring at his hands while picking at the strings, vibrating the night in songs of our youth. An inward smile tries to make it out, watching as he shakes his head *no* towards her.

Her eyes hold a surprised look, brows furrowed - she's not used to being told *no*.

A new stick makes it back towards them, she sucks it in, blowing the smoke into his waiting mouth. Holding it long, he lets out the plume of white into the deepening night. It instantly disappears as a gust of wind takes it away.

His eyes are slightly unfocused, yet he still doesn't look at me. I breathe a sigh of relief knowing he is no threat to our secret. I was afraid he would come back professing his love

for me, or something like that. He's not who I thought he might be.

With eyes half shut, he still can play with an artist's touch. Never missing a beat, even the further stoned he's getting.

I can see Tommie's eyes glancing now and then to Addie, who's sitting slightly to the back of the wolves. She's a quiet wolf, not what you would call a natural beauty. She has no self confidence. Her face has a quality that just disappears into the crowd - *easily forgettable*.

Tommie's taken her out a few times since he's been back.

A jealous uncontrolled lump rises in my throat with the thought of him and her together. Addie and Hazel are the only two wolves in our pack that have lost mates.

Remembering a few weeks ago when we were sitting at the breakfast table finishing our breakfast, Tommie finishing before me, my mother making a remark about how Addie seemed like a nice wolf for me. The second chance at a family.

My mother's not too fond of Hazel.

Tommie's shoulders stiffened slightly before looking at my mother confused. "Second chance at a family? I don't understand." His composure crumbling for a moment.

"Don't you know?" My mother's eyes watering slightly at the lie I knew was coming. She wiped the stray tear that dropped to her cheek. "Tate lost his mate a few years ago; he felt her die."

In that second his eyes found mine. He held them with a look that will always haunt me. His jaw clenched tight with a little tremble of his cheek.

Heartbreak.

I thought I could see just the faintest shine of a tear that wanted to make its way out of his eyes, before he turned his back to me. His hand gripping onto the counter top as if to steady his body from falling. "I'm sorry for your loss." The words cracking in his throat before he walked away from me.

My mother put her hand on his shoulder, giving it a squeeze before he made his way out of the kitchen. A confused look to her face when regrouping her thoughts. "He's such a caring male, always was. Did you see how

much pain he felt knowing your mate died? He seems to feel sorry for you. I don't understand why you males aren't better friends? Was it over a female? Did you steal someone he was interested in?"

"No, mom, I told you we just grew apart. He has his thing and I have mine."

She shook her head at my words. "Well, you better get used to being around him more now. After all, he's going to be your Beta."

That thought made my heart beat in my chest; having to be around him more. It's a good and very bad thing.

Some more wolves band around the fire, the gathering filling up with males who are slightly drunk. Someone bumps someone else, who then falls in Addie, and she hits the ground hard. Some of the wolves laugh at her and scarlet-red flushes on her cheeks in embarrassment. Tommie's up before another offers her a hand. Wilson is laughing louder than anyone else - always reveling in the hardship of others. Tommie gives him a small growl of

annoyance while brushing the dead grass from Addie's long black hair.

"Are you okay?" Tommie's concern has her smiling up at him.

It's good to see her smile, she rarely does, but it's not okay for her to smile at him - at what's mine. Again my jealousy comes in hard like a rogue wave that effortlessly crashes over my sense of reason.

The ebb of not wanting that male, then a flow of wishing it was his hands on me. I have to give my head a shake to clear these thoughts away.

Wilson and his friends are still laughing hard at Addie's discomfort. Standing, because Wilson needs someone to wipe that laugh off his lips, I take the first step forward.

"Let's get out of here. They're assholes, and I can't stand the stink of them."

Tommie's voice is louder than their laughter, which has all of them stopping with the insult he threw their way for all the other wolves to hear. He did that on purpose; he's

instigating a fight. They have been circling each other for the last few weeks, now it's coming to a head for all here to see.

Taking her hand, he leads her through their group. He could have gone another way but he takes the direct route into the middle of them, making the males move, giving him space. Wilson steps in front of his path, arms crossed in front of him.

"Is there a problem, Tommie? I didn't think we had issues." Wilson always direct and to the point, never one to back down from any form of disrespect.

Tommie standing tall, looking at him in the eyes, not giving any ground up either. I haven't seen Tommie fight in four years - I wonder if he still can. I remember him as a scrapper, but time changes wolves. The thought sinks in my stomach - what happens if he can't fight anymore? That somehow school has made him *softer*.

"No problems. Like I said, I couldn't stand the stink of assholes."

Wilson's fist connects with Tommie's jaw in a crack that has me sitting back down, hands holding onto the arm rests of the lawn chair. I can hear the faint crush of metal that's

squeezing in my grip - it's the only way to restrain myself so I don't jump in to help Tommie. A Beta shouldn't need an Alpha to fight his battles, even against another Beta.

It would look very odd if I tried to defend him.

When Tommie wipes away the blood from his split lip, I know that Wilson will have a hard fight in front of him. The crowd is backing up, making room for males to fight. It's the way. This is pack life, a pecking order; a hierarchy that needs to be worked out between the two Betas.

This was bound to happen *eventually.*

Tommie's just rushing the process.

Both of them with the grace of top predators, they circle the other looking for any weakness, anything that will give the advantage. None have a weakness - this should be a very evenly matched fight.

Fists start flying. I can't help but make my way in close, trying to fight my very nature that demands I protect my mate. It's an eternal battle of my fur versus skin, and I can't do anything that will show favoritism. My mate has to battle for the top position, the one that's just underneath *me.*

I can see the females all jockeying for a good position to take in the fight. Tommie's an enigma; being away for so long it's as if a new wolf entered into the pack life. Growls are growing deeper as both males trade hard punches, testosterone thickening the air from their pores. My mouth is watering with my want to taste his skin at the moment.

He's giving just as good as he's taking. Shirts being ripped off - the material easily torn by the claws of wolves. Gashes opening up in the skin, blood pouring on the ground.

With a renewed quickness, Tommie is on Wilson. Liquid smooth with a grappler's grace he hooks his legs, the big male toppling over him. Tommie takes the opportunity to lay punch after punch to Wilson's face. The females don't look away as Tommie makes Wilson submit to him. With his neck angled Tommie's way, he just conceded his rank to the top future Beta.

Darkening eyes that reflect the firelight look at me. His canines have descended slightly over his lips - it's an alluring sight. I nod my head towards him in recognition of the place that he just won on my left. He turns towards the crowd, a terrible threatening growl rumbling the air. The

females are licking their mouths, the males casting eyes to the ground not wanting to take on Tommie.

Grabbing Addie's hand, he leads her away from the group, the bulge in his pants from his win has him high off endorphins that must be pumping through his system.

While walking by me, our eyes meet - really meet, for just a fraction of a second to share between us. I see it then.

Want.

Need.

Hunger.

Taking a step back at how powerful he looks in that second, before his eyes focus back on what's in front of him, I watch as he claims his prize.

He takes Addie by the hair, angling her face towards his. He's looking at her, teeth still poking through gums. I hear a gasp from somewhere as his mouth descends on this willing female, biting on her mouth so that it opens for him. He's kissing her expertly, his tongue sweeping just the inside of her mouth. I smell want in the air. His hands are on her ass

as he picks her up and she wraps her legs around his waist. He carries her back to the house, lips tasting every inch of exposed skin, making my own needs known with the way I have to resist rubbing myself through my jeans.

Hazel's by my side watching *The Tommie Show.*

"He's not what I remember." Her voice is slightly breathless.

"Did you like that little show?" Turning to her, so my eyes don't have to watch my mate with someone else. Is this how he feels when he can hear me screw Hazel every night?

"He wasn't bad was he?" That's all she replies, taking my hand and walking me towards the house.

Going up the stairs, I can hear the bed shaking violently, almost as if it's to the point of collapse. The door to his room is open - another show that I have to witness. Hazel stops to watch. He's behind Addie who's on hands and knees while he's driving himself into her. His hand is between her legs as she trembles from his touch. Taking his wet fingers away, he begins to push one into her other hole while he's continuing to thrust himself into her wet one. A long pleasurable moan

is drawn out, low and soft from her open mouth. Her eyes are closed, taking everything he's giving to her.

Hazel's breath is coming out fast; she's getting excited by watching. Her ass is rubbing against my rock solid shaft.

Leaning into my chest her mouth tips towards my ear. "Do you like watching?" Her hand suddenly in contact with the zipper of my jeans.

"Yes," I lie. What I like is watching him nailing her from behind.

"I could talk to her, see if she's willing to join us? We could do a trade maybe? You could talk to Tommie, see if he would be interested?" She lets her words hang in the air only to be overpowered with Addie's grunt as he inserts another finger.

Her fingers are gripping the bed sheets tight in her hands, chest swaying while he's rocking her body. Her face has a look of utter euphoria with just a slight grimace.

Pleasure with a touch of pain

Hazel's hand now rubbing me through my jeans, I can't move away from the scene. They don't acknowledge us, caught up in their animal needs.

When my hand goes between Hazel's thighs, she doesn't protest, in fact she spreads herself just a little more for me. A whimper comes out of her mouth, not quite loud enough to disturb our real life movie.

Tommie pulls himself from inside her - he's glistening wet with Addie's juices all over him. I can't pull my eyes away from him. No matter how disgusted I am with myself, I can't look away. His eyes find mine as with a gentleness, he descends into her other hole, inch by slow inch. Watching him as he sinks deeper and deeper, until he's buried almost fully inside an entrance that isn't made for that kind of thing. His free hand is stimulating her most sensitive spot while she stills - focusing on her breathing. He pulls himself slightly out only to go back deeper this time, all of him inside her while he's looking at *me*.

Hazel takes my hand leading me away, her needs saturating the air. In no time, faster than I thought possible, the both of us are naked. Kissing her has me almost exploding before even being touched by her skillful hands.

Kissing her neck, down her chest, before spreading her legs wide for my tongue to taste her. I can smell his scent slowly creeping into my open room. The smell of Tommie has a taste of saltiness to it that lingers on my tongue, saturating the air thicker than her smell can. My mate's essence is making a disturbing appearance in my mind.

This is the first time I have ever smelled him in that *way*.

This is messing with my mind as the thickness of me buries deep into Hazel. She grunts with the force, holding onto my shoulders as I continue to dominate her. This is not about her at this moment, it's about me and my needs.

Feeling her nails embedding into my flesh, her teeth flash a warning before coming out. She's taking nips at my skin as her hips keep my pace, meeting me thrust for thrust. This is becoming one of the most satisfying experiences I have ever had.

Hazel's cries are soft as she starts to pulse tight around me, the inside of her clenching down rhythmically, pulling on my shaft before I bury my head into her neck. Balls pulling up so tight, it's that last possible second before

exploding that has me imagining I'm buried to the base inside of him.

That thought combined with his smell gives the most overwhelming, whimpering, toe curling release I have ever had. Even my asshole pulses with the pleasure.

Shame washes completely over me as I come down from the experience.

I'm not like that. I tell myself.

Chapter 6

Tommie.

Black mascara tears fall silently from the curve of Addie's cheek, dropping sadly from a face that's falling apart.

"Addie, did I hurt you?" Maybe I was too rough with her. She's sitting at the end of the bed, fingers playing with the corner of the sheet. Her shoulders are bent forward as she's looking at the ground, more tears dripping like little

raindrops for eyes that are too full of water to hold them any longer. Her makeup's all smudged, taking the edge of a sheet from her fingers, I wipe away the lingering marks clinging to her face. "What's the matter, Addie?" Her internal suffering is causing me great discomfort. I can hear my mate in the other room enjoying everything Hazel is offering him.

"You were my first since my mate." A little whimper from her throat constricts mine.

"Addie, I didn't know. You should have told me that. We could have just talked, I just thought you were into it." Now I feel like scum.

"No, it's okay, I wanted to do that. It's just now I feel guilty like I've cheated on him." She's constantly wiping away tears that won't stop. "I just didn't want to feel alone anymore, Tommie. I'm sorry this is so stupid. He's been dead three years and I'm acting like it just happened as if he's still alive." She takes a deep breath in, now looking for her clothes.

"You don't have to go, Addie, stay with me. I promise I won't touch you like that again. I'm lonely too. It feels good just to have someone maybe to talk to." Can she see how

lonely I am? Can she see that I'm in pain? Not on her level, but somewhere close.

She puts her hand on my shoulder. "I should go." Her voice is lowered in sadness. Watching her dress, she's hurried, not wanting to stay one more minute than she has to. Once dressed she halts at my door, turning towards me. "Why me, Tommie? Why choose me?"

"Why not?"

"Tommie, look at me. I'm not blind. I can see what I look like. You have your pick of females and you chose me. I'm not really anyone's option."

She's hurting my chest with her words about herself. "Addie -"

Stepping towards me, putting her fingers on my lips, stopping my words. "It's okay, Tommie, you don't have to say anything. I'll see you around, okay? You don't have to call me tomorrow, I won't expect your call. Males like you don't call females like me back." She gives me a quick kiss on the lips before walking out the door.

I should say something to her before she leaves. "For what it's worth, I think you're beautiful, Addie. Your mate was a very lucky male to have someone like you in his life."

She pauses with my words, turning around with a blush to her face. "Thanks, Tommie."

Ghosting out of my room, she leaves me by myself while I have to endure round two of my mates undeniable drive. Heading to the shower, I taking my time washing up, the water blocking out the sound of their lovemaking. Putting my head against the tile, I let the water run into my mouth before spitting it out at my feet. Trying to rid myself of the taste of someone else on my tongue. Closing my eyes, I try to think of other things that can occupy my brain while I stay in here until they finish. I remember when my teacher and I would go out, how all our dates were full of:

Teasing.

Gentle caresses.

Sultry glances.

He was a walking seduction. Knowing just the right words, just the right touch, to melt me, make me feel special.

Always our dates were a build up of what was to come. By the time we made it back to his place, I'd have had a raging hard on for hours. I couldn't wait to slip inside and have the door close behind us. He'd kiss me, full of passion and lust, both of us happy to be away from prying, watchful eyes.

After all - he was a teacher - we just couldn't flaunt our love for one another. We had to be discreet. I understood the importance of this; the need for secrecy, to keep this just between him and I.

We'd have a drink on the couch, roll one up as he touched me, places straight men would never touch another man. A graze to my upper thigh as his voice held me in rapture, he'd talk to me about everything and anything. Rubbing down the length of my back, feeling my vertebrae, slowly walking his fingers down my spine. Touching my underwear line with feather-light caresses.

A slight dip inside the material before he pulled his finger out, he would be looking at my face, watching my mouth, before leaning in and kissing me. Opening my mouth for his tongue to enter inside me, all I had to do was kiss him back the way he liked. That's all he asked of me. I was more than happy to comply with such simple demands.

Maybe his thumb would touch the outline of what's held between my thighs. Feeling his very familiar length through his clothes, eliciting an anticipated moan. The belt buckle that at first, I'd had a hard time with, undoing with the fingers of an expert. Our lips never leaving each others the whole time I unzipped him.

With no prompting from him anymore, my hand would travel on its own, exploring the length of him. In the beginning, I'd thought he was monster-sized, because I still hadn't been fully grown and I'd never seen a man's arousal before. I came to realize eventually that he was average for a human.

In no time the both of us would be naked, on the floor in the living room, unable to even make it to the bed. His hands all over me, his mouth sucking everywhere I had flesh. Teeth gently biting any raised areas. Back then, I still had hardly any chest hair and he'd loved that, it made me seem younger. *Perfect.*

When I went through my transition from juvenile to adult male, he'd made me shave my chest hair - it's a practice I still do to this day.

Once again I was the center of his attention, all I had to do was lay there and accept what he wanted. The almond oil making an appearance. "I want to watch you please yourself, Tommie."

He'd take my hand, squirting the oil on my palm, watching as I rubbed it all over my shaft. The sexiness of being watched as I masturbated was highly enjoyable to me. He loved looking at me pleasing myself, pumping myself up and down slowly, my hips starting to roll slightly with how good I could make myself feel.

He'd gently kiss my inner thigh while telling me the things he wanted to do, telling me the dirtiest places his tongue wanted to visit. These things he would say excited me so much, I had to focus on not going too fast. He taught me to enjoy the experience, to never rush things, let the feelings build up. I'd finally take him in my hands without any asking on his part. I'd slick his perfect cock up so it made it easier for me to feel him up and down. My hand slippery in the oil that had an exotic scent, a sensual aroma.

"I want to try something new, Tommie."

With those words, I knew that my comfort level would be tested, I'd be taken to a new level of *learning*.

"If you don't like it, I'll stop."

His words always making me believe that all I had to say is stop, and he would. I think he knew that the word would never leave my lips, not as turned on as he'd made me. he just couldn't rush things. I would feel the quickening of his breath all over my body as he kissed every inch of flesh. The nervousness of what he was about to do getting to him. Always a risk with anything new I would be learning.

He'd take the almond oil out again and really coat his hands, his fingers. Rubbing me up and down, letting the oil drip over my sack and gently massaging. Every once in a while, his fingers would brush up against my hole, before moving away to come back and brush up against it again. My breathing slightly shortening at the realization of what he wanted to do to me. His thick palm gripping the underside of my shaft, his warm mouth sucking me off, the tip of his tongue playing with my hole before licking down the big vein that was engorged thick on the underside.

In those moments, all I could focus on was how good he was making me feel. His well lubricated finger slowly entering inside me, his continued sucking while his finger lazily, delicately, pushed further inside. Not to cause pain *only pleasure.*

I could feel every inch of his finger go inside deeper and deeper. Not painful, but *wonderful,* and knowing how much he enjoyed it made it that much more satisfying. Thoroughly stimulating, while his mouth was banging the outside of me. Pushing as far as his finger would go, a soft moan of slight discomfort making it's way out of my mouth, *but I didn't tell him to stop.*

Soon my hips would thrust, trying to get myself as far into his mouth as possible, only to pull myself out again to get that incredible feeling of his finger inside me. Back and forth my rhythm became faster and faster, the build up of my release closing in fast.

My music filling the living room with my own personal moaning. Him telling me how sexy it was to have me groaning and grunting. Watching my face as I came down on his finger again to notice another joining the first, I'd tense up slightly, feeling the stretch of it, the invasion of

something once again foreign that I wasn't use to. He'd been persistent though - continuing with his strong, slow strokes from the base of me to the tip, his pace gently increasing in strength.

He'd held his fingers still to let me decide if I would take the both of them inside me. He'd left it up to me. All on my own with the next thrust of my hips into his mouth, pulling out to sink myself down on those two fingers which had his mouth turning up in a smile.

"You like me fingering you, Tommie?"

My shaft sliding back comfortably inside his mouth after he spoke those words to me. The whole situation so uncomfortable but so highly *erotic*, so pleasing that I was doing what he wanted me to do and how good it was making me feel.

I'd find him angled close to my mouth, just in-case I ever felt a need to slip him inside me. The explosion rocking through my whole body, something even now I'll never forget. My legs quivering with the feeling, and him swallowing every last drop greedily with a satisfied look on his face.

"Thank you, Tommie."

In time my body grew to crave this form of learning, I would always have the hardest, most mind blowing releases this way. I'd thought - *this is okay, as long as I don't have a real one up inside me. I'm not going to be like that. I won't be like that.*

I have a line.

A curving line that now allowed for wondering what he'd taste like in my mouth - A big jump in my education.

The water getting cold, finally stepping out of the shower, I dry off tying the towel around my waist. I got hard from the memory of my past. The bulge in the front of me can't be hidden. Walking out of the bathroom, Tate is there waiting for me.

"Try not to take so long again. It's the only bathroom up here we have. Others need to use it to."

He's trying so hard not to stare at me, not to let his eyes leave my gaze. He doesn't succeed, I let him take my body in. His breathing becoming shallower, I can hear his heart

beat in my ears. I walk past him without a word but I do brush my shoulder against his chest as I go by. It's just the lightest passing touch, almost as if it were by accident. I can feel my legs becoming unsteady with the real feel of my mate's skin against mine.

Shutting the door behind me, because I don't want him to think that I did it on purpose, I leave him with a wanting feeling.

A slow build up of need.

Chapter 7

Tate.

Sun leeches into the cracks between the blinds, the rays
warming my skin in light touches of early morning. Getting
out of the empty bed, I see Hazel must have left sometime
during the night. I don't think anything of it since she
doesn't regularly stay until the morning.

Walking out the door, I find Tommie taking the stairs
two at a time.

He's still somewhat sweaty, breathing hard, hair damp. He's shirtless. Muscles of his body flexing and bouncing as his legs take the stairs easily. I'm rooted to the spot. My own legs heavy, sinking into the wooden floor with the visual assault I'm taking in.

He see's me as he clears the last stair, his pace slowing to a complete stop. I'm standing just outside his door. We watch each other, neither of us making the first move. Time standing still with the burden we share.

Heavy silence.

Crushing.

Agonizing.

Choking.

Eyes travel all over him. Lips, neck, chest, legs. My ability to resist is being severely tested. His eyes stay focused on mine; they don't travel, they're fixed in one spot. It's me who takes the first step toward him. He holds himself steady, contradicting the tremors in my thighs. Another step and our distance becomes that much smaller. Standing in front of him, our bodies almost touching.

"What are you doing?" His hushed voice strains my skin. His gaze never leaving mine.

"I don't know." My eyes once again roaming. He's my visual treat that sickens me at the same time.

The thoughts I'm having, I can't decide if they're terrible or terrific.

For his part he lets me stare at him, he doesn't flinch away, no disgusted look on his face. He's just watching.

My face warming, I can actually feel the flush creeping along my neck to my cheeks. If he see's it, he doesn't acknowledge anything; he's calm. While I'm holding on by the barest mental string. *This is wrong, this isn't right.*

He smells like a summer breeze - warmth that heats me up from the inside out.

This has never happened before - just the two of us alone, *no witnesses.*

Usually we have so many faces around us, his head always turned away. All I'd be able to glimpse reduced to snatches of his bare back, or a tease of more flesh, but never

this. Full on Tommie who's just worked out, displaying himself for my eyes. I don't pretend that I don't notice him, because I notice *everything*.

The way his tongue teases with a simple flick over his lips, the moisture left behind in a glistening taunt. His chest wider than his hips, giving him that v-shape body that makes jeans hang off in artful enticement - one good pull and off they go. Long, lean legs that carry him with a forceful grace.

His face leaves its imprints on my lids at night.

I'm straight. But the look of him *curves* me. The nearness of our bodies has his skin's warmth starting to penetrate through the thin material of my t-shirt. Crackling connection the longer we hold our positions, electric current is pulsing through my body as our bond starts to strum its power between us. Troubling thoughts of a need to just touch him *whispering along the edges of reason.*

Touch him.

Light, amber eyes dilating, becoming darker, his desire now starting to drift over me in a wave of lust. It's just him and me.

Only us.

My gaze on his lips, then flickering back to his eyes. Stepping closer to him, a whisper of skin touching my shirt. Heart jack-hammering in my chest. The rush of blood in my ears, making my head feel lighter, slightly off balance. We're so close; a mere inch of separation. He takes my breath away when his head leans in, I feel his hand on my hip, pulling me towards him. We're touching now, but not pressing against one another. His breath on my neck, my muscles tensing.

Our lips almost touching, my reason taking flight replaced by forbidden desire.

Breathing faster.

"Tate."

Hazel's voice breaks the connection as she climbs up the stairs. Both of us *straighten up.*

Tommie has a small grin on his face before pulling away from me, his fingertips glide over my hip slowly before his touch is completely pulled away, leaving me with something suspiciously like emptiness. His hand goes through his hair as if it might be a nervous habit of his. I've seen him do this a

few times in my presence, it's a slightly boyish gesture and I would probably think it cute, if I was that way.

I let myself get caught off guard, it can't happen again.

I'm not that way.

"You're sweaty this morning." Hazel brushes by Tommie, her hand skimming the waistband on his shorts.

He backs away from her slightly, a low growl at the base of his throat, a sound that is vocal seduction. "I went for a run. You need the bathroom or can I take a shower?" He's asking me but looking at Hazel as she moves to stand beside me. His eyes are watching her hand as she traces her fingers over my shoulder, her hand disappearing down my back. I can feel the burn of fire from his stare before he pulls them away from my flesh.

She raises up on tiptoes to kiss the corner of my mouth, he watches, the side of his lips turning down. His posture not so straight, almost as if he slouches within himself just for a moment before he rights himself again. Her kiss doesn't affect me like the way his *almost* kiss does. "Go ahead, I was going to get something to eat. Hazel, let's go out for breakfast."

She's looking at Tommie as he edges towards the bathroom. "Tommie, you eat yet?"

He stiffens slightly.

"Why don't you come with us, more the merrier." Giving him a high-voltage smile.

"No, you guys go, I don't want to *intrude*."

Hazel looks slightly disappointed a tiny pout on her face. She has no affect on him. "Before you go in there, could I get a stick from you to hold me over for the day?"

He turns on her, getting close to us. "I don't want to share my stuff with you, Hazel."

She laughs this off as if he's joking, but from his tone he's not; he's serious. For some reason, I step slightly away from Hazel, creating a space between our bodies. She doesn't notice, but his eyes do.

"Don't be like that, Tommie. Listen," She steps slyly towards him. "I'll suck you off for a half bag."

His face looks shocked for a second before he recovers. This is her tactic; shock and awe. She does this often, never doing anything she says. It's all a bluff. Leaning into her body, he runs a finger along her collarbone, up along her neck, lightly along her cheek, before tracing her lips with the tip of his finger. She can't hide her excitement, I have a hard time suppressing the growl that's bubbling up inside me. "Hazel, two reasons why that won't happen. The first is: your mouth isn't big enough. The second: I don't think you have the skill level for the job."

I can't help the laugh that escapes out my mouth.

"So spicy, Tommie, I like that about you. Give me ten minutes to warm my jaw up and we'll see what I can shove in it." She begins to open her mouth really wide, stretching her jaw with a smile on her face.

Tommie just shakes his head while he starts to laugh at her slightly. Heading back into his room with a grumble, his bed is still messy, not made yet. Going into his top drawer, he pulls out a pre-rolled, handing it to her. "No more, Hazel, I mean it." He's looking annoyed at her.

"Thanks, Tommie." She's smelling the herb with giddiness, excitement. She always gets what she wants eventually. "Come out with us for breakfast. We'll wait for you."

He looks at me before turning his face to hers. "No, you guys go. Addie and I are going to hang out today."

"What are you doing with her?" My words fall out my mouth before I have time to stop them. They have a jealous edge to them.

"Hanging out for the day, hiking up to the lake."

His words feel light, casual, but I'm feeling green envy spreading inside me. "You need to be careful with Addie, she's fragile, don't hurt her." I mean it to be a warning; that I'm concerned with Addie's well being. But I just don't want them hanging out. I don't want her having him smiling.

He touches his head again, fingers running through his hair. "Don't worry about Addie, Tate. She's in good hands." He gives me his hard eyes, challenging me to say something else.

"That she is." Hazel's voice rises, and I look down at her, a slick smile on her face as if remembering how Tommie handled Addie last night.

"I just don't want her to get hurt by you." I try to sound like a big brother concerned for a sister.

"She won't, it's just nice sometimes having someone to hang out with." He shuts the bathroom door before I can say anything back, the water of the shower already running.

"I don't think Tommie likes me very much." Hazel going into Tommie's room, opening up the top drawer, getting a few more sticks before putting them in her pocket.

He won't be happy having his stash touched. "You shouldn't be doing that," A little warning to her.

"I'll have to owe him." She flashes a hopeful promise, eyes gleaming.

I think she has a crush on Tommie. "You like him don't you?"

"No." She says it too fast.

"You do, don't lie to me."

Her hard, marbled eyes look at me now, intent with coldness. Her light switch just turned on. "I don't like anyone, Tate, I just tolerate wolves. Would Tommie be fun? Yes, he would. That's it, just a little fun, nothing more." She puts the joint in her mouth before walking into my room, opening the window, lighting it, and I watch her pull in the first long inhale of the drug that she smokes more than Tommie. That's saying a lot. "What? Why are you looking at me like that." The hard edge of her voice hardly ever makes it out, only at her most honest does it surge to the forefront.

"Nothing, Hazel." I take the joint from her hands pulling my own needed relief into me. Hoping that maybe it will affect me too, make me not care about anything.

"I think we should have a lake day. It's the weekend, I'll make some calls and get a group together. What do you say we crash their little party?" After she says those words, she releases the smoke that she was holding in her lungs.

The bathroom door opens, a rush of steam billows out. From my view I can see him go into his room with just a towel on, drops of water still cling to his skin. Before closing

his door, his eyes find mine and hold me in my spot. Inhaling another lung-full, holding it in, he finally closes the door to my view of him. "Whatever, I don't care." Looking at the closed wooden door, upset my view has been blocked.

"What's up with you? Why the sudden interest in Addie, are you jealous?"

"What, jealous?" Giving a confused look.

"Are you interested in Addie?"

"No, I just don't want him to hurt her. She's been through a lot." A cough comes out my mouth as I exhale the smoke.

"If you are it's okay, just tell me and our arrangement will be done." She takes the joint out of my hand. "I don't want to stand in your way, Tate, of being happy."

"No, Hazel, I don't want her. Our arrangement is still good, I'll let you know when it isn't. Same goes for you, if you start liking someone you tell-"

"I'll never like anyone again, never. He was my only one. He died, and I just have to fill in time before I see him again.

All this is meaningless." She's a chaos of female emotion that I know nothing about.

I let her drift in her own world as I drift into mine.

Tommie comes out of his room, eyes trying to see straight, but looking like he's flying higher than me.

"Bye." His voice sounding far away already at the last step of the stairs.

By the time we hike to the edge of the lake it's already late afternoon. His backpack rests on a blanket that's spread out, with a cooler and half drunk drinks in plastic cups that the ice has melted in long ago. No one is around, but music plays on a small speaker. I think it's his phone that's beside it. *This must be his music playing.* I like the tune - it's indie but good. I see them then - on a paddle board - Addie's straddling the front of the board, legs dragging in the water, while Tommie's standing up paddling around the lake. She's facing him, the bottom of her t-shirt is wet while the rest of her is dry. She's looking at him, smiling with her eyes. He's just in a pair of swim shorts that show off his upper thighs

just above the knee, his quads are strong. With every stroke of the paddle, his abs flex, exerting with work.

Hazel lights another one up - never enough for her. Smoke 'em if you got 'em - that's her motto. She has her hand on her forehead shielding the sun from her eyes. More wolves start gathering at the edge of the lake. Music starts turning up, some of the males making a fire. I see that Addie's brother has come and he's not looking happy at the way Addie's looking at Tommie. He's agitated, his hackles raised.

I stretch out on the blanket that Hazel has laid out for us, right next to theirs. Tommie paddling to the shore only to meet with her brother's hard eyes, he stares him down til the brother looks away. Coming towards the blanket, he lays down right next to me. Tommie on his stomach, upper body raised on his forearms. We're almost touching again, his body so uncomfortably close. "Is this your music?"

He turns his head my way, giving me a smile, "Yes it is."

"I like it. This band is good."

His eyes light up as he starts to talk about how the next song after this one has the most incredible guitarist. His

voice rises up and down as he tells me of his favorite song from them, and how they wrote it in ten minutes. He's a music lover.

Some of the females gather around, crowding us in. Addie, on the outside pulling down her t-shirt, looks uncomfortable, not sure what to do. She's the only one not in a bikini - she's not the show off type.

Hazel's already in her bikini; red triangles barely covering anything. Very low bottoms that rise high on her ass cheeks. Again I look at Addie who's the absolute opposite of Hazel. Two different females with such identical stories. Finding their mates young, falling in love with the future ahead of them, only for it to be pulled away as if it never was there in the first place.

"Move." Tommie says this to the females on his blanket as his hand waves in Addie, patting the space beside him. She comes to lay down, head resting on her arms she closes her eyes. "You want a drink or anything?" His lips almost touch her ear. She just shakes her head with her eyes closed.

He starts at my feet. A warm path up my calves, hitting my thighs, his lingering stare on my stomach. I look at his

head - it's down as if he's looking at the ground - but really it's tilted my way.

Does he understand what he's doing to me?

How uncomfortable this is for me to be so close but unable to touch. To fulfill this building desire that's twisting my insides up.

My straight line is starting to bend his way.

Chapter 8

Tommie.

Scorched brain from a weekend of too much smoke. A layer of ash left behind in the suffocation.

The only thing left before I can just slip inside my room is Sunday dinner with the family - the first I've been required to sit at in years. When I was a pup, I loved gathering around the big table, talking and sharing our week with everyone.

Tate and I would always have our own side conversations going on.

Roast beef, chicken, mashed potatoes, carrots, gravy, desserts all made with love from our mothers. We would demolish the lot - helping ourselves to seconds because during the day we would be all over the woods together, exploring, running, playing, being what best friends were supposed to be.

Wherever he was, I was, and vice-versa.

When Tate and I first shifted, we had excuse after excuse never to go to Sunday dinner, avoiding one another at all costs. We went from one day being best friends to being each others worst *nightmares*.

Never talking, never being able to be in the same room together. I changed all my high school classes so that we didn't have to sit next to each other. I remember when he brought his first female home - I thought I would die. I honestly thought I was dying from what it did to me. I remember in the morning I couldn't get out of bed, I couldn't eat for days. Tate was able just to go on as if nothing happened. The second day in bed my mother had come to

see me, asking me what was going on. I think it was the very first time I just held onto her and cried. She held me to her, rubbing my back as if I was a small pup again. Of course, I couldn't tell her what was going on. I could never share my *secret* with anyone.

Always having to hide *that* part of me. It was something to be ashamed of.

Tate had walked by my open door as I wept in my mother's arms, looking at me while my mother just held me. Great shame washing over me because it was his arms that I wanted to be in, to be holding me, and that was the wrong way to think.

It's not our way.

My father coming up to my room with concern in his eyes - I hadn't been able to meet them. The guilt, the shame, the *oppression* of staying silent. We'd been taught that it's *not right*, it's not the way to the *moon*.

How could it not be the way to the moon if she was the one that paired us as mates? I would pray to her, ask her why, but she never answered me.

I never got an answer.

After a while it didn't hurt as much, it didn't cut as deep, hearing him in the next room. I got numb to it, developing tricks to become blind and deaf to it.

Becoming braver than what I really was, I brought Hazel home one night, leading her up to my room. I was so nervous - the vodka in my system already starting to fade. Her mate had recently died and now she was doing everything that even looked her way. I'd thought it would be easy. She was my first kiss - decidedly sloppy on my end.

Her, a practiced kisser, laughed at my effort. I remember just looking at her face while she was laughing and laughing at me. I'd told her to *"leave, get out!"* Shouting at her until she left, but not before she whispered *sorry*.

Looking back, I think she might have meant it.

Shutting my door to her, it was then that I'd made the decision to leave the pack - to go to school. I needed an out and that had probably saved my life. My parents not happy but understanding that something was affecting me deeply - even asking Tate if he knew what was wrong. Oh, of course

he'd feigned ignorance - he wasn't about to tell my parents or anyone else that we were mates.

The next Alpha having a male mate? *Unheard of*. Not that it just didn't happen often, more so that *never* an Alpha.

I think my Professor knew as soon as he saw me that first day of school. I wonder if we all have that look about us, a distinct smell that predators associated with *prey*.

There had been another wolf in my class. Shaved head, lean, lanky body, same age, not transitioned yet into adulthood. He sat at one end of class while I sat at the other. We would eye each other up on occasion, keeping our distance because we were both stranger wolves from different packs.

First time meets between different wolves could go very wrong. So we kept our distance at first from one another.

The male wolf that sat at the other end of class, I came to know as Carson - fourth born to an Alpha line. My opening was first born to a Beta line.

We would make some small talk but nothing serious *at first*.

The Professor, when handing my papers back to me, would make sure his fingertip brushed against my hand for a moment longer than appropriate. What I would brush off as *nothing*. That I'd just imagined things. He was my Professor - he wouldn't be interested in someone like me. Plus he was a man, not a wolf.

Within the first week he had me stay after class so he could go over something with me. He was the funny Professor - one with all the stories that made the class laugh. I would laugh. And I didn't remember the last time I'd laughed.

It was only in his class.

Slowly I'd started to make friends with other students. But they were humans, not my kind as I was told.

Stick to your kind.

That was ingrained into me from birth. If a human found out about us they were killed, the offending wolf killed. Our secret needed to stay a secret.

The teacher made me laugh. I would get up *wanting* to go to his early morning class, being sad when the period was over, having to wait to the next day to see him again. I should have known something was up when I saw him talking with a distraught older student who kept trying to touch him, trying to hug him in his office that first day he'd asked me to stop by and discuss my paper that I'd somehow failed. I never failed at anything. He'd closed the door, asking me to wait outside.

"Who's that?" The man's voice coming from behind the door. "Are you *screwing* him?" His voice cracking, choking on his sobs.

The Professor opening the door, asking if we could, *reschedule another day about the paper.* The man sitting in the chair with his red eyes, glaring me down as if he could kill me.

It was just a few days after this incident that I got invited to his office again. Going over my failed assignment. How I could improve with some extra tutoring from him. His hand sliding on my shoulder, a little squeeze which I never thought odd. I should have, but I didn't. He was my Professor, why would I think anything more than what it

was - a reassuring squeeze. He'd had his guitar in his office one day I'd just dropped by and I mentioned that I'd always wanted to learn to play. Those words had him visibly brightening.

"I could teach you?" His voice hardly containing the excitement.

My voice couldn't contain my happiness. "Really? That would be great."

Our guitar lessons at his house were at least three times a week. I couldn't believe how lucky I was - how he started to become my friend - that I didn't have to have very many other friends because he steadily consumed my free time.

The touching got more - a slight hug now and then, longer hugs which didn't bother me too much.

A hand on my thigh, more touching my knee as he placed my hands properly on the guitar. He had to be close to me to properly show me what he meant by hand placement. We'd talk about girls; if I had a girlfriend one night after a few glasses of whiskey. My first taste of the gold had me buzzed slightly. I'd admitted that I only kissed a girl once, and that she had laughed at me.

So began our lessons on how to please a girl. His wild college days and how it was important to put your partner's pleasure *first* before your own. He would sit close to me when he would talk to me about women.

He'd touch himself on occasion, which was a little weird, but to each their own I'd thought. He'd talk about eating out a girl, what a girl's insides felt like while pleasing her. It got me excited sometimes - hearing his stories - it turned me on. He'd asked if I pleasured myself a lot. I think I was taken back by this.

"It's okay, I do it all the time." He'd felt himself then, over the top of his jeans.

I think my breath stopped in my throat because I could see the bulge in his pants, but I didn't say anything because I had the same bulge in mine.

All his talking of women and jacking off really got to me. Nothing happened that night. I went home pleasing myself alone in my bed, trying to see a females face, but instead I would see his or Tates. Mostly Tate's face would be my go to for the finish.

This went on for a few weeks; him telling me about women and what they like, what he liked in bed. Us getting drunk. When I went into his office, the door closing behind me as he would lean over my shoulder, his hips against my back showing me something *new*.

Some part deep down knew that it wasn't right, that it was wrong, but I didn't care for the first time since my shift. I just didn't care.

He'd turned himself into my best friend. I'd laughed with him, we played games together, we started doing everything together. Of course, I knew that we had to keep this a *secret*, no one could know about us. He was a Professor, I was a student - his student.

He would go to obsessive lengths to ensure our secret was protected. Even with those rare occasions in his office, a risk was taken, I was always met with his nervousness - a man who could lose everything. After all, I was his student, *and teachers weren't suppose to be doing this.*

He would always comment on my tight ass, grabbing it in his hand while he kissed my neck, letting his tongue lick

my skin. To a wolf, that's the biggest turn on - having your neck kissed and sucked close to where a mark is left.

He knew what turned me on, how to approach me. He was such an expert, such a predator, that I had no chance with him. It wasn't until later, when we started to fight, that I understood what it was like to have love taken away from you. When I wouldn't try his *something new* anymore. When I couldn't bring myself to have him take me. I'd been an expert by then - using him the way my nature intended. He'd always wanted to be inside me, but I just couldn't, and by denying him that one thing he'd started to pull away from me - my best friend started to become *distant*.

On few occasions I would catch him talking to freshman, his smile was for them. For a moment, I'd contemplated letting him do that to me just so that I could keep our friendship, because without him I would be *lonely* again.

But I just couldn't do that.

"Tommie, are you listening to me." My mother's voice brings me out of my daydream, everyone at the table looking at me including my mate's eyes. Hazel at his side for

Sunday dinner, the spot next to me open. "I was saying that next weekend there's going to be a big pack get together with all the neighboring packs. Maybe you could take a sniff around. You never know, maybe your mate might be there?" Her face holds such hope of my future.

"Maybe Tate could go with you, have a look around." I can see Hazel visibly cringe with the Luna's deeper meaning. I don't think the Luna likes this female at her table for Sunday dinner.

"I have something to tell everyone." Tate's head snapping towards me - my words have him nervous. "I want everyone to understand this because I'm only saying this once. I won't talk about it again." My mother and father are looking at each other with concerned looks on their faces. I don't usually talk at dinner, so this has them paying attention. "I met my mate already, and I was rejected." The lie feels so thick coming off my tongue. I just can't have my mother always hoping that whenever I go out, I might find my mate. I need to just crush her hopes now instead of letting them bloom for the years to come. I keep my head up and shoulders back, trying to stop the shaking of my body. "My mate has obligations to the pack. I was made aware that

we have no future together, for me to move on with someone else."

"Tommie, maybe if we talk with the Alpha of her pack, they could talk to her."

Shaking my head no, my next words will be the nail in the coffin. "She's raising the Alpha's pups with the Alpha of her pack. She made it clear, no matter what, she will not leave those pups who call her mother. That she's raising them like her own, she won't abandon them. She's in love with him and their family they have together. She knew this day would come, she knew how hard it would be for me. She's in love, and I should move on with my life because I have no room in hers. She begged me to just walk away, and that's what I did. I won't stand in her way to the life she wants to live. I accepted it." It's then I feel the weight of my words. A tear comes down my face. My breath is hitching in my throat.

Tate's head is down, not looking in my direction.

"I would appreciate it if we never talk about this again." I try to clear my throat with the cry that's stuck inside it.

Even Hazel has tears dripping from her eyes. My mother's openly weeping now, my father holding her more closely.

The Luna and Alpha are looking at me as if my mate died.

Getting up, I leave the silent table taking the stairs two at the time. Shutting the door quietly, going into my top drawer, relighting a half-burnt blunt. I inhale the smoke with shaky hands. Looking out the open window, no one comes to check on me, no knock on the door.

It's just me again. Alone in my bedroom. Just taking in air.

Chapter 9

Tate.

Days fold into each other, weeks have passed and Tommie continues to avoid me, never looking me in the *eyes*.

He keeps his door open but never looks up when I pass by. I want to look at his eyes, I want to sit on the side of his bed and let him know that it's going to be *alright*.

Hazel told everyone about Tommie and his mate. They look at him differently now, they give him the same look they give me - *pity*.

Addie came over the next day, after he was done with work, waiting for him on the porch to get home. She made him some brownies with crushed walnuts on the top. I told her I would give them to him but she refused to hand the dessert over. Instead, she clutched them in her fingers waiting for the truck to pull into his spot.

Out of the corner of my eye, I could see both our mothers looking out of the window with smiles on their faces.

Watching the Tommie and Addie show.

He was surprised she was here, touching his head with his hand in nervousness. Loosening the tie around his neck, undoing the first button of his shirt collar, stretching the material with his finger as if it had been choking him all day.

For work he dresses professionally, appropriate. Suits always form-fitting and leaving the imagination running with what's underneath material that was tailored *just* for his body.

Immaculately imperfect; that's who he is.

Addie and Tommie stayed outside for a long time while they talked. Her hand going against his heart at times while his head hangs low, feeding her his side of the made up story. Addie stayed for dinner at his mother's insistence - sitting in the spot that was always left open because Tommie *never* brought anyone home for dinner. The whole time I had to sit and watch as they all fawned over Addie, even his father complementing her on her brownies which brought a blush to her face, her hand brushing the praise away as if she just didn't know how to take a compliment; embarrassed with nice words thrown her way.

She's a respectable candidate for the future Beta. They always liked Addie - even as a tiny pup she was likable - too bad she never felt the same way about herself. After dinner, watching them out the window while he walks her to the end of the driveway, they high-five before walking away in different directions.

He's wearing a *true smile* walking back to the house, it's the first time seeing this since before our shift.

It falls off his face instantly as he steps back inside.

Tommie always seems to be sitting on his bed listening to music, blocking out the world, the weed emptying his eyes. Dull and unfocused; that's how he's been living his life since he came back.

Tonight, he's just sitting on his bed, strumming his guitar, playing songs I know and waiting for me to finish up with my grooming.

"You ready?" Saying this has those thick fingers of his just hovering over the strings of the guitar not making another sound. He stops playing, looking up at me and holding my eyes for just a second more than *comfortable*. Looking away, I hear him stand to put the guitar on his soft mattress.

"I'm ready," Tommie says, while reaching into his top drawer. Grabbing the baggie with papers, he looks at it for a minute before putting it into his jean pocket. Taking his wallet, looking inside it, he pulls out a few bills before shoving them into his other pocket. *"I'm ready."* Tommie saying it more to himself while the corner of his mouth lifts up into a half lopsided smile, one that looks like he's not enthused to be going to this get-together tonight.

Our mothers found out that there will be three available females that they want us to check out. Out of *hundreds* of females - only three there are approachable.

We were told that we were to bring Hazel and Addie with us, so that they could sniff at the one male that's available for them. Out of hundreds and hundreds of wolves, these two females have *one* male wolf to look at.

"You play good, Tommie. I've always wanted to learn."

A corner-mouth smile tugs his lip upwards. "I could teach you if you want?"

The way he says it - as if it's no big deal. I can't see the harm in his offer. "Okay, that sounds good." Trying to sound and act casual, but he makes me feel anything but. "That's what you're wearing?"

Tommie looks as if he rolled out of bed yesterday. Faded grey t-shirt that fits him snugly, but not obscenely tight, lets everyone know that he has definition underneath if one were to want to pull his shirt off of him. Jeans that are old, worn threadbare in parts. All I would have to do is put my fingers on the thin material just above his knee and I'd be able to feel his skin. Black, faded converse, fraying at the

edges complete his outfit. Giving the impression that he just doesn't care what he looks like or what people will say about him. Putting a baseball cap on, little curls of hair peek out from the bottom, barely visible.

"What?" He looks down at himself, checking his outfit out.

"Nothing, lets go. We're already late. The females are waiting for us to pick them up."

Tommie follows me down the stairs. I can feel his breath touch the skin of my neck, before spreading over my back. It wants to curl around me, into my nose, breathing in his scent.

This is hard being so close to him.

"You have fun tonight." Our mothers meet us at the door.

"Tate, you look so nice tonight." His mother is always so nice to me. "Tommie, really? That's what you're wearing? You're suppose to make a good impression, not look like you don't care." His mother's tone is disbelief.

"I don't care, Mom - that's the thing. I don't care what they think of me."

Walking out the door, brushing against me as he does so. He's waiting for me to open the doors so he can get into the truck. It's the first time he's in my vehicle, it's the first time I get to take him for a *ride*.

Unlocking the doors, Tommie slides himself in. With the turn of the engine, his fingers start to play with the stations of the radio until he finds something he likes. Messing with all my pre-programmed stations. Pulling away from the house all that I can smell is him - all that's inside this cab of the truck is him and me.

Tommie sits with his legs spread, tapping his fingers on his inner thigh to the beat of the rhythm. His head and shoulders moving to the song's melody. Looking sideways at me he asks, "Do you mind if I smoke one?"

"I mind, I don't want to be smelling like that walking into the party. Lots of different packs will be there. We have to make an impression."

He's quiet looking out the window, his hand stops tapping his thighs. He looks frustrated.

"When we get Hazel, you can burn one with her - outside." That cheers him up slightly.

"Listen, Tommie, I know this is hard for you." Trying to start out with what really needs to be said in the silence.

"You don't know how hard it is, Tate, don't pretend you know because you don't." His voice changes, turning accusing, slightly *bitter*, his body angling away from me, looking out the passenger side window.

"You don't think I know? I do." My turn to throw my *bitterness* out for him to taste. Pulling the truck to the side of the road, putting it into park, I turn my body towards him. He still doesn't look at me. Putting my hand on his thigh, he takes a deep breath in. "Tommie, look at me."

It's slow motion; the way his shoulders turn towards me, the way his head follows. I can't help the way my eyes train on his lips.

The heat of his thigh seeping into the palm of my hand.

Questioning my *beliefs* in this moment. "It's just as hard for me, Tommie, even though it seems like I don't care, I do." His hand is on my hand now, the palm traveling to my arm

with the hand resting on his thigh. It travels up my forearm, to my bicep, feeling over my triceps.

It's a touch of a magnet; impossible to pull my arm away from his hand. It rests for a brief minute on my shoulder before it touches my neck in a way that has my muscles quivering. Fingers brushing my ear before wrapping behind my head. This is okay - because it's just him touching me. It's just his hand on me, nothing more will happen.

Leaning into me, mouth almost touching my ear. "You have no idea how hard it is for me." He pulls himself away, looking towards the window.

I don't say anything back to him. Instead, I start to drive to Hazel's house.

Tommie jumps out of the truck before it's in park, lighting a half-burnt one back up. Hazel approaches with a giant smile on her face, she's dressed just like Tommie except her outfit is tight, showing males all her curves - everything she has to offer. Hair loose, the sun loves her skin as it's kissed all golden, face framed in dark freckles making her look young and innocent. But we all know better than that.

Today, her eyes are more brown with just the faintest of green flakes to be seen.

Bewitching - if you were into that sort of thing.

Tommie just gives her a once over, not impressed with what she's presenting. Taking the stick from his hand, she inhales long, savoring the taste. Leaning up against the truck, looking at Tommie but not saying a word, she doesn't give the stick back. Instead, he has to take it away from her.

"Hazel?"

"Yes, Tommie?" The smoke blows out her mouth up into the air.

"Have you been touching my stuff?"

"Me? Not me, Tommie." She looks him in the eyes, not flinching. She is the best liar I know.

He holds her stare looking at her face; looking for something. "Your eyes look pretty today, Hazel." He says it out of nowhere.

"My eyes? I never thought of you as someone who likes eyes, Tommie, I pegged you more for an ass man."

The smoke he was holding coughs out. She takes the opportunity to take the stick out of his hand, inhaling longer than last time. The weed starting to make her lids half open, matching the way Tommie's lids are.

"You're right, Hazel, I am an ass man. I like a firm, tight ass. I like it to have good tone." He looks down making a big show of what he's staring at. "That's why I complimented your eyes, not your ass."

"Tommie, not nice. I never had a complaint about my ass."

Tommie looks at me now. "They lie to you, Hazel." He takes the stick out of her hand, inhaling on it again. Holding it in his lungs. He looks sexy standing there in his ball cap smoking, pissing off Hazel. "Let's go get Addie."

"She's coming? I thought it would be just the three of us." Hazel already has a pout on her lips.

"I invited her," Tommie says, while he puts the rest of the weed in his mouth swallowing the roach down, "After

you." Tommie holding the door open for Hazel to jump in, smacking her ass. "See, look at it shake when I hit it. Not tight at all."

"Tommie, that hurt." She says it while sitting down in the seat.

"Hazel, if you touch my stuff again, that little tap will be nothing like the way I'll make it hurt. That's your final warning. Trust me, Hazel, I can make it hurt real bad."

His teeth descend showing male canine that has me squirming in my pants. I think she is just as turned on with the red that's creeping on her neck, turning her cheeks crimson. For once she doesn't say anything back. Tommie jumps out of the truck once we make it to Addie's brother's house. He knocks on the door waiting for it to open.

"Do you think I have a nice ass?" She's just staring at the front door of the house, her voice is slightly off.

"Hazel, you have a nice ass he's just upset with you because you're stealing his *stuff*."

She doesn't look like she believes me. Addie's brother answers the door looking Tommie up and down, standing,

blocking the entrance with his body. Tommie steps close to him saying something low. Addie slides around her brother's body, pushing him back inside. Tommie says something else that has her brother taking a step towards him. Addie grabs Tommie by the hand pulling him away, while Tommie is looking back at her brother, before his attention swings back towards Addie. He smiles sweetly at her, brushing her bangs out of her eyes. Giving her a satisfied once over.

Addie's dressed nice, nothing too tight, everything very respectful, but nothing that catches or holds the eye.

Forgettable.

Opening the door for her so that she can come inside, Tommie closes it behind her before he comes to the other side and sits behind me in the back seat. He touches my shoulder, leaning in, "Let's go."

"How are you, Addie?"

She has her eyes on him, looking at Tommie who's watching me when I look in the rear view mirror. I contemplate switching the angle on the mirror, but I can't bring myself to change the *view.*

"I'm good, Tate, you?"

"I'm good, sorry for running late."

"That's okay, my brother just got home anyways. I wouldn't have been able to leave - I was watching my nieces for them."

"Didn't you tell him what time we were picking you up?" Tommie sounds mad.

"I told him." Her voice drops lower.

"You're always watching your nieces for them, they have parents."

"I don't mind, I love them, it's not like it's a burden."

"Yeah, but don't you feel like sometimes they're using you?"

I can even feel how uncomfortable Addie is with his words.

"No, Tommie, I don't feel used." Her head hangs down.

"Sorry, Addie, I didn't mean to sound that way. It's just you're young, you should be going out having fun not stuck in a house full of pups pretending to be their parent."

"Sometimes it's nice pretending." She looks into his eyes, and Hazel takes a deep breath in, rolling the window down lighting her own hand rolled.

"I knew it!" Tommie reaching over the seat towards Hazel, trying to grab his joint from her. His body coming over the seat aggressively.

"Tommie, stop!" One hand on the steering wheel, the other hand trying to shove him away from Hazel who's laughing at him. Her laugh isn't nice - it's mocking him.

My hand on his stomach that's flexed with the position he's in - I can't help feeling the muscles, my finger brushing the band of his boxers that are just barely above the denim material.

He stills.

No movement, a little groan comes out his mouth, very faint to the ears.

My finger just barely brushing his zipper while pushing him away. He sits back down in his seat looking flushed.

Taking deep breaths in.

I have to keep my eyes open, but I want to close them with the way his skin feels underneath my hand.

"Don't be so mad, Tommie, I'll share with you," Hazel says so nicely to him as if she's doing him a favor.

"Hazel, I'm going to make you never touch my stuff again. Do you understand this?" He's leaning into her ear, and she's shivering for some reason. "I'm going teach you that you don't touch someone else's *property*." Leaning back into his seat, he watches her spark it up.

"Promises, promises. I'm not sure you have a good enough follow through to teach any lesson that's worth remembering, Tommie." She doesn't pass when she inhales instead she hoards the smoke all for herself. The ride is a lot longer than it seems.

None of us are talking anymore, Tommie growling on occasion as he watches her smoke the whole thing, popping the roach in her mouth and swallowing it down with a sly

smile on her face. She looks into Tommie's eyes, challenging him to do something.

"Thanks again for inviting me out with you." Addie's voice breaks the tension.

A delicate hand placed on his shoulder that I'm having a hard time looking away from. It's hard keeping one eye on the road and the other eye on her hand that is now drawing the tiniest little circles on the material of his thin shirt. She actually leans in, smelling his shirt, before pulling away embarrassed. He looks at her finger, at her eyes, and he smiles. And I watch Addie, seeing her eyes brighten, looking at Tommie, looking at *my Tommie*.

Parking the car, most of the mate-less members of our pack are already inside, mingling, sniffing around for their prospect.

"What does everyone want to drink? First round on me." Tommie takes out a crumpled bill from his pocket.

"Whiskey and coke, make mine a double," Hazel calls out, already scoping out the scene.

Sweaty bodies on the dance floor, music vibrating my own chest. "I'll take a beer."

Addie's the next to respond. "I'll take a beer."

He walks away, getting our drinks from the bar that's packed, leaving Addie and I to find a seat.

"So, you like Tommie?" I can't help wanting to know. A small amount of jealousy I have to control while sitting this close to a female who could give him things I can't.

"He's nice." She doesn't give much away.

"He is, but you never answered the question."

"He's not him." Her brightness has left her face, replaced with a grief that I knew nothing about before. Her jaw clenches, a little tiny vibration in her cheek. "I need to go to the bathroom."

Standing, she leaves the table as Tommie approaches setting several cups of whiskey down. He hands me my beer, the tip of his finger touches mine. Slowly he pulls his finger away, letting it caress my skin before tipping his glass

to his mouth and draining it in a few swallows, going for the next. Hazel comes back with a scowl on her face.

"What's wrong?"

She points in the direction of a wolf who's leaning against the wall in the far corner, a scowl on his face, tipping a beer to his lips. He looks as if he's homeless. Uninterested in his surroundings. "That's who's mate died, look at him, he's a mess. That's who your mom told me about. That I should keep an open mind for. I think your mom hates me, Tate." Sitting down she takes two cups for herself, drinking both down faster than Tommie did his first.

"He probably has a great personality, Hazel, just your type." Tommie leans down into her ear before he takes the next cup of whiskey, draining it down.

"Your round, Hazel, make mine triples. I want four if I have to be here for this." He sits down beside me, not touching but almost touching. His thigh could brush against mine if I just move a fraction of an inch.

"Tommie!"

An excited male voice has Tommie turning his half drunk head in the direction the sound is coming from. "Carson." A giant smile spreads across my males face. They give a hug to one another before pulling apart. "How are you?" Tommie seems interested in his answer.

"Good, yourself?"

This wolf's eyes are not looking around, just focused on Tommie. I'm not liking this vibe and I'm not really sure why, but I don't like this wolf for some reason.

"I'm good, it's nice to see you again, Carson. Tate, this is Carson, he went to school with me, this is Addie and Hazel."

Introductions made - preliminaries of meeting new wolves. Standing up so I can stretch myself to my full height, before approaching this male. He shakes my hand the human way before looking at the females, bowing slightly without touching either one of them.

"Wait, Hazel and Addie?" Looking with a smile, "Cash come here." That male that's been leaning against the wall grits his teeth with having been called to come forward. "That's my brother Cash, my mother told me if I was to meet you females first I was to introduce you to my brother."

He takes his slow time coming, putting his finished beer on a table full of wolves before approaching a younger wolf, taking his beer out of his hand saying, "Thanks, Crane," patting his shaved head with a large hand before the younger wolf smacks it away.

"Cash, this is Tommie - I went to school with him, Addie and Hazel." He turns to me but forgets my name I can see it in his eyes.

"Tate." Putting my hand out to this wolf who's grip is firm and focused. I give him my grip back, looking at each other before he looks away towards the females.

Eyes falling on and off Addie quickly, she has a soft, welcoming smile waiting for him if he would have lingered on her face, but he doesn't, instead his focus is on Hazel, looking into her eyes.

Addie's smile *falters* with being dismissed without even been given a chance to say hi.

It's sad she can't hold anyone's attention except for Tommies. I don't know what holds him to her.

"Hazel, your name suits you, you have pretty eyes."

Tommie chokes on his drink, spitting it out on the floor, laughing at Hazel - he can hardly catch his breath, trying to pull a lungful of air in. Wheezing on his laughter, he says, "See, Hazel, it's all about your eyes. You need to trust me that I will always tell you the truth. Anyone else need another?" Tommie turns over his empty glass, everyone holds a drink up for him to get them another.

"I'll help you." Carson walks to the bar with him, touching his upper arm against Tommie's who looks down at it before looking at Carson with a new found interest that wasn't there before. They're talking and laughing to one another, Tommie reaching into his pocket and pulling out crumpled money, Carson says something to the bartender who just pours drinks and shots on a round serving platter without taking any money from Tommie.

Carson gets another tray full of drinks, weaving their way through the crowd without spilling the full glasses, they put it on the table. Hazel reaches with both hands, draining the first quickly before the second one makes a quick disappearance.

Cash watches this female gulp liquor like a star player for the drinking team.

I have to endure Hazel and Tommie and the rest of them all getting wasted until some popular song comes on.

"Dance with me, Tommie?" Hazel leaning into Tommie who's leaning away.

"Come on, Addie, I like this song." Taking her hand and leading her away from the table

"You like this song?" Cash looking at Hazel who's pouting slightly.

"I do."

"Then let's dance."

Putting his beer down, Carson looks all kinds of shocked. This leaves me alone with a wolf who I'm not sure I like too much.

"So, Tate, are Tommie and that female together?" Looking at how Tommie is moving the female all over the dance floor as if he owns it.

"No, he's not with anyone. Why?" Trying to control my voice.

"I might have a friend who may be interested in him if he was looking for some fun."

"He's not looking." This wolf just keeps eyeing up Tommie, and not in a way I want to witness. "What about you? Do you have anyone you're interested in?" Asking a question to this wolf who's raising my hackles up.

"Maybe."

His eyes are lingering on Tommie's movements. I can feel my hands clenching into fists underneath the table.

"See you around, Tate." Carson is saying it as if I will be seeing more of him.

"Bye." That's all I can manage to say out loud, anything more will have me shoving my fist in this strange wolf's mouth. I have to watch Tommie dancing with Addie, twisting and turning her body to the music. He's a good dancer - not afraid to show off his skills. When he's not dancing, Carson has Tommie's ear, curving into him so that Carson's body is bent slightly towards Tommie.

Hazel and that wolf have another dance before she stalks back towards the table. "He has pups - I don't screw

around with wolves that have pups." Her mood sours even more, watching Addie being lead by Tommie in the most alluring way. She drinks the rest of Tommie's glass, turning it upside down on the table.

By the end of the night, Tommie and Carson are discussing getting together in a few weeks for a camping trip. *That will never happen.*

Cash comes up saying goodbye to Hazel, nothing is thrown Addie's way, who's face once again falls, I give her back a pat. It's a quick touch before I pull my hand away. While driving back to our pack, I want to pepper Tommie with questions about this male wolf who was eyeing him up like candy, but I refrain from it. Too suspicious on my part, this has to be done without other ears around.

Dropping Addie at her house, Tommie walks her to the door, no kiss goodnight - instead a high five before he jogs back to the truck.

Hazel turning up the music, she doesn't want the party to stop, and continues to dance in the front seat, raising her hands in the air. Dropping her off, she turns to the both of

us, "Come inside, I have drinks, smokes, and anything else you might have a taste for."

Tommie opens the door, getting out and looking at me with a shrug of his shoulder as he follows her inside.

Closing my door, walking into her house, a nervousness comes over me as if my body is already understanding exactly what's going to happen.

Chapter 10

Tommie.

Hazel's place is small. Nothing grand about it - very minimalist furnishing.

Everything in here has a proper place and is extremely clean, for some reason, I thought her place would be filthy.

Turning on her stereo, I grab glasses, pouring drinks as she dances to the rhythm.

Tossing me a bag of her own weed she says, "Papers in the draw, with the scissors," over her shoulder as she kisses Tate when he enters the house.

No looking around the house for him; he knows this place very well. Tate makes himself comfortable on the couch, on the opposite end to where I'm sitting, watching me roll with expert hands - I think I can even do it with my eyes closed if I wanted to.

Lighting a few candles, Hazel turns off the lights, our faces suddenly thrown in shadows of flame. The flickers seduce in a glow, dancing on our bodies. The music a haunting vibration of sound. When she hands me my glass, her fingers linger on mine for a moment longer than she should.

Her eyes find mine, teeth pulling her bottom lip. Yet she sits beside Tate, her side pressed up against his. Bringing his glass to his lips, the ice hits the sides before the first touch of amber slowly makes its way down his throat.

He's looking at me the whole time, and I can't look away from him.

Taking a drink of my own, its heat licking the side of my tongue, it's expensive quality - smooth but very *dangerous*.

"Do you remember the time we kissed, Tommie?" Her honeyed eyes look at me in the shadowed light. She drinks her dark amber down, finishing her glass before us, putting it on the coffee table.

"I remember it." Holding the stick between my lips.

Lighting.

Inhaling.

Relaxing.

Reaching out, giving her the rolled perfection to take her pleasure from. "You laughed at me, do you remember that, *Hazel*. The first girl I ever kissed and you laughed at me."

"I'm sure you're better now." Inhaling it, she's looking at me how I look at Tate; needful, eyes wandering in pleasure.

"I am." Saying it while her hunger starts to grow, eyes screaming what she wants as she's looking down between

my legs. "If you weren't Tates, I could show you what I've learned." Smiling at her while I blow the smoke out.

Tate takes the joint from her, inhaling longer than us, filling his lungs before he passes it back to Hazel. Her lips going around the end gently, making sure not to get it too wet before taking another long drag and inhaling hard

The movement of her body towards me is a slow crawl. Music swaying her hips, even though she's on hands and knees. A female who thinks herself a Master - just playing with a toy. Unfortunately for her, she's going to be taught a few hard lessons of her own.

"We have an agreement; he's not mine and I'm not his." Her lips touch my ears, nose against my jaw line, tracing its edges.

Whiskey jaded eyes catch the candles light, dancing flames stare back at me.

"Can I touch her?" I look at Tate for permission.

"Isn't that why we're here?" He takes another sip from his glass before finishing it in one long pull. Fingers wrapping around the bottle and pouring himself another.

Getting close to my lips, Hazel blows the smoke into my lungs. Taking it all, my lips press lightly on hers, tongue gently licking hers before pulling away. She smiles with the realization that at least I know how to kiss now.

That will be the last time my lips touch hers. A drunken promise made to myself.

Getting off the couch, she turns the music up so we can feel the percussion in our chest, the noise deafening the sound of breathing.

Her lids are just like ours - half open.

The song is slow and gentle, the way she moves is a story about seduction, hips weaving and curving.

Smoke creating a hazy film over eyes that are relaxed. Sinking into the cushion, finishing my drink, while watching Hazel toss her hair and arch her back. A sultry swirl of the lower body.

Feminine Seduction.

Body warming on the inside, while a trail of heat burns my skin where Tate is looking. Turning my head towards

him, his glass is at his lips finishing taking another drink, the liquid at the ice line now.

He has a controlled look to him; no nervousness, just watching me watch Hazel. Touching my head with an awkwardness that just came over me all of a sudden, the corner of his mouth lifts as if he saw something he liked.

Another smooth song that takes over from the last has my own shoulders and neck bounce with the beat. Fingers starting from my elbow, walking down my forearms, entwining my hand, trying to pull me up to a standing position.

"Dance with me, Tommie, you didn't dance with me all night." She takes my hat off, running her fingers through my hair, messing it up. "You need a haircut," Whispering in my ear, teeth pulling on the lobe while her hand is touching my thigh. The feeling of eyes burning into the spots that Hazel's hand is touching. Her chest brushing against my shoulder as she leans down over my body. "Dance with me." Again trying to pull me up from my sitting position.

Relenting I give into her.

Whiskey courage.

He's smoking the rest of the weed while watching us dance. Hips pressing against hips, hands on her flesh, on her waist, guiding her rhythm the way I want her to move. My shirt raising when her hands touch my bare chest, while we dance as one movement, letting the music take us away. "I'm taking this off," Saying this while looking Hazel in the eyes. Without question, her arms slowly raise, letting the shirt lift off her body, exposing black lace that my eyes appreciate. Hardened peaks barely visible through the material.

She's a beautiful female, with all the qualities a male would love. If you were *that* way.

Still swaying with the music, my thumb brushes against one nipple. She closes her eyes with a soft moan.

"Take off your shirt."

I do what she wants, reaching over my head and pulling it up and off. Now it's her thumb brushing against my nipple before her tongue swipes at it playfully.

Nipping at my skin.

While she explores my flesh with her mouth, Tate watches, legs spread slightly apart on the couch.

She's starting to kiss the hollow of my neck where her tiptoe height will allow. Her hips pushing against mine with her closeness. I can't hide my excitement from her.

"Do you want to fuck her, Tommie?" Tate's eyes touch to mine. The way he says my name is low, deep vibrations in his low based tone.

A hand on my zipper, not pulling it down, but feeling me through the material, Hazel gives me her appreciative murmur of approval with what I have inside my jeans.

"I am going to fuck her, Tate." Watching him carefully, fully engrossed in his reaction to me. Unable to hide the sound of my own pleasure as Hazel's hand rubs me through material that I have every intention of taking off soon. Bending my head down, licking her shoulder while my eyes are on him. Fingers start to trace down the points in her spine.

With a exhaled breath out, he slowly gets up from the couch, making his way towards us. A powerful male that commands eyes on him and my gaze surrenders to the beast - loving the sight of him turned on. "Do you like having

Tommie touch you?" Pulling her hair firmly but not to hurt, because no grimace is on her face - only pleasure.

Her chin angles to the ceiling when it's his turn to trace his tongue over the spot I just licked. Pressed up firmly behind her, the strap of her bra lowers with a fingertip pushing it down. Her eyes are closed, goosebumps on flesh. His eyes hold mine while the next strap is lowered down. Chest heaving with her breath that's becoming shorter, more excited.

Lust swirling in the air, it's thick with a sweet taste that lingers on the tip of your tongue.

It feels good not to hide what his closeness does to me.

Taking her hand, he leads the way towards the bedroom. Eyes reflecting the light of the single candle that's lit on the dresser. It's been burning a long time with the amount of wax that's liquefied in the see-through container.

Music still playing, just more softly, we can now hear each other breathing, little gasps of sound coming from Hazel's mouth as he removes her bra. Dipping his head low, he takes a nipple in his mouth, tongue flicking over the end.

He knows her body well.

Hazel's hands pull his shirt off of him. Exposing his chest to me - even in the soft glow of the single candle, I can see the flexing and rippling of muscles that scream to be touched.

Watching his palm gliding up the curve of her back before tangling in her hair. *I want it to be me that he's touching.*

My turn to come close to her, pressing myself against her backside. Hands on hips, she rocks herself into my hardness. Stimulating me with the gentle roll of her body.

Grinding.

Pressing.

Enticing.

She's very aware of what she's doing to me. With a little whimper from my mouth, she presses her ass harder into my hips, grinding in slow-motion crazy.

His hand is holding her hair high above her head, exposing the long line of her neck. I suck on her flesh,

leaving my mark on her - one that says *I was here*. I can feel her melting in this moment, legs shaking. For right now, it's all about Hazel, hands roaming her body, nibbling her earlobes. Kisses trailing down her spine, paying special attention to every bone, between each gap in her ribs.

She is the center of our attention.

Every female wants to feel like a princess, and that's how we're treating her; like the special female she is.

Fingers are not fumbling with the zipper - I let it go down slow, not rushing this. A digit slides into her underwear line, pressing, not caressing. Just a pressure letting her understand I know exactly where to touch her. A gasp of breath from her, when Tate's fingers meet mine.

His is the desire to please as it starts to rub her in little circles. Taking my hand away from her center, I pull her jeans down, taking her underwear with them. While my head is low, I decide to lick her while he's making her moan. My tongue's tasting, sweeping against her while gliding along his finger that's stopped moving. Letting my tongue run the length of his finger from nail bed to knuckle, before running back up to his finger tip. Again I lick his finger from

tip to bottom, before putting it all in my mouth, allowing my teeth to gently scrape against the edges, pulling away to look at him as his finger comes out of my mouth, licking my lips at the taste.

His teeth are descending slightly, heartbeat rapidly increasing.

Her hands are entwined in his hair, pulling Tate towards her waiting mouth. Kissing deeply, tongue's tasting each other. He's looking at me the entire time while she's in heaven with hands.

Touching.

Caressing.

Grabbing.

Needful flesh.

Hazel's expert hands finding my button, opening my jeans up and exposing my boxer line. Heat from eyes that aren't looking away from what she's releasing.

"I want to see you, Tommie." Hazel's low voice full of her lust breaks the rhythm of our breathing.

Pulling away slightly, I let my jeans fall from my body with just a slight pull down. Stepping out of them, I'm left in boxers that are tight on my thighs. The material too confining, restrictive.

Her eyes are glued on my prize, while I watch him watching me.

Thumbs are hooking just on the inside of the material, pulling them down, revealing what I have for her - for him if he would let me.

When her hand grips me strong and sure, I know she's a master.

"Your turn, Tate." Her face turning towards him, I can't look away from this show.

She's still got me in her hand, up and down, slow, long strokes that are making my legs quiver in her grip. He starts with his zipper - pulling it down, while her thumb rubs the tip of me each time she strokes upwards. His pants are falling, pooling at his feet before he steps out of them.

Kissing her neck, watching Tate take the very last of his clothing off between the three of us.

Even if I wanted to, there is no way from pulling my sight away from my mate's naked form, full grown Alpha male who's thick, hard and so excited.

She continues with her expert assault on me, her up and down motion that has my legs starting to flex and shake. Having to take her hand away from me because I want to explode at this moment with the sight of him. A full grown male in all aspects of the word.

Hard but smooth; he's trimmed well. Nothing messy about him.

"On the bed, Hazel."

She obeys his voice instantly as if she's used to his demands. Pulling me with her by the hand. Tossing the pillows up the bed, she sits me down first, high up on the pillows while she kneels in front of me. Licking me from the base to the tip, she glides her tongue back down inch by slow inch. Eyes are almost closing with the sensation of his gaze on my body and her tongue teasing me.

"Open up, Hazel." Tapping her on the hinge of her jaw so that she can accommodate me. Looking up with my head just between her lips, she gives me a slight smile before descending to a few inches from the base - no gag reflex with this female.

Hands in her hair, guiding her motion up and down, my legs spread while I watch Tate as he watches her mouth please me.

Tate starts kissing down her body, pulling her legs apart, opening her wider, slipping a finger inside. Another hard moan vibrating against my shaft that's in her wet mouth. Once his tongue starts to taste her, she almost stops pleasing me.

"Concentrate, Hazel," I admonish, keeping her focused on the job in front of her, not what's happening behind her.

Her cheeks are dimpling, providing suction like she's a skilled tradesman. Her tongue running up and down the sensitive underside of my shaft, licking away the clear liquid that's leaking out, her free hand in Tate's hair, playing with it.

Feeling the rise of my release, not wanting to end this prematurely, I have to slide myself out of her wet mouth with a groan. My body is sliding down on the bed, touching Tate's. My thighs at his head level while I take her hard nipple in my mouth, sucking on it before going to the other one, biting gently with teeth that are trying to descend.

My mate only a few glorious inches away from me.

His hand now on my bare thigh, his palm pressing into me before he takes it away. His body now shimmying upwards to her other raised peak, both our hands are between her legs as her hips move in a motion of their own.

Moans filling the room with her falsetto voice.

Her body trembling so bad, as our fingers are in every hole, stretching her, pleasing her, filling her up.

Her body stills and I can see the curling of her toes, even with my two fingers buried deeply in her ass I can feel the spasms of her inner core. A rush of scent is coming off her, saturating the air in a female's pleasing smell.

It still isn't as powerful as his aroused smell.

"What do you want from us, Hazel?" Tate asks, up at her lips, kissing her, while I run my palm along the side of him.

He closes his eyes with a moan while I press myself into the side of Hazel.

"I want the both of you inside me."

Her wish is our command. Picking her up, so she's on hands and knees, I enter her from behind slowly. She's tight, lubricated with her own body's arousal. My finger on her other hole, just rubbing around the outer edge.

Hips are falling in love with hips.

Meeting my thrusts, bending her head low, watching as she grabs Tate's shaft at the base while he guides himself into her mouth, thrusting himself into her while I rock her body from behind.

She's in rhythm with my motion.

A finger in her other opening makes her moan low and deep, almost a whimper quality to it.

A Growl coming out of her chest and Tate's eyes find mine as he thrusts himself more. Wishing it was me, he was thrusting into.

Can he see my desire for him?

Back and forth we switch positions in fear that we might go too early.

Her ass so used to my fingers that have been stretching, she pushes herself more on them, trying to get more inside herself. Pulling out of her wet entrance, I position to enter her other hole. Holding myself at the base, I put firm pressure at her opening. Her moans are slowing down slightly, breathing becoming more focused with the strain she is feeling.

"Relax, Hazel." My voice is low in her ear as I open her up inch by inch. Kissing her neck the entire time, my fingers circling the sensitive swollen area between her legs, making her shudder underneath my touch.

She doesn't let Tate slip out from her mouth, she just holds herself still before she can move slowly over the length of me. It's not long before I feel her move her hips back and

forth, comfortable with the new feeling of being stretched to fit me inside her.

In and almost out before going back inside to the base. Back and forth motion has her sounding out her uncomfortable pleasurable pain.

The night rolls on to its final stages, our princess being fully satisfied many times over. Pulling out from behind her now fully used ass, I pick Hazel up, while Tate's rock-hard shaft falls from her mouth. Laying on his back, it takes all my control not to slip it through my own lips,.

Turning Hazel to face me, I put her on Tate's lap as he slides comfortably back inside her ass. She starts to ride him looking at me - mouth half open, eyes fully saturated in her pleasures. Pushing her down, so she's laying flat on top of Tate, he kisses her neck, hands roaming all over her body. Holding her legs wide apart, I watch as he thrusts himself into her, all the way to the base before coming out to push himself back in.

Getting closer towards her entrance, she looks at me for just a moment while I wait for consent to enter. A slight nod is all it takes.

Without fear now of causing her pain, I enter her as deep as I can. Her hand pressing on my chest for just a moment. I can feel him inside her through the little membrane that separates her two holes. His strokes shortening with the way Hazel's body is tensing up.

A hesitant whimper comes from her throat, but the feeling this is giving me is too much.

It's not about Hazel anymore, my need to be gentle is over with the feeling of him against me.

Tate's strong fingers grip into my hips, pulling me into her. His nails digging into my flesh, poking through skin.

There is no need to disguise the moan, it's loud and long. Kissing her neck, his lips are so close.

Sucking and pulling skin into my mouth, trailing kisses over her collarbone. His mouth on the same spots I was just on, pulling the trail of my kisses into his mouth.

She peaks again while the both of us are buried so deeply inside her.

Both our bodies rocking into hers.

The strength of two fully grown male wolves taking her at the same time is causing whimpers of pain, of pleasure, to tumble out of her mouth.

We're pounding into her; this is our moment now.

Between Tate and me, nails embedded into my hips pulling me into her, and I imagine it's him I'm trusting into. She's holding onto my shoulders, head on my chest as the both of us tense up, our moaning becoming more pronounced as we start spilling ourselves to coat the inside of her.

Both eyes locked on the others, dilated slightly, even our breath is held in our lungs while the waves course through us. He's so close, my fingers on his jawline, holding his face in my hands while my essence is pouring out in deep spasms from my body. I can feel him jerking inside her, twitching as his pulse races underneath my finger pressed to his neck.

Taking a deep breath as the pleasure starts to become manageable, he licks his lips, looking at mine that are inches away from him.

Hazel still tucked in between our sweaty bodies.

Slowly.

Tentatively.

Dreamlike.

A gasp from his mouth when placing my trembling lips on his, so soft, without trying to scare him away.

This one honest touch between us stirs my soul.

Renewed pleasure builds inside me.

My hand wraps around the back of his neck, pulling him into me, my tongue traces his lips and I rock myself inside her again.

With a surprise, he parts his lips, letting my tongue inside.

The barest moan slips out for me to taste.

This is our moment, for just a moment.

Before having to pulling away fast once we feel her moving between us. Looking down at Hazel, I face his lie as he looks at me.

Facing his ugly truth.

Chapter 11

Tate.

Sunday morning quiet. Nothing but the soft, gentle breathing of both their bodies pressed in close to mine. Hazel tucked in tight, her leg over the top of my stomach, her face against my ribs. Tommie's arm flung over the top of my chest, head on my arm that's slightly numb with his weight. A leg is thrown over Hazel's waist resting on my

hip. He's almost laying over top of her, as If trying to get close to me in his sleep.

With an unsteady hand reaching out, the tip of my finger traces his cheek, the rise of his lip line.

The temptation of him is bending my lines.

Tommie leans into it, a sigh escaping his mouth before stirring awake. His hair is messy, so I brush the strands away from his eyes. I want to see those eyes. Visions of last night are coming back to me - it's just something about the way he moved, the way our eyes locked together. A natural instinct wants me to pull him in tighter to me but Hazel is blocking his body from mine.

The rush of that one kiss stirs something that's on a basic level of chemical need.

Hazel's waking up. My hand has to pull away from Tommie, looking down at her, kissing her forehead. Looking back at him, saddened eyes watch the spot I just kissed. He can't cover up his emotions so he chooses to look away.

Hazel smiles up at me. In the dawn's early morning light, without her put-on face, she looks real with smooth, fragile skin, eyes that aren't hazy with the dope she smokes.

"Go back to sleep," Hazel mumbles tired words into my side, head nuzzling back into me.

When I look at Tommie's eyes, they hold a hopelessness in them; a defeat.

"I should go." The flatness of his tone just sounds so empty.

Hazel reaches behind her pulling him closer into her naked body. "Stay, Tommie."

She tries to turn her head to look at him but he's out of bed already, looking for wrinkled clothes on the floor. His bare ass facing me while pulling up his boxers. He looks as if he can't wait to get out of here.

"Are you alright, Tommie?" I can't hide the concern in my voice.

He doesn't look at me while doing the button up of his jeans. "I'm fine. I'm just going to walk home. You two," A

crack in his voice hurts my ears, "Enjoy your day." He flings the last words out, leaving the room.

The front door slams shut, while Hazel has a confused look on her face. "What's his problem?"

"I don't know." Trying really hard to sound as if I *don't* know. "How was your night, Hazel, did you enjoy yourself?" Trying to deflect her question.

"I did." Her body rolls on top of mine, her lips kissing down my neck.

I've been hard for a while now, she must think it's because of her. Reaching between my legs, she slides herself down my shaft with a small hum. Both of us make a little groan when pushing deeper inside her as she squeezes around me. Eyes closing. Slowly, lazily stirring ourselves awake. Unhurried rise and fall between her thighs, her hips starting to lower with the rise of mine. Pushing more of me into her. "Are you sore?" Asking before the softness of this turns more intense.

"Not really." An exhaled answer.

Fingers now dig into the fleshy part of her ass, pulling her down hard on top of me. Another upward thrust has a gasp come out of her mouth. This won't take long; the smell of him is everywhere. She straddles my groin, letting me see her chest bounce with each roll of my hips. Breathing deeper, the feeling intensifies. Becoming more pleasurable, her back arching, head thrown back, hair on my thighs swinging wildly now. Each movement of our bodies bringing me closer. Her throat composing sounds of pleasure, while I continue to pound at her flesh the way she likes.

The more pain, the more pleasure it brings her.

Claws sink into the soft flesh of her inner thighs, drawing out little beads of blood that my lines make. Her clenching rhythm from within tells me I can't let go.

Growling pleasure intensifies, muscles tensing up. In the seconds before I pump myself into her, it's not me inside *her* but in *his* ass; a primal, honest drive into him. I almost call out his name as the first streams erupt out. Holding her there, letting the spasms subside before trying to pull out.

"Don't get out of me, stay inside."

She likes when I just hold her like this. Cheek on my chest, her arms laying limp at her side. "Why don't you like to me to get out of you, Hazel?" Always a question I wondered about.

"I like the fullness of having someone inside me, when you get out of me, I just feel empty. I just don't like feeling *empty*. Does that make sense?" What's empty is her voice - hollow without real sound.

"It does, Hazel." Not wanting to ask any more questions because I can't stomach the answers to them. Closing my eyes again because it's still very early.

Stroking her hair in my hand, I keep myself inside her for as long as I can, until I hear her soft breathing again. Sleeping on me like a child that just loves to be held.

The brightness of the sun hitting my eyes makes me groan, the room slowly heating up with the heat of the coming day. Hazel still sleeping soundly. "I'm going to go." Untangling our bodies from one another.

"Shut the blinds." Her head is going underneath the pillow, blocking the light out.

Feeling hung over, the dryness in my throat doesn't leave me after several glasses of water. The ride home feels fuzzy; I'm in my fog. Walking in the front door my mother greets me with a hug, her nose scrunching up, a look of fear overcoming her for a shadow of a minute, before a hardness in her eyes take over.

"You need to wash yourself, Tate." Her hard words elevating it's pitch to sound disgusted with the way I must smell. "We have guests coming for dinner tonight, I expect you there." She gives me one of her serious looks, eyes drilling into mine. I don't have any argument for them. "When you talk to Hazel, tell her I expect her there too. It seems she has sparked an interest in a male wolf who's available to be claimed. The family wants a meet and greet - nothing official. They're also bringing a few more available wolves with them who weren't at the party for you to meet. The females can be claimed as well."

Hope. That's what is staring out from eyes that just want her son with a female.

"Mom, I told you - I'm not ready for that yet."

"Tate, you can't just live your life like this, there's so much more that you're missing out on. If you just would give a female a real chance instead of dismissing everything about them before you meet them, see who they are."

"Mom, I told you I just can't."

"It hurts me to see you this way, I can see how much pain you're in every day. You hardly smile, it's as if you're just ghosting through life." Now her lashes fill up with tears that start to drip out of eyes that love me.

But if I tell her why I'm so unhappy, then those tears are going to turn into disgust because I know how she views males likes myself; *moon-cursed*, an *abomination* of nature. My father would disown me - their love would be gone for me, and I love my parents. My world would be taken away from me the instant my mouth was to tell my secret out loud. "Mom, I'll come to dinner, I'll keep an open mind alright, I'll do it for you." Giving her a quick hug before walking up the stairs. My back bent with the secret I can't tell to anyone except Tommie - he's the only one I could talk to about this.

The bedroom door is closed tight, I can't even get a glimpse of him. I can tell he's in there because I hear the

rhythmic breathing of sleep. After showering, his door's still closed with him behind it, it's as if he's trying to shut me out. Before I can knock on his door, the knock on the front door stops me from going inside his room. Taking the stairs two at a time, my mother beats me there, opening it up wide.

Addie is standing there, a blush creeping over her face. I have to restrain the growl that's trying to work its way out of my chest.

"Hi, Luna Eva, how are you?" Her hands are wringing with nerves, why is she nervous?

"Hi, Addie." My mother's smile is full on. Pleased to see this female that I'm starting to really dislike.

"Hi, Tate." She gives me a friendly wave.

"Addie." Putting my hands in my pockets because my claws want to come out just to take a little swipe at that face of hers. She's the plainest female I have ever met. Nothing stands out about her, and I don't understand Tommie hanging around her.

"Is Tommie home?" Her voice is even just plain sounding, nothing standing out to draw interest.

"He's sleeping." Saying it quickly to her so she can just go.

"Oh, well can you tell him I was here?"

Taking the door edge in my hand, I go to shut it. "Will do, bye, Addie." My mother is giving me a look to stop being so rude.

"Tate, go wake him up. Tell him he has a visitor." She smiles at Addie, and I just want to glare at the both of them.

Dragging my feet up the step, opening his door without knocking, his pillow is over his head. He's on top of his covers, only in his boxers that stretch across his upper thighs. He smells clean as if he had a long, steaming shower before going to bed.

He scrubbed me off his skin.

"What?" He doesn't move or shift his body. His words are muffled from the pillow over his face.

"Addie's here - my mother told me to get you up."

He gives a low groan, but the pillow gets pulled from his face. He keeps his eyes closed, and I take a step towards him. He's rubbing his right side grimacing slightly. "I think my liver light's on. I can't drink like that for a while." His body is slow to sit up, feet hanging over the side of the bed while he scratches his head. A stretch of arms high in the air flexes his abs. I can't help looking at him. His back muscles are shifting like a landslide of moving flesh, rippling and flexing.

The movement of him is alluring.

Getting up he adjusts himself in his boxers, not looking at me.

"Tommie, about last night." Fingers are curling over his biceps to stop him from looking for clothes in his drawer. His whole body stills, eyes on my hands.

Electric feel of flesh that sparks against my nerve endings.

"What about last night?" Now his whole body stands straighter, his shoulders back. Waiting on me.

"I don't think that should happen again. I think that if Hazel gives the invite, you should turn her down."

His lips draw tight across his face. "Is this what you want, Tate?" Now it's his turn to curl his hand around my bicep. Pulling me against him. Palm on my flesh, fingers slightly going inside my underwear line, just past the edge. I can feel the tightening of my belly. Flushing, hot breath coming out faster. The rising of my chest, trying to control a gasp. Blood rushing in my ears, it sounds as if the tide is rushing inside of me, covering me up in our bonds depth.

His lips on my collarbone, tongue tracing its length until I feel a scrape of teeth against my neck - where his mark *could* be placed. "Should I stop, Tate?" Voice teasing, enticing my resolve. He doesn't wait for my answer, continuing with his physical assault on my body. A hand is slowly going down over my shorts, rubbing me through the thin material.

Pleasure bringer.

The first moan tumbles out with his hand working up and down in his own motion, the sensation almost too much.

"Tell me to stop and I will." Words pressed against my neck, hot, heavy, daring me to say the word.

This isn't right.

"Tommie." My mother's voice is calling up for him.

The both of us tense up before we pull away from each other, creating much-needed breathing room, I think out of the both of us I'm breathing the hardest.

Watching Tommie just grab whatever the first thing his hands land on, he does his jeans up while walking down the stairs.

"I'll do whatever I want, Tate, just remember that. I will do whoever I want to do, just like you. After all, it's expected out of me."

That earns him a rumble from my chest; the wolf is not appreciative of his little display towards me. He doesn't even flinch, instead, acting as if it never happened. I can't help but follow, watching on the step. Leaning against the wall, trying so hard not to throw death stares as Addie blushes at Tommie. My mother giving them privacy, but I don't.

"Hi, Addie, what's up." His hand is going into his hair. Why is he nervous?

"Hi, Tommie, so I was wondering if you still wanted to go with me to that festival this afternoon. I know that the band you were talking about is playing at two. So I thought if you were still interested, but I understand if you don't want to." Clearly, this is painful for her to ask him. She's all fidgety, skittish almost. She can't even look at him in the eye.

Tommie is just looking at her blank for a minute searching his thoughts before a smile comes over his face. "That's right they are playing today. Give me a minute, let me get my keys and wallet." He walks past, brushing against me while he runs up the stairs. Getting his keys, shoving his wallet in his back pocket.

"When are you going to be home?"

He stops before going out the door. "Does it matter, Tate? Say hi to Hazel for me."

He doesn't look at me, instead his hand is on the curve of her back, leading her outside, and Addie couldn't be any *happier*.

Chapter 12

Tommie.

Vibrations of sound resonate outwards from shaking speakers, hitting the crowd in waves of melodies that you can't help but close your eyes to, letting the music move you this way and that.

"You like music don't you, Tommie?" Addie's on tiptoes trying to reach my ear with her voice.

"It's gotten me through a lot, Addie." Music has been my savior at times, some songs just hitting the right places at the right times.

"Me too, Tommie, I know exactly what you're talking about." Melancholy eyes looking away while her body sways with the way the sound affects her, the sea of people compressed tightly with the main band going on in a few minutes.

Addie's voice starting to rise up with the rest of the people, singing the lyrics as if she knows them well. Her eyes even close while her lips curve upwards unhindered by her life.

"You know this song?" Surprised she knows this sort of band. Didn't peg her for a lover of music.

"This is one of my favorites they sing." Addie has to stretch upwards to reach my ear again. The degree of sound is becoming more intense.

"Wait for it, close your eyes, Tommie, so you can feel it." She smiles at me, "Trust me, it's awesome."

Humoring her, while the first chord of the acoustic come out. Goosebumps; that's what it's doing to me. The corner of my lip lifts into a smile, the guitar leading my rhythm of movement. Addie giving me a look as if saying, *told you so.*

"They're good." Wrapping her up in my arms, so she's standing in front of me, we let the music just rock us. She moves *with me*, following the way my hips lead her body, the gentle shuffle from one foot to the other. After the song is finished, I give her a twirl which puts a smile on her face. The crowd's starting to becoming more packed with the main act taking the stage. A crush of bodies pressing in on us, pushing us further back into the sea of people.

"Do you mind if I smoke one before they start?" Her eyes falling on the stick I'm already putting it in my mouth just waiting on her approval.

"Why do you smoke, Tommie?"

Her eyes don't hold judgment but sadness for me, a pity for me. I hate pity. Here she is with problems beyond me, and she's looking at me as if I have more than her. "It keeps me level, Addie." Pulling the first sweet, toxic smoke into my lungs, holding it in for as long as I can before I blow it upwards into the sky. Some people around looking at me as if I should puff, puff, pass. *I don't share my stuff,* is the look I give those wanting eyes around me.

Remembering the first time I smoked one, how could I forget? It's a memory I will always have, it's the time I crossed a hard line for me and I became a pole sucker.

The day was bright, warm, the both of us happy just to get away for the weekend, alone without anyone knowing who we were. We drove along winding roads that took an extra hour, but he wanted to show me important landmarks along the way. The closer we got to our destination, an eagerness settled over him. Gripping the steering wheel a little too hard, his eyes struggling to keep his vision on the road instead of me. The hotel was impressive - never having stayed in such opulence I was impressed by him.

Charm.

Pomp.

Fuss.

He set our mood, the both of us black suit and tie, he even had me get a haircut for the occasion. Looking back, was it because he wanted to see what I would be doing to him without hair getting in the way of his view?

At dinner he encouraged me to try a new dish I would never have thought of ordering. He was having an in-depth conversation with the sommelier about the wine we would drink at dinner. He was knowledgeable about all the finer things in life, constantly teaching and explaining things to me. By this time in our relationship I was able to play chess with him, and on occasion, I could even beat him, which he found *odd*. Also, our guitar lessons had stopped because I could play better than him *now*. He would drink wine while I played for him, encouraging me to try out for open auditions for local bands, he told me I was good enough now to play professionally.

During dinner, discussing issues about society, where before I thought I had no opinion on worldly things he would force me to think, to have an opinion on things that I never realized I had. We could hold great discussions about ideas but what I loved the most was just *talking with him*. He made me feel special and that I was *important* in this world and my voice was meant to be *heard*.

When we got back to the hotel, behind the closed door of our room was the first time I ever saw pot, it would eventually become my *saving grace*.

He took out a baggie from his suitcase opening it up, letting me smell it.

"That's quality, Tommie, not the garbage those college kids smoke. It doesn't hurt to spend the extra money for quality, Tommie, always remember that." A small pair of scissors and paper were already on the table.

Watching him roll one up, an expert with nimble fingers when he tried showing me how to do it. I was clumsy, lacking the skill he had, in time I would be able to spin one up faster than him.

Sitting on the couch together, he took the first pull before handing it to me. This was the first time I had tried this, a little nervous about how I would feel but I trusted that he wouldn't give me something that would hurt me.

Inhaling just like him, pulling the smoke deep into my lungs, coughing it out quickly because it burnt slightly. It didn't take long for my lids to start feeling heavy. It was the calmness that struck me more than anything; the way I thought everything was *alright*. While I could feel my body sinking into the cushion, *relaxed*.

"Tommie, why don't you take that off for me."

The music turned up slightly, it's exotic tone not missed by the music lover in me, rising to stand in-front of him. Looking back at this, he must have chosen the suit I was wearing for this exact purpose - to watch me take it off.

Starting with my suit jacket, letting it fall to the floor, the top button of my shirt fell first, while he sipped on his wine, licking his lips and watching me. His eyes were only focused on me, and I loved it.

Center of his attention.

I understood the sexiness of being watched, the importance of not rushing what I was doing, letting him get the full visual of me.

"Come here, Tommie."

He sparked another one up, giving it to me first, while I pulled the smoke into my lungs he unzipped and pulled me out to slip that wet mouth around me.

The Professor commenting on how I felt inside his mouth, how smooth my shaft was, how big I'm starting to get. He was unable to fully take me all the way in like he had done so many times before.

A smile on my lips saying. *"I'm going through a growth spurt."*

His eyes didn't smile back at me.

He would get me right to the edge before stopping, letting me calm down slightly then right back at it, over and over again, working me up to the point I was almost begging him to finish me off. At this point his clothes no longer covered his body, my hands taking off every piece of material he wore, slowly kissing his lips, chest, stomach, and his thighs. Getting so close to his prize.

My hard lines that I never thought of crossing started to become blurred with curvature.

He placed himself close to my mouth, it's a sight I became used to. Nothing wrong with the feel of him as my hand worked him up and down. He taught me about my body; what part of my anatomy held the most sensation. How normal it was to receive pleasure, and also to *give it*.

Pumping me up and down while I watched him, his tongue, mouth, engulfing me the best he could. Up and down from tip to bottom, pulling one ball into his mouth

then both of them. My eyes almost rolling back into my head.

Flicking.

Licking.

Sucking.

When he swallowed the last drop I had to offer him, he still continued to stroke me with the palm of his hand gripped around me, it felt so good I didn't want him to stop. Ready for round two - I could always go again, which he found *amazing*. It was something he could never do.

"Taste me, Tommie."

His simple request spoken an octave lower than normal. Looking into his eyes, my mouth descended downwards to the tip of him. A hesitation on my part for just a second before I took him into me. Holding him at his base like he did so many times to me. I let my tongue run along the dilated vein on his shaft - it had a smooth texture to it with a slight after taste of saltiness.

"Tommie, that feels so good."

He practically moaned it out while his hips started his own up and down motion. It didn't take long, it felt more like seconds before I got a tap to my head as he pulled himself out, releasing all over my chest. Thinking back, he probably did that so I didn't get scared off. Eventually, in time, he never pulled himself out of my mouth, letting me have all of him.

"Thank you, Tommie."

Bringing me to his mouth, we kissed for a few more minutes - his reward to me.

That night, after he finished me off again, we slept in the same bed together wrapped in each other's arms and with my fading high, I'd had to admit to myself that going down on a guy wasn't as bad as I'd thought it would be, that it wasn't as disgusting as I'd thought it was.

A promise to myself made that it was as far as I would take it. I wasn't going to fuck him, and I would never let him get himself inside me. That would never happen because I wasn't like that, and I started to chuckle out loud for him to hear me.

"What are you laughing at?" His voice sleepy in my ears.

"Myself," Replying back in a laugh, before kissing his chest goodnight.

"Tommie, where you at?" Addie is waving her hand in front of my face.

"Sorry, Addie, I was gone for a moment." Laughing slightly at zoning out. "Let's go to the front." The lead singer is taking the stage.

Gripping her hand in mine, pulling her forward, she hesitates, "We're wolves, Addie, it's time to take our place at the front of the stage." Pulling her out slightly, very gently. "Time for these people to move aside." Letting the wolf come just barely under the surface, creating a current of static power around us. It stands the hair on the back of the human's necks. They're feeling something, they just don't know what it is. They give way to us, not understanding that at the moment, that feeling is prey being stalked by something much more dangerous than them.

With ease, we make our way to the front along with all the other wolves that are there. Giving them nods of our heads in recognition of our kind but other than that we stay away from unknown wolves - too much fighting involved.

The band starts playing, Addie starts to sing, her voice is magical. It's got a uniqueness to it; a haunting quality. We stay in the first row, dancing, bouncing around, singing along to the songs until the afternoon comes to a close.

"Addie, thanks. This was something I needed."

Smiling up at me, stopping for just a moment so the crowd has to go around us. "I had a fun time too, Tommie. I felt alive today, for just a few hours I felt good." Her hand goes to my heart. "Thank you." Turning from me, I still see the tear that trails down her cheek as she tries to wipe it away without me noticing.

"I'm glad we're friends, Addie." Giving her a high five that she catches with her hand, squeezes, letting it go a second longer than what a high five is meant to be. Her eyes are holding something that I just can't make out before she looks away again without saying a word.

Walking towards the truck, the phone starts to ring.

"Hello?"

"Tommie, when are you going to be home?" My mother's voice worried.

"The concert just finished now, we're just heading home."

"Good, make sure Addie comes for dinner, the Luna said she has to come. There's another wolf going to be there that she didn't meet at the party yesterday. You just never know." Her voice sounds full of possibilities for Addie.

"Will do. Bye, Mom."

"Bye, and hurry up."

Putting the phone back in my pocket, giving Addie my best smile. "The Luna wants you over for dinner, apparently there was an eligible wolf that wasn't at the party last night who's coming for dinner." Trying to make my voice sound light as if it's no big deal so she doesn't feel the pressure of meeting a strange wolf who could be a potential partner for her.

"Oh." That's all she gets out of her mouth while I see a heaviness slump her shoulders down.

"It's not that bad, Addie. I'll be there with you, it's just a little look and see. Nothing more, nothing *official*." She maintains a straight line lip, not pleased with the turn of events, but doesn't argue about going or saying anything negative. She holds everything inside her. Her brother's waiting for us on the front lawn drinking a beer when we pull into her driveway. "Do you need a ride back to my house?"

"No, I'll get there. I just have to get ready. I'll see you soon. Thanks again, Tommie."

Addie is hurrying out of the truck before I can open the door for her. Walking her to the door, passing her brother, he gives us a growl of annoyance. A high five is exchanged, but she goes in for a little more - a quick hug, before turning away from me, closing the door behind her. I wait until she's inside before facing her scowling brother who's now standing, breathing down my neck.

"What's your problem?" Coming to stand right up to him.

"You, you're my problem, sniffing around my sister. Screwing her like she's some throwaway female you can use and lose, she's not like that. She's a good wolf who deserves an even better male, and you aren't that male."

Now my turn to step right in this wolf's face. Chest pressing against each other. "Your sister and I are friends, hanging out, that's all." The vibration of sound rattles both of our bodies.

"She's been through a lot and doesn't need to get her hopes up by someone like you."

It's a hard punch he takes to his face, knocking him down. His nose is opening up as if a tap of blood was just turned on. He's faster than expected; he could give most wolves a good fight. Except I'm not the *usual*. A swift hit to his ribs breaks them with a crack, he takes a knee to the ground, wheezing, trying to pull in a much need breath. I've gotten his blood all over my shirt. I understand where he's coming from; if I had a sister I wouldn't like me either, but we are just friends. "Your sister is my friend, nothing more. I wouldn't hurt her. If you come at me again like that, I'll show you what someone like me can do to someone like you." Bending down slightly so I'm still taller, "Understand?"

I wait for him to argue within himself before his head nods in understanding. My mood just soured. Grumbling the whole time driving home, it only gets worse when I see Hazel's car in the driveway. That's her usual spot, I need to start parking my truck there, just to show her that I can take her spot anytime I want. Pulling the door open, my mother's voice yells out to me.

"Tommie, go get dressed they should be here soon."

I want to punch the wall, I'm vibrating now. I need to smoke another one so I can just calm down.

Hazel is coming out of Tate's room, looks like she's in a hurry until she sees me. Gripping the handle of the bathroom door, opening it, trying desperately to close it before I have to smell him all over her.

"Tommie." Her cheerful voice makes my spine shiver, not in a good way. I'm really not in the mood to deal with them at the moment.

"Why do you have blood all over your shirt?" She's sniffing at it.

Tate now stands in front of me. Looking all over my body. He's upset. "What happened?" A muffled voice growls out between the three of us. Hazel is looking at Tate in a weird way.

"Nothing. I need to take a shower." Trying to close the door on both their faces, Hazel stops its progress with her foot, I could just crush it in the door so easily, but I have restraint.

"Are you hurt?" Tate is trying hard not to look concerned, but he's failing miserably.

"No." I don't meet his eyes, trying to close the door on the sight of them.

"Do you need any help in there, Tommie? I could wash your back, you can wash mine. Maybe Tate could watch this time? Stand in the corner."

Smirking, looking at Hazel who is deadly serious. Tate scowls, shaking his head *no* behind Hazel.

"Hazel, I already had a piece of that, I won't be coming back for seconds. The piece you gave me left a bad taste in

my mouth. I like quality, Hazel, you just aren't up to my standards, sorry."

Smiling at me, she says nothing else letting the door close. It's a quick shower, contemplating about if I should wrist one off. Deciding I don't have enough time before dinner and to smoke a joint.

I pick smoking.

Walking out of the bathroom making sure my towel is low around my hips, let him see me. Males are such visual creatures. Let my male have a good look at what he could have if he'd just let go of what he thinks is normal. His eyes don't even leave my body. Keeping the door open so he can watch if he wants to. Going into my top drawer to pull out the dime bag I just bought yesterday, it's gone along with my flavored paper. A little note is left in its place. It's a torn piece of paper from a notebook on my desk.

Bet you want a piece of me now, you know where I live.

Hazel.

This day needs to end now. She just screwed my mate, and now she's screwing with me. This female needs to be taught a lesson to not touch my stuff.

"I told her not to take it, told her you would be mad." He's leaning against the door frame, eyes wandering all over my chest. He's getting used to seeing me this way, in a state of half-dress. At first, he would look away, but now he can't pull his eyes off me.

"Tell her to stay out of my room, Tate. I mean it, I'm not in the mood for her games. She's going to get hurt."

"That's what she wants, just remember that." He's watching me take off my towel, drying my body with it. I can feel everywhere his eyes roam. Now he's starting to look uncomfortable but doesn't look away.

Pulling out a pair of boxers, stepping into them quickly so my completely naked flesh doesn't freak him out too much. It's just him and me, no buffer in between.

Baby steps with my Alpha.

"What happened today, Tommie? Whose blood was that?"

"It's Addie's brothers, he's upset she's hanging out with me. Said some words I didn't agree with so I hit him." Pulling my pants up, leaving them open so I can feel his eyes now and then linger on what's available if he wants it.

"Can you blame him? Addie's a good female, you're going to hurt her if you keep going places with her, hanging out with her, she's going to get the wrong idea of you guys."

"She's just my friend, we're just hanging out. She's lonely, and so am I. Is it wrong to have a friend to go out with? Is it wrong not to want to be lonely? What's so wrong with what I'm doing and so right about what you're doing? You can screw Hazel in the next room, while I have to listen to every groan, every grunt, every whimper you make, but I can't have a friend because they will get the wrong impression?" Putting on my shirt, taking the towel, drying my hair with it.

Lifting up the window, searching for a half burnt roach, anything will do at this moment. Finding one, the first inhaled breath has me naturally relaxing. I can feel my edge floating away with each exhaled breath I let out. Taking another pull, holding it for as long as my lungs will allow.

"Tommie, it's just something you have to get used to. I'll always have a female in my room. It's expected of me. I'm just doing what's expected of me. It doesn't mean anything, she's not the face I'm looking at while kissing her." He takes a step closer to me.

"Boys, come on down, they're here."

The Luna's voice on the bottom of the staircase calling up to us has Tate shaking his head. He reaches for my hand-rolled that's almost done. Taking it from me, a long inhale, holding it inside his lungs before grabbing the back of my neck, lips almost touching mine as he blows the smoke back into my lungs.

He eats the rest of it.

"I need it more than you right now. Trust me, this is going to be awkwardly painful for all of us."

Tate heads out the door slowly as I follow behind. His walk is slow, feet dragging until he reaches the bottom steps. His whole posture changes into the future Alpha he's going to be, I stand just slightly behind him - the future Beta I have to be.

Both of us camouflaging, while we smile towards the group of wolves who take our breath away. The coldest color of blue, almost white, stare at the both of us - she's still the most enchanting she-wolf I have ever seen.

Chapter 13

Tate.

White eyes with just the faintest of blue hit mine. I should have taken a breath in before looking at her because now, I can't seem to pull the air into my lungs that are screaming to breathe.

Moon blessed. I thought it was just rumors; crazy wolves talking about crazier things. But when I see the large male, with the exact same eyes as hers putting a hand on her shoulder, I know without a doubt I am witnessing history. Never again in my lifetime or maybe even in my pup's lifetime will we ever see this again.

I stumble on that thought as if I just mentally tripped - I will never be able to have pups with Tommie, pups are not in my *future*.

Some wolves are living blessed while others are left as wandering curses.

Walking toward the entourage that's gathered at the front door, I stand with my parents.The entryway is filling up with wolf after wolf, my mother had said that this was not an official visit, but this looks anything but unofficial. Hazel's going to *freak out*.

"Welcome, please come in." My mother's tone is inviting. Greetings being given from my mother to put everyone at ease, she goes to the wolf with the almost white eyes, embracing her, pressing their cheeks against one another, taking each other's scent in. My father's face has an ease about him, nodding his head to each wolf who enters.

The homeless looking wolf, who actually looks slightly cleaned up, is wearing an easy outfit of faded jeans and black t-shirt, hair pulled into a loose bun. His beard is trimmed up so it doesn't look so *wild*. He's scanning the

room expecting to find Hazel here; he won't find her yet, she likes to make her *deliberate* entrance to this kind of thing.

I wonder what kind of show she will put on for him, all I know is it will be a show stopper whatever she plans. There will be no doubt that this wolf and his official looking entourage will want a second meet and greet.

Bringing up the rear is that wolf who had Tommie's ear all night last night. He's scanning the room until he finds Tommie, who's standing slightly behind his parents. They nod their heads to one another in acknowledgment with light smiles on their faces.

"I brought a small gift for you, and thank you so much for letting all of us come today." The one with the eyes of the moon speaks out, handing my mother two jars of dark honey.

"The color is beautiful." She's holding the jars to the light inspecting the quality that's inside the glass.

"It's *wildflower* honey, my mate has several beehives on our territory that she takes care of in her spare time." The male with the same colored eyes as this *Moon Blessed* female gently laughs out.

Now my father steps up to him without ill tone, just an appraisal that this male meets. "You've grown since the last time I saw you. How's your mother and father doing?" They shake hands the human way.

"Good, they wanted to come but Cash," looking the male who's still looking around for Hazel, "thought it best they stay home, this isn't official."

"Understandable. This is my son Tate." My father's hand on my shoulder.

"Dallas."

We shake hands the human way. His grip is firm, confident, and I squeeze it back just like my father has taught me to do. Head up, eyes looking into his quickly without intent to fight.

This is a meet and greet.

"This is my mate Rya." His large hand touches her back.

Nodding her way I can't seem to pull my eyes from hers. The draw to them is an easy presence.

"My brothers Cash and Carson." Pointing to them both, he takes a hand and reaches behind his mate pulling out a female who has been hidden behind her. "This is Treajure."

My mother tries to stifle the gasp of air. Our group stills at this female who has met silver *intimately*. A face that's entirely scarred with lines that crisscross her skin, glasses on her face that enhance the size of earthy eyes. Her head bends low, slipping her glasses down the bridge of her nose before she picks her head back up. A finger pushing her glasses back in place. What's shining out of her are the *ruby* studs that she's wearing in her ears.

"Is she from your pack?" My father's stance starts to bristle slightly, looking at Dallas with different eyes *now*. Judgmental eyes that speak volumes that he does not like what he's seeing standing there.

"She's part of our pack now."

Those words settle my father's ruffling up the ridge of fur along his spine. "What pack did she come from?" It's as if my father is going to hunt down the pack that did that to this female. This is the one thing that is absolute in our pack: you do not hurt females, no matter what, no male hand will

be raised to one without my father's wrath falling down hard on the male that does.

"We don't know - she doesn't talk much." Rya is pressed against her back with a small kiss to the back of her head.

"It's nice to have you here, Treajure, please feel at home in our house." Now my mom's pressing her cheek against this female who's face holds nightmares about real pain.

"This is Cottom."

Another male with a shaved head nods to us, he's also looking around the room for females who haven't shown up yet.

"And this is Cara."

A female whose eyes find mine, trying to hold them but I look away. I will give no hope when there is none to be given to a female who looks like she needs it in her life. I can't lead the lost on. That's the thing with all these wolves who lost mates; they all look the same.

Ghosting through life just below the living.

Now my father is leading them to our dining room that only gets used if we are having a large amount of guests inside. The leaves of the table are extending the space, making it longer and wider than usual to accommodate everyone.

While everyone walks by me I give them a nod of my head, except for that wolf who can't stop side-eyeing Tommie - he gets no nod from me.

My father is pulling out the chair for the large male to sit at a place of honor at the opposite end to him.

Once is everyone is sitting at their places, Cara - the female dressed in red - sits opposite me, right beside Tommie who slightly moves away from her while he pushes his chair into the table. It's a very subtle move on his part, but noticeable to the female who puts her head down.

A knock on the front door has all of them sitting up a little straighter in their chairs as they hear female voices. Walking into the dining room, Hazel and Addie both come through at the same time.

One trying to dull herself down while the other is trying to fix herself up.

Chestnut competing with pine fight for the small space in Hazel's eyes.

Her most stunning quality, except her lids are half-closed and faded out. She's dressed in her hippie sabotage wear; they're in for the Hazel Show today. Long hair hanging loosely over her shoulders, she looks around the room without any *warmth*.

Addie has just a dusting of make-up on - for her that's a lot. Soft, blue eyes that hold no other color, looking at the gathered crowd, a nervousness settling in as she starts to fidget with the box she's carrying. The shoulder strap to her summer dress falls off her collar slightly, her eyes looking for Tommies, and when she finds them, a cinnamon color tints her cheeks before she looks at the floor.

Hazel came empty handed on purpose; she hates making good first impressions, not wanting to get anyone's hopes up about what she has to offer them. Nothing; that's what she's telling this wolf who's inquiring about her.

My mother going over to Addie taking the box out of her hands.

"I bought my wine." Addie's voice holds a nervousness whenever she has to speak out loud in groups, her discomfort sounds out in a shaking voice.

"What a treat for us." Placing the box on the hutch before turning to the group of wolves.

"This is Addie and Hazel." My mother makes the unofficial introduction.

The male wolf at the end of the table stands, "I'm Dallas, this is my mate Rya."

She gives a wave watching the two females standing in the entrance way.

"This is Cottom."

The male wolf stands up with a little bow before sitting back down.

"Treajure and Cara."

Both sets of eyes of Hazel and Addie stop on Treajure's face when she turns around to nod her head at them. They

cannot hold the discomfort on their faces with seeing what I try not to look at.

"My brothers Carson and Cash."

Hazel's eyes fall on Cash, a start of a slow smile tugs the corner of his lip upwards while she gives him nothing his way.

"I thought that this was an unofficial visit?" Hazel's subtle slur of speech looking around at all the company. Wasted gestures of finger point accusations scream my way. She would never dare come at my mother this hard so she chooses me to lay blame on.

Cash stands up taking her hard eye focus on him. "They insisted on coming, if it was up to me, I'd be alone with you right now."

I sit back in my chair, watching the show about to start.

"Really?" Her voice sounds fake as she takes a seat in the empty spot across from him, that's Addie's cue to take her seat across from the other male who doesn't even look in her direction - all focus on Hazel.

"Would anyone like some wine?" My mother's trying to give Hazel a hard eye but she won't look at my mother.

Opening the bottles up and setting them on the table, Hazel grabs a bottle, pouring herself such a cup full that once she's done, she has to lean over the glass and take a sip from the edge, the loud slurp sitting heavy in the silence while everyone is watching her. Once she can pick up the glass without spilling its contents she drinks it all down in a sloppy show, pouring another glass, keeping the bottle right next to her.

The food is being served by Tommie's mom. Platters being placed on the table while Hazel just pushes her plate away from her, preferring to drink her dinner instead.

Tommie is pouring himself a glass of pale, yellow wine, he tips the glass to his nose taking a long smell before swirling it around watching the vortex it creates in the cup. Holding it up to the light he inspects the way it slowly fingers down the sides of the glass. Smelling it again before taking a small sip, he lets it swish around his mouth before swallowing, it's as if he's a connoisseur of wine.

"Addie, this is so good!" Saying out loud for all the wolves to hear. "You made this yourself?" He seems shocked but *impressed*.

"Yes, it's my grandmother's recipe, but I made it." Her lips pressing against themselves trying hard not to smile at the compliment she received, her neck turning a lighter shade of cinnamon that's creeping up her face.

Rya is going to the bottle of wine pouring herself a half-full glass. Putting it to her nose and inhaling. "What kind of wine is this?" Her voice lets her curiosity show.

"Honeydew wine, it's made with the leftover fruit I have in my garden. I have honeydew wine, apple wine, and pear wine." All eyes are on Addie now, looking at her. She bends her shoulders forward with all the sudden interest in her that she's not used to having.

"It's delicious." Slurred out voice coming from Hazel whose eyes are becoming glassy with finishing her second glass - she must have taken something else before coming.

"So, Tommie, what are you doing now?" Carson turning into his line of sight trying to take eyes off of Hazel.

"I'm working in the investment division in our pack."

"Really? I thought you were being recruited hard by that firm in the city."

"I decided not to go with them. It wasn't a good fit."

"Did you go to the same school as Tommie?" Tommie's mom looking at Carson.

"We went to school together, even had a few classes together. We did some training as well." Tommie's hand going through his hair looking uncomfortable, his neck holds just a blushing of pink.

"You look familiar have we met, maybe at graduation?" Rya is looking at Tommie with focused eyes.

"I didn't go to graduation, I skipped it." Tommie not looking her way.

I have my elbows on the table leaning into the conversation.

"That's right you did skip grad, I can't believe you missed it, he graduated top of his class." Carson just giving out information on Tommie that we had no idea about.

"Tommie, you graduated top of your class?" Now his mother is looking at him with concerned eyes.

"It's no big deal." Tommie trying to brush off how big a deal it really is.

"Maybe I've seen you somewhere else before?" Rya's voice determined to place him in her mind.

"It could have been at our house, he was there once." Carson just spewing details about Tommie's life we never knew he had.

"You went to their territory with him?" I couldn't stop the question coming from my mouth if I wanted to.

"What's that supposed to mean - with him?" It's a defensive voice Cash's tone takes on.

"Nothing, I'm just surprised that's all. I never knew he had friends outside the pack." Thinking to myself how much time did they spend around each other? I'm getting

uncomfortable with my thought of them together, how were they together?

That sickens my stomach enough to not want to eat. Tommie's not like that is he? He looks like the straightest wolf you'd ever meet.

"Did you ever have your head shaved?" Rya's delicate voice ushers out, while his fingers run through his hair clearly uncomfortable with the conversation.

"Yes, I shaved it all off once." Tommie's shoulders straighten out.

"Well, actually I shaved your head with the clipper." Carson says with a tone that is off.

Tommie laughing awkwardly, "I guess you did." They both give each other a quick eye before looking away.

"You shaved his head." My voice matches my eyes, hard and disgusted at this male that now I'm seeing in a new light.

"I did." Carson looking at Tommie whose red-faced now.

"I looked funny." Laughing to himself, trying to laugh off the conversation.

"You did." Both males regarding the other laughing out slightly with their memory.

"That's it." Rya snaps her fingers. "You were at the basement party one night and-" Eyes going round, she shuts her mouth after that, not finishing her sentence, looking between Tommie and Carson.

"Why did you shaved your head?" Hazel's drunken focus is on Tommie who seems unimpressed with her.

"It tells their pack females I was available to them. The males shave their heads until they meet someone they are interested in but when they find their mates then they let their hair grow out. The females wear red showing that they are willing to entertain a male." Tommie is saying all this as if he knows how this pack runs, as if he has had a lot of in-depth knowledge of Carson's pack.

"You shave your heads if you're available?" Hazel's question to Cash.

"We do." His strong answer-back.

"Then why isn't your head shaved?" Accusing eyes his way.

"Because I'm not available *yet*." He's giving her his truth back.

"Then why all this if you aren't available." Hazel looking around at all the unofficial company at the table.

"I'm here because of your eyes." She regards him, taking another long drink to finish the glass before they fall on Tommie's eyes. He gives her a quick wink with a sideways smile while taking a drink from his glass.

"So my eyes brought you here, not me."

He's silent for a short moment before answering. "Yes." His one worded answer quick out of his mouth, he doesn't even bother to explain anything else.

"What a waste of my time." Point blank to his face, her coldness fumigating the wolves around the table with her icy chills.

"This was a mistake, I apologize for taking up your time and my family's time. Obviously, you aren't who I thought

you could be." Cash is standing up leaving without even touching his food.

"That's alright; I'll send you my bill in the mail because unlike you, my time means something." She slurs out to him with relief sinking in fast as she wobbles sideways on her seat.

Tommie stands up, digging deep into his pocket, pulling out a five-dollar bill and tossing it on the table. "Here, I'll cover his bill, I expect change back because your time really doesn't have much value now does it? Look at you." His face is scrunched up with what he's seeing sitting in front of him. "You really have no respect for yourself do you?"

Tommie is new to the Hazel show that he's watching for the first time and actually, she was being very calm compared to how she normally is.

Everyone watches open mouthed, not saying a word, just watching Tommie.

Turning his back on all of us before walking away, his steps are heavy on the wooden staircase, letting his anger at Hazel sound out for all of us to hear. I see him out of the corner of the window shifting into fur, launching himself off

the porch and running into the woods before disappearing from sight.

"He's just mad I stole his stuff, don't pay him any attention, his thong is riding up his ass." She reaches for the bill on the table putting it in her pocket. "I won't be giving him any change because I'm worth the whole five." Taking two full bottles off the table, one in each hand. She gives a little bow to everyone. Walking slightly sideways before leaving the house, tipping the bottle to her mouth while walking down the driveway before Cash approaches her once again. She's speaking with her hands to him, he swipes at the bottle while her middle finger goes up in his face.

A one-sided war of words descends on Cash while he stands there taking all she is offering him. What I notice is that the scarred wolf is also intently watching the display outside, her eyes even squinting in her glasses taking in the show. She can't pull her eyes off of Cash, even when Dallas is calling her name saying it's *time to go.*

Chapter 14

Tommie.

Back leaning against a tree, watching her head fall down
on her chest, before she jerks herself awake remembering the
bottle she's holding. Tipping it to her mouth, drinking the
rest down, before it falls out of her hand landing beside her.

Hazel almost made it inside her house. Passing out just
before she reached her back door, underneath an apple tree
that's loaded with fruit that's almost *ripe* enough to eat.

Dusk is falling fast; the light barely making it between the trees as the sun sets itself down for the night and our moon's momentum grows brighter in the sun's retreat.

Contemplating.

Should I let Hazel stay there, passed out against the apple tree, only to get eaten by the hordes of mosquitoes that are now buzzing the air in annoyance?

Shifting from fur to skin, my decision grumbles at my thoughts.

When lifting her up, she doesn't even open her eyes. Like a rag doll limp in my arms when I carry her inside the darkened house. Looking down at my feet that are caked in mud, I smile as I take that first step on her clean floors, making a mess of them with my trail of *dirt*. The kitchen holds no smells in the air; no food has been prepared here for a long time. Walking towards her room, noticing the hall empty of any pictures on the wall. Everything is bare - even the color of the paint is a dull-grey, almost *colorless*.

No life exists inside this home.

Setting her on the bed, leaving her shoes on because the soles have mud clinging to them - I want her to have to clean up her bed in the morning. It's just not the usual clean-up she's used to.

Looking through her dresser drawers for my bag of pot, I can't find it. What I do find, is a drawer dedicated to Tate's clothes, all folded nice and neat as if his belongings have their own special place. Socks, underwear, shirts, and pants. I wonder if I look in her bathroom, will I find his toothbrush there too?

Walking into the bathroom, finding his toothbrush right beside hers is a small blow to my gut, but really what did I expect? He has his life that he's been living here, and I was living my life there.

His dirty, white shirt is resting on top of the laundry pile. Picking it up, it holds mascara stains on the left-hand corner of it, as if she's been crying into his heart. Tossing it back down, walking through her small house, nothing stands out. There is nothing that says a female or male lives here, a *hollowness* inside the four walls.

The smell in her living room is a dead giveaway that my stuff is here. Opening the drawer of the cabinet I find it, only half of it remains. She smoked more in an hour than I can smoke all day long.

Sitting my bare ass on her couch, I spin one up with her paper which I now claim as mine. The first inhaled breath filling my lungs is burning sweet. Letting the smoke fog me up in a haze. Taking another toke while my mind takes a seat inside itself.

Deep relaxation.

One of my favorite practices when I started to transition from juvenile wolf to adult wolf was working out, smoking a big fat one then zoning out in the sauna for thirty minutes being completely mind-numb.

That's the first time I met Carson and Jake - the two wolves that shared some of the same classes. For the most part, they stayed on their side of the room, and I stayed on mine. Lines were drawn like territory; they didn't cross onto mine, and I stayed away from theirs. A head nod would be our only acknowledgment to one another. We knew names, but that's it, no other history would be discussed.

Sitting in the hazy hotness of the sauna on top of a towel, relaxing, letting the scent of him seep out of my pores. After all, I was going home for the weekend, I couldn't take any chances of smelling like the man that had been saturating up my life. I'd found out from my mother that Tate was going away for the weekend with his Dad, so I'd thought it would be perfect timing to go home. I hadn't seen him in two years at that time, but every curve of his face had embedded itself into my mind - if I let myself think of him on those rare occasions that I wanted to *torture* myself.

Sitting as far back as possible from the door, after just ladling water on the lava rocks, creating the hissing steam of water turning to vapor instantly. Sweat trickling down my back, inhaling the boiling temperature to rid myself of any scent that would be incriminating.

They both entered inside with a rush of cool air seeping quickly in. Carson's hands on Jake's hips, pushing him inside with his chest. It's then that I saw him dip his head down, kissing quickly to his right shoulder, the back of his neck, a low murmured growl from his chest vibrating his sound into the smaller male in front of him. They must have thought no one else was inside. They were laughing until they saw me through the steam cloud, both freezing up.

Hackles up, both were posturing defensively toward me, eyes of wolves flashing out. Standing up, walking towards the both of them, maintaining direct eye contact with the one who's head is shaved. He would be the one to take out first - his sidekick held no threat.

Wrapping the towel around my waist, getting closer to them. Carson puffing himself up while I did the same.

Tension building with the uneasiness of stranger wolves approaching closely for the first time is dance worthy. The posturing of body, the smelling of the air to taste the texture of mood. Dominance has to be developed, it was just the way with males in confined spaces.

Hierarchy of pack rule - we weren't pack, but we were living in the same space.

Testosterone releasing pheromones from under the skin into the air, sweeping around us. The distinct quality the scent holds on a purely primitive level, our wolves' *nature* understands.

He didn't back down and neither did I. A flash of teeth telling me he wasn't afraid to bite, showing him the same courtesy back. A forward step of motion from the both of us

brought our bodies to almost touching. He was almost as tall as me; good breeding line in him. You could tell with the way he handled himself.

The wolf inside making his assertion known with the tumbling vibration of sound coming from my chest.

He wasn't one to back down from my first real challenge.

Chest holding his flexing tension, pumping muscles full of adrenaline, fight or flight. He didn't look like a runner.

"Do we have a problem?" I was the first to cut into the masculine show with my eyes fixed on his.

"No problem." His hard stare held but I could see a small quiver of muscle in his neck with the effort he maintained.

"Good, I'm Tommie."

"I know. I'm Carson this is Jake." Quiet assessment of one another again but the degree of mood was dialed down slightly; not so *combustible*.

Walking backward, going to the same spot I came from; I didn't want them to think they were intimidating enough for me to leave. Getting comfortable again, my back lent against the wall of heated wood.

They took their own positions - Carson sitting on the highest bench while Jake went for the lower bench. They didn't sit close together; they attempted appropriate space between them.

"Where are you from?" Directing my question to Carson.

"Up north, about a six-hour drive from here."

His voice had a depth to it, masculinity at its finest that perked my interest slightly, which disturbed me because I had a man that held my interest.

"Where are you from?" He engaged me in small talk.

"Northwest of here, about a three-hour drive." Being vague just like him.

"What about you?" Asking the male with a light tan to his face.

"Around." Jake didn't meet my eyes when he said this, just looking at his bare feet. He had hair like mine except a few inches longer, curling slightly less at the ends, and few shades lighter.

The lull in conversation held for a good ten minutes, enough time for the scent of him to excrete out of me from pores that were then empty of any smell except for my own. A little trick learned that all juveniles did to hide scent from prying parents. A good hot, steaming shower wipes away all traces of any activity that needs to be hidden.

Before walking out the door, turning to the both of them. "Just so you know - it's none of my business. I won't tell anyone about you two."

Relief in both their eyes, I could even see the faint exhaled breath out of Carson's lungs. There was no denying what I saw - males just don't kiss other male's shoulders or necks when they are just friends. I also felt relief - that I was not the only one; that there were others like me, just hidden, out of sight, closeted.

"If you want, you can train with us, I know how hard it must be for you to be by yourself. We come here this time

every day so if you want to work out or spar a few rounds drop by anytime." Carson's *open* invitation to a stranger wolf. But with time we would get to know each other very *well*.

Getting up off Hazel's couch, letting the hand-rolled dangle from my lips, making my way to the bathroom because I want to take a dump in her toilet. Getting nice and comfortable, letting my bowels spill inside the porcelain white. Sitting there finishing smoking the rest of my stick. I'm in no hurry; I want to make sure I empty myself completely before wiping. Not bothering to flush the toilet, I leave the lid up, I want her to see what kind of presents I can leave for her. Nothing like waking up hung over and smelling someone else's shit first thing in the morning, it's a whole other experience having to see it as well.

After washing my hands I go to the fridge, there is barely anything that is edible. A white take-out container is the only thing on the shelf beside beer, wine, vodka, and whiskey. The hard liquor is extreme quality, I don't even know some of the labels, but the labels I do know are ones

that the Professor had in his house - nothing but the finest he would drink even if he had to save up to buy a bottle.

Taking a container out and a bottle of pop, opening it up, leaving the cap on the counter. Scooping out most of the pasta in a bowl, putting the almost empty container back in the fridge for her to find, hardly a bite left. A smile lights my face up. Nothing worse than thinking you have something to eat when really someone else ate in on you and the package is still there, reminding you how good it could have been.

I hated when Carson did that to me.

Heating up the food in the microwave, drinking the pop from the container, making my way back to her couch, turning on the TV. I'm going to linger on her furniture, hopefully I wiped good enough - don't want that kind of smell to saturate into the fabric of her couch. When I'm done eating the pasta I leave the bowl on the table, my fork beside it. I almost finish the pop completely, leaving behind just a swallow, except all that's left is my backwash.

Going to the drawer that holds Tate's clothes. Hazel still passed out except she's in a fetal position, the mud all over her blankets, ruining her sheets. That has me chuckling -

she'll wake up in her *dirt*. Putting them on, they hold no smell to them just laundry detergent clean. The pants are just a touch loose compared to the way I like my pants to fit. The shirt doesn't stretch the way it does across his chest.

The walk home is long, dragging my feet the whole way there. Once inside the house it's dark, everyone going to bed because Monday is a new week of work. Opening the door to my room, Tate's sitting on my bed waiting up for me. He's been reading one of my books that would take me away from this world into my fantasy land when I was younger; when I had to endure him in the next room with someone else.

Does he realize that my new fantasy is what's right in front of me now?

"I have some questions for you, Tommie." A serious face for a serious talk.

"Are you sure you're ready for the answers, Tate?"

Chapter 15

Tate.

Adding to the already dog-eared pages of the book that has become one of my favorites from his collection - the well-worn edges tell that this tale has been loved by the both of us.

Common interest.

"Have you been reading my books?"

Tommie's eyes pointedly on my hand that's putting the novel back in its proper place, the nerve ending in my fingertips heating up, to the point my hand tremors as if electricity is streaming through me in a current I can't control.

"I started coming into your room about a year after you left for university, just looking around. I couldn't stop the compulsion inside me. Laying on your bed as I am now. I'm not much of a reader, but you have some good stories here. So I decided to give one a try. This book, I always come back to, I'm not sure why but I like it."

"That's my favorite one, I read that over and over again when you had Hazel in your room. It didn't drown out all the sound, but I managed to slip away for a while until you were finished with her." A proclamation is spoken low. He keeps his eyes on mine, not looking away.

"I'm sorry you had to go through that." He doesn't say anything back, but his face is frowning slightly before his mouth opens to speak.

"What about now, are you sorry for me going through that all over again?"

"I told you that you have to get used to it, that this is the way it's going to be. I need a female in my bed, I'm sorry that it hurts you."

"No, you're not, or else you wouldn't do it." Tommie looking at me with his judgment.

"What would you like me to do? Tell me, what do you want me to do, Tommie!" Trying to keep the rise of my voice down.

"Nothing." His eyes looking away out the window into the late, summer night darkness.

"Like I said, Tommie, I have some questions for you."

"Are you sure you're ready for the answers, Tate?" Tommie doesn't look at me as he pulls a bag from his pocket, reaching into his top drawer and taking scissors out. He begins to cut up a small green dud into tiny pieces, crumbling them in his fingers before spinning it up, hardly even looking at what he's doing.

His attention now on *me*.

"I wouldn't ask if I wasn't ready. By the way - nice clothes." Eyeing my clothes on his body.

"You like these? Found them in your drawer at Hazel's house. Must be nice having your drawer there. It's like you live there part-time, am I right?" Curiosity's edge in his voice, waiting for an answer.

"I have my drawer there, like I said, we have an arrangement."

"An arrangement? More like a relationship, because one doesn't have a designated drawer at someone's house if they don't have a relationship with that someone." Observations are coming out hard from his voice.

"Hazel's my friend, Tommie." Looking him in the eyes, he stares right back at me, challenging me for truth.

"Sure she is, Tate." The words slipping from lips that are holding his hand rolled, lighting it up he takes the first savored breath in before he opens the window, blowing the cloud of white into the night air that's filtering out the oppressive inside.

"Why were you at her house?" A little anxiety is creeping along my rib-cage, enough to alter my breathing for a moment.

"I put her to bed." Laughing to himself with a wickedly tempting smile that graces his face. His hand is going through his hair while he chuckles again, not looking at me - he's looking at his dirty feet, laughing again. He takes another pull from his stick with a purpose as the atmosphere

of him is changing, becoming the relaxed side of Tommie. Sinking into the chair he's sitting on, his legs spread comfortably, the valley of his chest is exposed slightly because the collar of his shirt hangs lower that it's supposed to.

I avert my eyes from the perversion his sight causes me. It's hard to stomach wanting to see another male's chest, what's worse is the compulsion creeping inside to touch him.

"You mind?"

Tommie is leaning off the seat to grab the bottle from the edge of the desk, his collar dips down further exposing a smooth chest that's tight. Putting the bottle to his lips, he doesn't wait for my answer, drinking down a good portion that remains while his eyes drift slowly over my body, his eyes caressing every inch. I can hear his slow heart-beat in his chest beating to a rhythm that makes me want to sway his way.

"That's really good wine." Saying it more to himself than me, while he stretches once again to put the bottle close to me. Another quick look down his shirt before I refocus my mind, chastising myself. "Ask your questions." Blowing out

the words with the smoke that was just in his lungs. Drooping lids, a slow smile spreading across his face, his hand going into his hair before resting it down at his side.

"Why didn't you tell your parents you graduated with top honors?"

"It wasn't important." A shrug of the shoulder as if he couldn't care less.

"Did you enjoy school, being away from here?"

"At first I was lonely, but then I met someone and loved it. Learned a lot about myself and the best part - I was away from you." The intensity rises when he mentions his *someone*.

"Is that why you hardly came home, because you met someone or you wanted to avoid me? You know the first year you never came home until I left for a weekend away with Hazel, we would always go somewhere if she wasn't away with her business. I could smell you all over the place, it was the first time I came into your room. My mother found me in the morning sleeping in your bed. She freaked out, asking why I was in your bed, asking questions I knew she never wanted the real answer for. I made something up that settled her fur down. Said I fell asleep reading a book,

and thank the moon one was open beside my head. She didn't question me anymore after that. I did find something out about you then; you only came home when I was gone. So I would make it a point to leave so at least your mom wasn't so sad, she missed you so much. She would just look at your empty spot at the table and sometimes she would cry, but your father always said that you would be back soon, until you were in your third year. Then that conversation started to change between them."

"My mom was crying?" His face falls.

"She was, your parents sounded as if you might not come back home after graduation, they were worried about you. Were you thinking of joining another pack?" My heart rate is increasing.

"I was thinking about staying in the city, not joining another pack. I had a change of heart six months before graduation; I just couldn't stay there anymore." His lips press together tight, shoulders fall slightly.

"You had someone in the city. Were you in love with her?" That hurt my gut to ask, but I need to know.

"Yes, I did have someone, and I thought I was in love." He's straightening out his body, less loose, a tension taking over in muscles that are flexing slightly.

"You loved someone?"

"Yes, I did." He's looking straight in my eyes, and I see sadness there in his face.

"What was she like?" I don't even want to know, but I have this fascination inside me to hurt myself. I'm the one tensing with the blow that's going to come.

"He was amazing." Tommie's just watching my eyes, waiting still, I think he even is holding his breath. My breath is caught in my throat.

"He?" Bile's acid path is rising inside my throat, burning its heat upwards.

"He."

Tommie's one-word confirmation has me rising off the bed, I can't hide everything I'm feeling in this moment, it would have been easier if it was a female, but a male is too much to take in. "You were in love with a male. Who is he?

Was he that wolf who has been side-eyeing you tonight? Is that the wolf, the one you went to school with?" Taking the bottle of wine off the desk his taste still lingers around the edge of the rim, while I finish the rest of it. Somehow it doesn't make things better; it just amplifies them.

It's as if the only sound I hear is the rushing beat of my heart swooshing in my ears, sounding like the oceans pounding surf.

"Carson?" He takes another long drag of a stick that's becoming shorter and shorter, he's the picture of calm now while I'm losing my mind. "He's a good friend, we did fool around together. But he wasn't the one I was in love with. I loved a man." He starts to stand up off the chair as if reading the language my body is telling him. "He was a human."

It's without thought that I put hands on his shirt, squeezing the fabric in fists that's pulling him closer to me. The timbre of my wolf's voice is filling the room in its low growl. A snap of teeth his way shows just how unhappy the wolf is about this turn of events. Jealousy in the most vivid green I have ever seen is taking over. "You let a human man have you?" My face is almost touching his, he just looks at

me, at my lips. A calmness almost on the border of fickleness he now possesses.

"He never had me completely, I had a line I never crossed." Words sounding like whispers, because the thudding in my heart is still echoing in my ears. Tommie's hand slides up from my hip in slow motion purgatory, gliding over the side of my ribs, the palm on my shoulder feeling my flesh until it's around the back of my neck. His thumb just on the back of my hairline. He steps into my space, "I'm going to kiss you." The decibel of his voice is dropping in a lover's low tone.

Paralysis.

Energy dripping in the air that's falling all around us.

The first touch of lips, bodies nudging closer, less space.

A gasp.

Lips are moving slowly, I can't pull away from him while his lips start to consume what's *His*.

Tremors pulse like sporadic shivers in flesh that feels alive. I don't smell him anymore; all I smell is the scent of desire that's filling the small space.

A hand slips underneath my shirt, just staying on the edge where jeans meet skin before he draws my hips into his. A whimper from the base of his throat before his tongue licks the space between my lips, seeking entrance in. When I feel that wet tongue against mine, it's hard to not get lost in this.

Immoral thoughts have me pushing him away hard, because I can't go further than what I'm fantasizing about in this moment.

"I'm not like that." Saying it more to myself, telling myself who I am. My hand wiping off my mouth, walking out of his bedroom.

"I know, Tate, but remember I was just like you once."

Tommie's voice reaching me in the hallway as I make it to my bedroom, closing the door behind me.

My straight line just altered from its path.

Chapter 16

Tommie.

Hazel's been standing in the doorway for a while now as the Luna's voice drifts into the kitchen, the octaves of her violence clearly shown towards the she-wolf whose episode she didn't care for.

No appreciation for the Hazel show yesterday - the Luna is no fan and she's letting Hazel get her brutal critique about it.

"You will call that wolf and apologize for your rudeness, Hazel. I can tolerate a lot of things, but I will not tolerate our pack looking bad in front of another pack. Do you understand, Hazel?" A pausing voice from the Luna. "Hazel, tell me you understand." A creeping edge of a harsher tone singling for Hazel to do as she's told.

"I understand." Spoken with the direction of understanding, no other answer would be satisfactory to the Luna's ears.

"Good, here's Cash's phone number. I expect you to call him sometime today. Make your apology believable, almost as if my hand is around your throat, squeezing it. I'm a patient Luna, Hazel, but my patience can only go so far. Next time, you'll face me if you do that at my table again."

Putting my dish in the sink, the Luna going outside, slamming the door behind her, leaving Hazel in the house that's becoming a hushed quiet.

Walking past the entrance of the house, Hazel's just standing there, holding a piece of paper in her hand. Eyes emotionless, almost a numb quality to them, just straight ahead without any movement until I come into view.

Painted gum-drop lips, her artist touch making her cheeks a shade of soft, blushing crimson to match some of her hair that's been highlighted naturally by the sun. A master of makeup, applying the neutral mattes of eye shadow to bring out her green with brown flecks of irises to life. She looks beautiful to the eyes of wolves and men who don't know her.

"How was your sleep last night, Hazel?" Giving her a smile that shows dimples. The Professor always commented on it - saying how attractive it is to see on me.

Her lips turning up in a self-satisfied way. Almost as if she's smiling to a secret no one knows about but her. The look she gives me is a strange, border-line interest, her composure is without flaw.

"Interesting." She pulls on the strap from her purse with a manicured hand that starts to cut into her shoulder, pulling her loose blouse to the side and revealing a hint of a sheer, pastel-pink bra.

"Really, how?" Trying not to sound so eager to hear her story of waking up in a mess.

Footsteps walking down the stairs has Tate coming towards us, freshly showered, smelling clean. His hair still slightly damp, wild and unruly. I want to put my fingers through it and comb it down for him.

Hazel's the one that does it for me, her fingers running through it while her eyes find his. "I thought you would be ready by now. I'm running late, we need to go." She stands on tiptoe to place a kiss on his mouth, except he turns his head slightly, so her lips fall on the corner of his. The atmosphere changes in the room, the air getting thick and hard to breathe in. Hazel taking a step backward, "Is everything alright?" Her hand going on his hip, my eyes falling on that thumb that's resting on the band of his shorts.

"Nothing's wrong." Bending his head down, he places a lingering kiss on her mouth while taking a quick glance at me, making sure I'm observing this.

Their exchange is a slow torture.

Watching him pull her into him, pressing himself against her body. His hand is traveling up the length of her back before it rests on the base of her neck.

The angle of him is straight and unbending.

Pulling away from her lips, he traces them with his thumb, an intimate moment he's giving me a front row seat to. A female gasp invades my ears when his hand goes underneath her short skirt, showing me more of her thigh.

"Go upstairs, I don't want to see that." Disgust is dripping with every word spoken from my mouth. It's Tate I'm looking at, trying to hide the hurting madness my soul feels.

If she were a male, I would crush her skull in my hands.

The pull from his hand for her to follow him upstairs is blatantly obvious.

"We can't, I'll miss my flight."

"Alright." Saying it as if he's disappointed in the fact they don't have time for a quickie before she leaves.

"Let me just put on a shirt and get some stuff." Running back up the stairs, he leaves Hazel and me alone.

I can't help but circle her slightly, a footstep placed softly on the wooden floor that doesn't make a sound, bristling up towards a female that I can't compete against.

She's the body type he wants.

"Where are you going?" I need to talk or else a growl will come out, her body turning and keeping mine directly in front of her as if she understands I'm stalking prey.

"Vegas, I'll be gone a week. It's for work." Her eyes tracking my movement, no amusement in them, that left when I took the second purposeful step closer to her.

"What do you do there?" Her hand now has a shake to it as she opens her purse, digging around and pulling out a business card then handing it to me.

My third step brings me right in front of her, grabbing the card, claws barely contained from poking the edge of fingertip skin.

Looking at the card, it's Hazel's face in sepia, ghost-like features haunt the image except for her eyes. They have the ability to change their frequency. Brown more prominent as green takes the back seat to the depth of them.

Her number on the left-hand corner. Nothing else on it.

"I've started my own *Entertainment* business, I'm into my own *self-promotion*. I found I have a quality about me that men will pay big money for." Her shoulders square up as if she's preparing for my verbal assault about work.

"People pay you?" Looking shocked at the fact she can charge money for what she has, not at the fact she sells herself to the highest bidder. Putting the card into my pants pocket.

"Yes, they do." Spitting it out at me clearly ruffled up. Her polished exterior is wearing thin.

"Do they ever ask for their money back?"

Her mouth opens from my words before she shuts it tight. "Never, in fact, I'm one of the highest paid out there. I have a certain ability that makes my clientele keep coming back for more. In fact, not only do they pay me, they give me gifts." Her hand is raising showing me her platinum watch. "I think it's the same brand as your watch, Tommie," Her head angling to the side with a smile that says she understands what these gifts were for. "Am I right?" Looking down at my present that's glaring at me hard. "I know for a fact you could never afford that, Tommie, also how do you

afford all the suits you wear for work? They're tailored just for your body. That's an expensive quality that you don't have the bank for. What kind of part-time job could you hold to afford quality like that?" Her voice finger-pointing my way.

Looking at my watch, how could I ever forget what I received it for?

We'd just smoked a packed bowl, watching a movie on his couch before the first crushing all-consuming kiss and the love that followed had me doing things I never thought I would do.

My education was about to take a giant footstep forward, my hard line easily *broken*.

"Do that little show I like, Tommie." The Professor always one for the visual loved me undressing for him. The exhilaration in his eyes the wonderful smile on his face as I let my hand undo the top button of my shirt like I had been *trained* to do.

No rushing, he liked the art of slowly removing material from the body. He would feel himself over the top of his pants, rubbing himself at the show. Wandering eyes taking me in, making me feel,

Good.

Sexy.

Wanted.

Once free of any material, he would hand me the almond oil and to this day, I will always associate that with the Professor.

"I've been thinking of you all day long, Tommie." I think he knew how much I loved hearing that he *thought* about me, that I was *important* enough to be cared about. His hand going to the collar of his shirt, loosening it up but not taking it off, he liked when I *undressed him.*

Gripping myself in my hand while the oil did its job, easily gliding up and down with eyes that are glued to me. I knew the importance he placed for what was between my legs.

Standing up, I would start with his collar button, slowly with nimble fingers, undoing them one after another, hand sweeping over his chest. My tongue licking, sucking his flesh as if he was a wolf. His belt easily pulled off, loving the sound it made as it slid past fabric forcefully.

Laying on top of me, grinding those hips into mine, his hand an expert at bringing all kinds of pleasure to me. That time he had the both of us in his hand, working each other against the sensitive underside - my most pleasurable spot I found out.

"Spread your legs."

By then I craved this form of my *education*. His hand pleasing the both of us together as he reached around with his other well lubricated one. A large index finger slipping inside me, at first uncomfortable, but he had a way of making it feel wonderful. A whimper from my mouth as he pushed past the barrier that made the finger comfortable inside me. Several long, thick inches of finger dipping in and out, over and over again. Made my thighs shake as he continued to rub us up and down together.

He must have been hoping to stretch me enough to accommodate a much thicker, bigger part of his anatomy.

Bending down so he could kiss my lips, his hands stopped, I was just on edge, barely hanging on. He'd been doing that a lot; just stopping and not finishing me off. He liked to hold himself against me, the tip of him against my hole. He'd try to push himself inside, but I would have no part of that. Usually throwing him off, an argument following, so he had to resort to new ideas of thought on how to get himself inside me.

"I want to feel you inside me." A whispering plea so seductive I think I moaned from the voice he used.

He held himself still, letting me decide if I was ready for that.

The tip of my cock right at his lubricated entrance.

I was so tuned up I was almost like a vibrating string.

Deciding to bend that line.

The tip of me pushing into him slowly, trying not to cause the Professor any pain.

Looking me in the eyes again. "No need to be gentle."

In a flash doing exactly what he said, groaning as I completely thrust my entire length inside him, feeling him opening inch by inch, until I was fully surrounded, tight by the inside of him that was dripping with oil.

His hand on my waist, a long breath out, before his hips started to roll with my movement.

Tight.

Warm.

Beautiful.

It was better that anything I'd learned so far. While I was thrusting myself up, he was coming down hard, our moans filling the room.

"Do you like doing this to me, Tommie? Watch yourself screw me."

I looked between my legs, watching him rise and fall down on me while he had himself in his hand.

"I like this." Saying words while giving him a hard angle thrust upwards, making the Professor give me a deep downward moan that comes from a man's chest, showing me he appreciated the hard movements.

My *nature's* needs started to surface with the way my progression of transitioning was coming along.

Moans becoming more pronounced, almost growl like, chest rumbling, my hips slamming into him. He couldn't keep up with the pace, just holding onto my shoulders trying to ride me.

His moans turned into whimpers with my steady rhythm that didn't care if I was hurting him, just a *need* to come to *completion* was all my nature was thinking of.

Body tensing one last time, spilling the contents into him as deep as I could get.

"You're absolutely unbelievable." A glistening of sweat on his brow let me know just how much of an exertion it was to him. That familiar smile I had come to *love*. *"Thank you, Tommie."* His face looking almost relieved things went his way. Kissing me with all the *passion* he felt, that I *craved*.

His voice sounding so proud - as much as for a student getting straight A's. The praise he was throwing my way, the compliments *puffing* me out. Laying naked together we talked about what just happened and how *normal* it was to be doing that, nothing *shameful* at expressing love for one another.

Sobbing in his arms saying to myself, *"I'm not like that"* and a small voice in my head whispering back, *"But we are."*

The Professor took my face in his hands, *"It's nothing to be ashamed of, Tommie, we are who we are."* He got up from the floor, going into his bedroom, coming out with a black box lined in deep grey with the writing of the brand on it.

"I wanted to give this to you for a while now. I think this is a perfect time."

Opening the lid up, a platinum watch sitting secured in the inside of a velvet casing. I knew instinctively it had a quality of richness to it.

"A man should always have a good watch."

The professor's watch matching mine except mine was newer, by many years.

"Tommie?" Hazel's voice is bringing me out from my history lesson on *who I am*.

A shake of my head to clear my thoughts before answering her question, I'm trying to remember what she asked, about how I could afford my watch.

"I had a good part time job, did security for a *wolf* who owned property just outside the city on the weekends if he needed some extra wolves around. He paid well, probably better than what you make."

"Better than what I make?" The words of her voice have a tickling quality as if she's amused by my words. "You can't afford my rates, Tommie."

"Don't worry, Hazel, like I said - I won't be coming back for seconds. Not worth my time, your skill level is primary at best. No real *master of skin* are you?

"Tommie, you aren't into the kind of service I provide. It's a niche market I have going for me."

"What's that?" Asking with an interest in what she can actually offer someone.

"She can take a lot of pain." Tate is walking down the steps throwing the words out, while his arm goes around her shoulder. "Let's go."

Watching them walk away towards her car that's parked right next to mine. She turns her head to look at me with that secret smile of hers before I see her shoulders shake with a laugh. Tate is opening the passenger door for her to get in. Closing it shut, he doesn't look at me as he gets into the driver's side, backing up and pulling ahead before the car disappears from my line of sight.

Looking for my keys on the counter, I must have left them in my truck. Putting my suit jacket on that is tailored just for me, another one of his lessons - pay the money to get a suit tailored, it will give quality to your appearance. He not only schooled me on how to suck cock but he also gave me good life advice about the *little things that say big things about you.*

Walking outside, breathing in the morning air, the heat so oppressive, so stifling, it hurts the lungs to breathe it in.

The gentle wind does nothing to cool the scorching air, no clouds in the sky just the sun beating on the ground, cooking the landscape with is rays.

A white paper underneath my wiper blade. Taking the sheet and unfolding it.

You forgot your crap at my house, thought I'd be nice and return it to you. It took a while to round it all up, but I managed to get most of it.

Sorry about the container - it was the only thing I could find that was empty.

I might have spilled a little on your seat, I apologize for that. Should be easy to clean off the leather.

Hazel.

Trying to open my truck door it's locked, a white take-out container with its lid open on my seat, its contents are a disgusting mess of what I let loose in her toilet, more liquid than solid. So full that even when I do go to move it, I will make a mess of things, the temperature of the day will only bake it, saturating it's stink into the material of the truck that I don't think will ever come out.

"Hazel!" Yelling it into the air, no way to get inside my truck because I don't have a spare key.

Music from a system is thumping up the driveway. A black minivan that's been tricked out is playing some deep base and pulls up beside me. Limo-tint black windows roll down.

The wolf who was at dinner last night regards me with a solemn expression, the wolf driving looks like an older version of him, behind them sits two empty car seats, in the further back sits that female wolf with the thick glasses whose face tells about her *education on silver.*

"Tommie, right?" The male wolf pulls my eyes away from the small creature who just looks out the landscape with a worried expression.

"Cash right?" Saying the question right back at him.

"Right, this is my brother Caleb." The male gives a slight head nod my way.

"I was wondering if you could tell me where Hazel lives?"

"Why?" Questioning out.

"I just wanted to apologize to her for yesterday. Clearly, I made her uncomfortable."

Laughing at this because Hazel doesn't get uncomfortable.

"No you didn't, she doesn't rattle easily. She's not here anyways, she left for Vegas on business."

His face falls slightly. "Do you have a number I can call her at?" He seems too eager to have her number in a voice that rushes out.

"As a matter of fact, I do." Reaching into my pocket pulling out her card, handing it to him.

He stares at it for a moment, a finger tracing each eye before the larger male takes it out of his hand. He takes a long look before looking at his brother in the eyes, throwing the card at the male's chest, shaking his head.

"Tommie." Addie's voice behind me, she's on her bike, double riding a small pup in front of her and a slightly older one who is standing on the pegs on the back wheel.

Addie coming to a stop in front of the open window looking inside at the back.

"Hello, Cash, hi, Treajure." Their names coming easily from a polite mouth. She remembers names well.

"Hi." Cash clearly unable to remember her name, Addie's eyes fall to the ground.

"Addie, her name's Addie. You just met her last night."

"I knew that." He's trying to seem as if he did remember.

"What are you doing here?" Turning to her because I'm done with Cash. He can't even be bothered to remember her name.

"I brought them for a swim, they get crazy if they are cooped up in the house too long,"

The oldest one jumps off, already racing to the back yard, helping the little one off the handlebars, short legs running as fast as she can, chasing her brother.

"Gotta go, nice seeing you again, Cash and Treajure." Addie gives a little wave before placing her bike at the side of the house following the path the pups took.

"Cash, you should call Hazel. Tell her I gave you the card. Make sure she doesn't charge you full price, not worth it, trust me. She likes to be haggled with." They give me a confused look before their window rolls up, pulling out the spot, they drive away.

Nothing makes me happier then sending the wolf who looks like he lives under a bridge in the middle of a swamp Hazel's way.

Chapter 17

Tate.

Hazel's laugh.

It's not her ordinary laugh; it doesn't hold any blemishes or broken eyes. It's real, with tears threatening the corners. The good, belly-shaking noise that rocks into your soul.

"What's so funny, Hazel?"

Pulling away from the main house, she pulls out a pre-rolled, lighting it up, taking that first inhaled breath, a pause

of sound before releasing it into the tight space fogging up the interior. I'm the one to roll down the window; she could care less how she smells to others.

"I left something for Tommie in his truck as a thank you for helping me to bed last night." She says it through laughing lips that tremble with the vibration of her glee. Another inhaled breath that she holds in for as long as she can before little coughing puffs of white go out her window for the air to consume.

"You shouldn't screw with him, Hazel." Looking at her hard before eyes going back to the road.

"Why? It's fun. Besides, Tommie's harmless." Words laced with that light laughter again. He has a way of making her laugh when no others can, including *me*.

"I'm just saying I don't think he likes you very much." She turns her over-dramatic shocked Hazel eyes my way where each color is battling to dominate the other.

"He doesn't like me? Say it's not so." She starts laughing except now she's starting to fade into her world, sinking into the seat looking out the window.

"I don't think he does."

"Now you're an expert of what he likes, are you his best friend all of a sudden?" Her face pointed towards the roadside watching the scenery blur by.

"No, I'm just saying he told me you need to stay away from him and not touch his stuff." Looking at what she's inhaling I can tell its Tommie's quality she's smoking and not her usual.

"So Tommie doesn't like me around him, or to play with his stuff, good to know." A little half smirk that curls the side of her lip.

"Hazel, I mean it, don't play with him, He's not the usual."

"I know he's not the usual - that's why I like to mess with him, he's intriguing to me. Something about him that I need to figure out. Did you see his watch? That's at least fifteen grand he's wearing on his arm." She raises her arm up showing me her watch. "It's the same as mine, except I have diamonds and his doesn't. The suits he wears are all quality names that are tailored to him, more money than most make in a day just for one. What did he do when he was in school?

Because I'm telling you, he had someone taking care of *his ass*."

Hazel is pulling another lungful of her smoky wisdom inside her. It's big breaths that I need to pull into my lungs because I'm trapped in my own thoughts about Tommie, and I have no choice but to be mute on the subject of him. "So what are you saying about Tommie, Hazel?" A tiny fear that she might find out about him.

"I'm just saying, things don't add up with him. He leaves for four years, hardly comes home, now all of a sudden he's home looking like *old money*. I can always spot old money, Tate, it isn't hard. They're not flashy - they don't pick me up in Ferrari's or Lambo's - they pick me up with a driver in a town car, sleek black with limo tint. It's just an understated look about them."

Hazel switching the stations looking for some melody she can sing to, while I try not to come undone at my seams. Trying those relaxation techniques I've been doing since knowing Tommie is mine. Counting back from ten, blowing out air slowly because my chest feels as if it's heaving from the inside as I try to repress my legion of feelings.

"Are you alright?" Hazel's lazy eyes are looking at me, the green has won over brown at this moment.

"I'm just thinking about something." The grip on the steering wheel can hardly handle the strain of my nature's strength.

"Do you need me to relax you?"

Her hand is going to my thigh just above my knee, palm making its way upwards. Fingers are going inside the band pulling me out. This is what I like, female fingers on me, not *males*, not *Tommie's*. "Yes." The word barely audible because my jaw is clenched tight, refusing to open up.

Hazel undoes her seat belt, leaning over, her mouth bringing me to life inside her wet entrance. This is what I like - a female's mouth taking me in.

She knows exactly what to do, after all, we've been at this a long time. My turn to sink into the seat, concentrating on driving but feeling those lips descending the length of me, then pulling back up with suction. Her tongue flicking and dancing along the underside, sucking the blood filled veins in her mouth, my favorite technique she uses.

I remember the first time she did this to me in the shed with the broken knob on the door, it was at a bonfire - Tommie was there in the background sitting where the light just barely reaches the edges of the perimeter. He still had the lingering bruises all over his face from his fight earlier in the day. The juveniles were relentlessly attacking him because he was small, runtish in a way. He saw me go in there with her because his eyes were on my back until the door half shut behind us. When I came out, he was gone. I made sure when I did go home I wiped myself off with a towel before showering, leaving it in the corner for him to smell in the morning when he woke up.

He had to be made to understand I wanted no part of him. It wasn't easy to do but it had to be done.

I remember the time he brought a female to his room - it was Hazel. I remember listening to them with my ear to the door unable to stop myself, trying to *calm* myself. Hearing her laughing at him, while he was screaming for her to get out, to leave. I remember her coming to my room after that looking shaken up slightly. *"Do me a favor, Tate, tell Tommie I'm sorry for laughing at him."* I never did tell Tommie that. I made sure Hazel wasn't laughing that night, her moans were so loud I thought she would wake my parents up from the

other side of the house. Tommie didn't get out of bed the next day.

He refused to look at me after that. Always making excuses never to be around me. He started to fold into himself.

It's almost as if he went into his own world, his grades improving while he isolated himself more and more, books becoming his best friend, instead of me. Still, he had to fight every day, and there was nothing I could do to help him; he needed to fight his own battles with those pack males, a pecking order of things.

Hierarchy.

He would give as good as he got, both sides ending up bloodied and bruised. On one occasion where they got the better of him and severely injured him, his father and mine taking him for private fighting lessons, hours of honing his skills underneath their watchful eye.

He still got his ass kicked on the daily, but now he would pick just one target instead of fighting the gang and he would be merciless with that one wolf until the fighting got less and less and they left him alone because he was too much of an effort to take down. He might have been the

smallest runt, but he now had the skills to really do great damage if a wolf wasn't careful about defending themselves. Also, if he found one of his tormentors alone he would make an example out of them to their friends. It would earn him a group beating but he would smile the whole time at the wolf through it all.

His father was always telling him that he was a late bloomer - it wasn't until he was twenty that he started growing and filling out the way Betas do.

The car weaving slightly into the other lane as I think of *Tommie*.

Hazel is making little sounds in the back of her throat that vibrate against my now fully awakened cock.

Looking down at her, this is what I like, I need to keep telling myself.

Is it? The voice inside my head is answering back.

Pulling over to the side of the road because I'm going to prove to myself that this is *what I like*, plus my concentration is all over the place making driving difficult. In the confined space, climbing over until I'm on top of her, reclining the

seat back. Pulling her panties to the side I enter her swiftly, grabbing her hips, nails digging into her flesh causing a whimper of pain from her throat.

She likes that - for me to just enter her without any work from me. She likes the pain of it, the roughness of not being turned on is what makes it enjoyable in the beginning for Hazel.

Canines out, holding her by the delicate flesh of her neck, no puncturing skin but hard enough where she stills as if her life is in danger. It's quick without kisses, just me taking her with a need to prove to myself that I am a male who likes females. She's just the vessel I need to empty myself into, to prove to myself that I like *females*.

A shudder is raking her spine, her insides squeezing me tight, clenching around me. A groan is escaping her throat as she continues to squeeze around me. She likes it this way the best - no kissing just getting used for my singular purpose.

One time I tried to show her love, I tried to show her very gentle, it was a mistake on my part. Hazel refusing to speak to me for weeks, saying our arrangement is off, to find someone else because she was not meant to be loved, or

shown love. After that I just fucked her and she likes it that way.

Her legs wrapped tight around my hips while I fill her up completely. The both of us stilling, our breathing heavy, the only thing that could be heard against the traffic buzzing by.

"Are you alright?" Her question to me again.

"Yes." Getting off her, tucking myself back inside my shorts while she takes a tissue out of her purse cleaning me out of her before throwing it out the open window.

It's quiet now in the car while I pull back onto the road. Neither of us has much to say, so we don't say anything, *it's our way when one of us needs something from the other.*

Cellphone rings wake her eyes up.

"It's work." Her fingers are turning down the radio, while I roll the windows up.

"Hello." Hazel is pulling out an appointment book from the bag that's at her feet.

"This is Hazel." A moment of pause.

"I don't see anyone new without a referral." Shutting the book in her hand going to put it away before it stops midair.

"Tommie referred you? Who is this?" Her face scrunches up in disgust while listening to the voice on the other end. Why would he refer someone to her?

"Cash? You're the wolf from yesterday aren't you? What do you want?" Reopening her book back up to the pages that are full of written names on hourly appointments, some time frames have been reserved for hours. "I am." Her serious tone being used, a shadow passes over her face while going underneath an overpass. Her feature shade slightly. She listens to him quietly tapping her finger on the armrest. "I'm unavailable to you. I have no appointments left. Booked solid for the week. Find some other she-wolf, I don't play with your kind. Plus, you don't have the bills for me." The laughter that now holds her cries out, "He said what? I'm not in the discount business, I don't do specials." Her voice holds the insult.

Tapping her on the shoulder, "Apologize to the wolf." My mother will have her throat if she doesn't do as she was

told. Hazel shoots me the finger and mouths a curse under breath.

"You know what I'll book you for Saturday, at seven pm, that's prime time and its premium rates. I'm only doing it because I was told to apologize to you for my behavior, *Wolf*." Another pause in conversation as she listens to him on the other line. "I take credit cards. Don't worry it's billed discretely. No one will ever know you had to pay for it." Another hard laugh. "No discounts! Tommie has no idea what he's talking about. He doesn't know me or my work, but I promise after we're done you will have a new understanding of what I do."

Even her finger is pointing in the air with how ruffled she is becoming.

"Wolf, you listen to me, I'll tell you how it's going to go for you. Either you're going to have me look into your eyes while you please yourself at the end of the bed or you're going to have me ride you while looking in your eyes. You're going to pretend it's her until you're finished, then what's going to happen is you're going to feel really guilty because I bet this is your first time touching someone after she died. You're going to start to cry because everyone starts

to cry after. It's extra if I have to hold you while you sob in my arms, I don't do anything for free. I have myself to support. Just remember that I'm not a holder. So you still want to book with me, *Wolf*?"

She's holding the pen in her hand waiting for a response.

"Alright, I'll pen you in, now you've just got to find me. Vegas is a big place good luck." She hangs up the phone putting it into her bag while putting Cash's name beside the seven pm slot.

"Tommie gave him my card." She's not very happy at all. "He told him I'm not worth my full asking price to ask for a discount."

The laugh comes out, I can't hide it. "He did what?"

"You heard me, your boy is going to be paying big time for this." She pulls out her lipstick while pulling the sun visor down revealing a mirror. Slightly turning my head her way watching her apply her color to lips that are taken an oaken red hue.

She starts to fix herself up the closer to the airport we get.

Auburn hair being pinned up loosely so it looks like you can just take one out and everything will tumble down. An avalanche of curls that almost touch her belly button.

"Hey do you mind taking my car for an oil change, it's due?"

"No problem."

"Could you also go to my house and close the window tonight? I had to air the place out."

"Alright, anything else?"

"No." Pulling up to the drop off at the airport. She holds her carry on in her hands because that's the only thing she needs when she goes to Vegas. She likes to travel light, that way nothing is ever lost.

With a wave goodbye, she walks towards the door, not looking back while I pull away.

The drive back to the pack seems longer somehow. A heaviness settling inside my rib-cage, it's an unsettling feeling.

Pulling into Hazel's unofficial parking spot, Tommie's truck still in its spot except his window is busted with glass lying all around it.

Walking into the house my mom is making sandwiches, her nose taking in my scent, shaking her head slightly but not saying a word. She doesn't have to say anything out loud - her face says it all. Our fights have gotten old, the same thing over and over again. She doesn't approve who I do, but as long as it's a female she will cast her judgment in quiet.

Looking out the back window, I see Tommie on the edge of the pool sitting beside Addie who's in a bikini without a shirt covering her. Their legs in the water while the pups splash and play in the shallow end. She's looking into his face smiling and nodding her head at what he's saying to her. A touch to his shoulder, it's quick, light before she pulls her hand away.

Walking outside because I want Tommie to smell me. I don't want him to get the wrong impression of us.

I'm not like that - he might be, but I will never be.

Both heads are turning my way, his nose sniffing the air, eyes are finding mine, holding for a minute before he rises at the edge of the pool, doing a massive cannonball in the center of it. The splash is so big that it raises the whole water line up and out of the pool. The pups are screaming and floating in the waves he's created.

He's underneath the water, holding himself at the bottom until I think he wants to drown himself.

Chapter 18

Tommie.

Disappointment holds its own language.

Did my professor hold such feelings when he would hear my first no? My first shove of a hand on his chest to stop his teaching midway through his *lesson plan*?

I'm sure he felt such things but he never let on, he just acknowledged my reluctance with an all too knowing look

at what a hard time I was having within myself. He would talk to me at those times, asking why I was nervous, what was holding me back, trying to talk me through my fears of what I was figuring out about myself.

There's nothing scarier than learning your deep truths.

Saying this to me while getting the almond oil out, squirting some on his hands before they started to massage my back, trying to get the tension out. Me on my stomach, him pressing himself against my ass cheeks. It was starting to be a common practice - letting me get used to the weight of him on my back, to get used to the slip and slide of his shaft against the crack of my ass. Hands slick with oil all over my shoulders, spine, ribs, the feeling overwhelming. He talked me through it, telling me how amazing I felt against him, how it was alright because it's done with two people who care for each other.

He never mentioned *love*.

By then he knew what I loved to hear, *keywords* that always brought a fulfilling smile to my face and a willingness to my body.

To trust him - that he would be so gentle with me, he always had a way of making it so pleasurable, so exciting, and I believed with time he would have made even that something that I would love. Except, it was one hard line I just could not cross *with him.*

I just couldn't do that. But thinking back, was my hard line crossed when I let his mouth touch mine? Or was it when I allowed him to feel me up? Maybe the line was crossed when his open mouth went down on me until I filled up his stomach. My hard line was crossed when I put him into my mouth thinking *I won't go further than this,* but somehow my lines were getting more curved with time. For sure a hard line was jumped over when I allowed fingers inside me, and even a bigger crossed when I entered him for the first time, thinking *this is it, nothing further than fucking him.*

Seeing as I would not open myself up to him, he had laid down on his back with his hips at my head, by this time I knew what he wanted. Taking him in my mouth, I knew the purpose and the technique that he loved. I was a very good student - the best he ever had, telling me this while I traveled my tongue down the tender underside of him. I felt pride in myself that I could bring him as much pleasure as

he brought me. After all, it's not only important to get pleasure, but also to give it as good as you get it.

Once he was completely satisfied and empty, licked good and clean, I gave him my first spoken command, *"Turn over."* My voice growing deeper with my transitioning from juvenile to adult.

I could see the slight shock on his face, but he did as I instructed without hesitation. Getting on his hands and knees with a small arch to his back. I made sure to coat myself up good with his almond oil, not because I was afraid that I would cause him pain, I just liked how easy it was to slide myself in and out of him.

Descending deeper and deeper with every stroke of my hips, his breath coming in short intakes, the only thing that alerted me that maybe he felt some discomfort because after all, I was growing at an unprecedented rate. I could feel him stretching to accommodate what I had. No longer could he take all of me inside his mouth. I'd outgrown every article of clothing I had. I always thought my Professor was above average for a human, but I realize now that he was just average in height and everything else.

As my tempo increased, his hand went to my hip to ease my pace but I was too into it. Besides, he should have been used to it - his ass was in constant use then. With my hormones flooding my system, for a transitioning male wolf, all that goes through you are the three F's - food, fighting, and fucking and not in any particular order.

That was the first time my nature also made an upfront appearance, fingertips starting to turn to sharpened claw with a need to puncture flesh, teeth trying elongate with a need to just take a little bite. I knew better than that though - humans don't heal from wolf bites, they die.

A low rumbled growl made its way out of my chest.

"What was that?" His question had a slight fear that something was not right. I could smell the subtle hint of it against his flesh.

"Nothing." Almost growling the words out, he'd tried to turn his head around. Taking the back of his neck in my hand I pointed his face to the ground, so he had no hope of turning to see my slightly shifted face. The force of my next thrusts shook his entire body, and I heard my first whimper from his throat, yet I couldn't stop exerting my will over his.

The strong consume the weak...hierarchy of nature.

Taking him hard, fast, and without any mercy. Exploding inside him, his thighs shaking so bad, his body gave out while I stayed inside him, pressed against his back. I couldn't take myself out, not even when the last drop squirted out.

I wasn't ready for the session to be over, I could go multiple times but him, he could only go just *once*.

Sitting at the bottom of the pool.

Calm.

Detached.

Silent.

Temporal bliss without scent. The caress of peace seduces me to stay under for just a moment more until the world starts to blur itself away.

The pool filter is humming its tune until the stillness is broken. Addie approaches in her dive, hair waving behind her like one of those mermaid movies you see on TV. She sits with me at the bottom, regarding me with eyes that look like two sad blue moons in a face that held a question as to why I might be down here all by myself.

Smiling while I let a little bubble of air out, taking her hand while with my feet I push off the bottom and pull the both of us up to the surface. Heads break out of the water, while my lungs pull in a breath of air.

Her hand is going into my hair before she dunks me underwater again. Seeing her legs kick frantically away from me, I can hear her giggling once my head comes out of the water, she's already on the side of the pool. Taking her ankle, she's hanging to the edge with a fingertip grip, it's too easy to break that hold she has.

Bringing her close to me with an evil smirk she shakes her head 'no' trying once again to swim away, I just hold her to my chest before dunking her underwater, holding her down for a moment before letting her rise up then back down quickly before letting her go.

Taking a gulp of water, she spits it at my face before laughing away. Feeling Tate's eyes on me, he's sitting at the table eating a sandwich with the two pups beside him. They have their water wings on and are dripping wet with their mouths full of food.

He's putting more food on their plates, Addie walking towards the table taking a seat away from him. As soon as her hand goes to take a sandwich from the plate, he lifts a raised lip towards her with a growl before her hand pulls away quickly. Shoulders are sinking, she sits there quietly looking down at the ground.

"Sorry, Addie, I didn't mean that. Go ahead, take some food." Tate looking confused at what he just did.

She doesn't move a muscle, she doesn't look up, she's just *frozen*. "It's time to go." A trembled voice spoken softly to the pups who voice their complaints at leaving too soon.

"You don't have to go, Addie." Sitting next to her, a hand on her back soothing down her shaking flesh. Giving Tate a hard regard at how unnecessary that was.

"No, we've been here long enough. Can you tell the Luna thank you for letting us come for a swim, the pups

love it." She starts to get up while the pups stomp their displeasure at having to leave the fun.

"Shouldn't you be at work?" Tate doesn't look at me while he talks, instead, he's helping one of the pups take off their water wings before throwing them in the bin.

"I can work from my computer, had some truck issue's this morning. Need to get the window replaced."

He doesn't reply instead getting the towel he dries off the young one as if he's in a hurry to have them gone.

"Addie, I can take you home if you want?"

"No, it's alright. I have my bike."

"Then I can ride with you. I think I still have mine somewhere." Getting up, walking into the shed, my old bike still hanging up where I put it long ago. Wiping the dust and spider webs off of it, testing the tires that still hold air surprisingly. It's small but can hold the weight of me. "Get on." Talking to the male who's got a giant smile on his face. He gets on the pegs just like Tate used to. I would ride him to school like this until we shifted for the first time.

Those were good times for me, before the shift. I couldn't have asked for a better friend.

All that stopped instantly, he chose to drive to school from then on while I chose to leave early on my bike so I could avoid him. This had both a good and bad impact on me. I didn't have to see him, but now the juvenile males thought that Tate and I were not friends anymore and they descended in hoards to attack me, fight me. A future Beta who was a runt; they were embarrassed by how I looked, they were embarrassed that I was so small, that the pack would be laughed at if I was allowed to take the Beta position in the *future*. I was no Beta they would say while driving fists into my face. The incessant teasing almost drove me to drop out of school, except I understood that school was my only way out of the situation I was in. Because back then I doubted myself, thinking I was never going to grow, I'd never be *normal*.

"Hey, I remember that bike!" Addie's face lightening up with a memory. Tate's face darkening. "You two always would ride to school together on it when you were kids." Neither Tate or I replying to the comment, but our eyes connect for a second and holds. It's a punishing current of true spine-tingling bliss that momentarily stuns me still.

"Let's go." The young male taps my shoulder anxious for his ride to begin.

Without delay, I start to take myself away from my mate who's scent stinks of his pleasures with Hazel.

The need to get away from that smell, because there is a driving desire to rectify who he smells like.

Stopping at my truck and grabbing a stick and lighter before shoving it in my swim shorts that have dried instantly in the heat. It's not a long ride to Addie's house, but I do try to jump as many curbs as I can because the pup behind me loves it. I doubt Addie jumps curbs with her granny bike, except it's fitted with pegs on the back wheel, specifically put on for double riding.

"'Do you double ride them?' Asking a question that brings a grin to her face.

"I like taking them for rides around town in the evening, it's nice to ride around with someone else sometimes." Addie's grin falters and falls with a slump of her shoulders.

"If you ever feel like it, I'd let you double ride me anytime you want. You can take me for a ride." The tiny

female on her handlebars smiling ear to ear, just enjoying the ride.

"I'm not sure the bike could take both our weight."

"I'm sure it could hold us." Taking a tight turn, the pup on my back grabbing onto my shirt so he doesn't fall off. Addie takes the turn just as tight. The granny bike is deceiving, it can take tight turns as if it's a dirt bike.

Once at her house the kids run inside while Addie and I are left to talk in the front yard.

"I do remember that bike, Tommie."

"Really? I didn't even know you knew I existed in high school."

"Oh I knew who you were, I just never really needed to talk to you. I had a mate, and he never liked me speaking to any males beside him."

"He was possessive of you wasn't he?"

"He was." A tickle of a smile making her lips curve up.

Pulling out the stick, lightening it up because I have to go home now. Inhaling the much-needed smoke into my lungs, holding it in for as long as I can hold my breath before blowing it out and up, so I don't get any on Addie. She puts her bike on the side of the house while I lay mine on the grass.

"Why do you smoke so much?" Her nonjudgmental voice is just asking a question that she wants an answer to.

"It keeps me even, Addie, I need it to stay straight up here in my head. It makes my life manageable, even bearable."

"Is it because your mate rejected you?"

"Something like that, I don't like talking about it, Addie." Looking away from her while trying to inhale the whole pre-rolled in one long breath. A hand on my bare shoulder, with a little squeeze of her delicate fingers before her body presses into mine holding me to her.

Closing my eyes hard because she's bringing out emotions that need to be kept hidden deep inside me.

Pulling away from her, she's got tears in her eyes.

"Hey, what's wrong?" Looking at her in confusion.

"I just feel so bad for you."

"Don't feel bad, I'm fine. Listen this weekend that's coming up do you want to go into the city with me? I need to pick up some stuff and we could stay overnight, get a room, catch a concert, dinner, go to a club? What do you say?"

"I'm not sure." She's backing away from me slightly.

"It would be fun. When was the last time you went away for the weekend?"

"I've never have been away." Her statement shocks me.

"You've never left the pack territory?"

"I have no reason to."

"Well now you do, it will be fun, you need to live a little, Addie, just because your mate died doesn't mean he doesn't want you to live, to get out there and explore what the world has to offer you." She's looking at me now with big eyes of light blue.

"Alright, I'll go, but we aren't sleeping together, separate beds."

"Addie, I wasn't asking for that. I just want company, and I think you would be the perfect company for me."

Contemplation, eyes regard me as if she is having a talk with her inner self, weighing the pros and cons of my offer.

"I'll treat, you just need to bring yourself and some clothes." Trying to make my offer more enticing. She seems the type of female that doesn't care for fancy dinners but I think she deserves one.

Inhale, exhale, a hesitation of speech out of a slightly open mouth.

"Alright, Tommie, I'll go with you." Her hand holds a slight shake to it before she holds them together in front of her.

"Addie, it's going to be fun, friends having fun. Nothing more to it."

"Nothing more?" her eyes are questioning me before looking away.

"Nothing more I promise." My hand now on my heart with my oath.

"It does sound fun."

"Good, I'll pick you up Friday after work, be ready for me."

"I'll be ready for you, Tommie." Saying this as she walks into the house, closing the door behind her.

Finishing my smoke before heading off on a bike that's way too small for my body. It's a fun ride home, soaring high as a kite in my mind, nothing bothering me now except when I pull into the driveway Tate's there getting into his truck, he still hasn't washed off their scent from his body.

Tate has a way of flattening my optimism with his realism how things will be between the two of us.

It's my job to educate him in a better way of thinking.

Chapter 19

Tate.

Tommie is coming in hot before he slams on the brakes to his bike, skidding sideways, kicking up rocks and dirt before a fine cloud of dust settles on my shirt. Stopping just an inch in front of the truck.

"See that? Still got it!" Jumping off the bike with a stupid smile on his face before walking away from me.

When Tommie's back is all I can see, he has me remembering what we were like before our shift. We would try to out do the other one on our bikes until I would jump

on his pegs, hanging onto his shoulders. I was able to squeeze a little harder, get closer to him when he did that. I was able to lean into his ear and tell him to do it again. He'd nod his head to me, standing on the pedals, pumping his legs so we'd take the jump faster, which again allowed me to hold onto him just a little tighter. Sometimes we would fall, our bodies landing on top of the other. I would wrestle him then. Pinning him underneath my body until he begged me to let him up. I never wanted to get off him, even back then.

Understanding deep down it's not right to feel that desire for a male.

Tommie's getting further and further *away from me.*

It's impossible to draw my eyes from his line of sight.

The muscles in his back, shifting effortlessly with each step he takes away. He's got that strong, athletic grace without being overly muscular.

Dry mouth making it hard to swallow, this heat is making me think crazy things. *I need Hazel.*

When he disappears behind the house, I can't let the image of him go, compulsion's whispering shoving me

forward to follow his retreating body. He's in the shed putting the bike away, closing it behind him. With a glint in his eye, he takes a running leap, flipping fast from the shallow end edge of the pool into the deep end, creating a splash so big he soaks me in the *wake of him*

I'd been standing too close to the *edge*.

When he surfaces from the water, he's laughing to himself because my face holds no laughter.

"You smell much better now." Tommie's prominent blue eyes find mine his laughter gone as the water drips off my face.

Effortlessly he lifts himself out of the pool, so he's standing in front of me dripping wet. Eyes are trying to focus on just one bead of water making its path down his chest before soaking into the material of his shorts that are clinging to his body. Nothing left to the imagination, fabric stuck to upper thighs before he fixes them loose.

Taking a towel from the lounge chair, he lays down with it covering his eyes and nose. Pulling down his shorts slightly off his hips, so they ride low on his waist just above

his base. He's trimmed down with just the faintest line of new hair growth.

Tiny receptors in my body are indulging in everything that he's displaying. This is just teasingly cruel.

Forbidden sin.

The Tommie show is challenging me into a moral dilemma where my eyes refuse to look away from the main act.

"It's okay to look, nothing's wrong with looking, Tate." Tommie is speaking as if he understands my thought at this moment.

I should leave, but I can't pull myself away, so I sit on the lounge chair that's right beside him. His face remains covered by the towel except for his lips.

I want to touch.

Ebb of desire stirring inside, the flow of morality leaving me with every passing second.

Pheromones are releasing from pores that are openly spreading lust's scent everywhere on a purely physical level. A rumble of a growl from the animal inside makes his skin goose-bump as if he's cold, but the heat is stifling, and *oppressive*.

"You can touch me."

It would be so easy to reach out, let the palm of my hand feel the shape of his chest. The only male I could ever touch in that way.

If I were that way.

"I can't." Spoken so low I even have a hard time understanding what I just said.

A sickness building inside the longer my eyes dwell on the one thing that I shouldn't want.

His lips are parting effortlessly, tongue coming out, licking them wet. Hands are at the side of his body as if he's relaxing into his *down-tempo beat*.

He's shivering my lines.

"Tate, it's alright to look if that's all you can do right now."

Still, he lays there with the towel over his face, hiding from me. Curiosity about his years away, what's he's done, give me that taste of jealousy that I'm starting to get too familiar with. Only with him do I ever get these thoughts.

I've never been jealous before, not of anything or anyone, but now this male laying out in the sun as if he doesn't have a care in the world makes me see all kinds of the green edges jealousy can hold.

He's the enigma, my mystery that keeps me wondering about the puzzle of him. He's intriguing to me in a way I feel guilty of spending so many waking hours just thinking of *him*.

"How many men?" Blurting it out as if it's my right to know his details.

"One."

"Did you fuck him." It's not a picture I want to see.

"Of course I did."

Bile is creeping slowly up before I swallow the acid of it back down, the sourness of it lingers at the back of my throat. The taste of it is stuck. Why am I having trouble with this? Why am I asking questions that I have no desire to hear the answer to but can't help to ask anyway?

"Is he the one who owned your ass?"

His hand goes to the towel, pulling it off his face, which is turned my way now. Eyes on mine. "What did you say?" His jaw is tightening, his easy going manner starting to fading away.

"You heard me. I said, did he own your ass? Hazel said that you must have had someone owning you because you could never afford the stuff you wear on your own."

"Hazel said this?" His hands are turning into fists.

"She just made some observations about you. Is it true? Were you one of those boys?"

"Maybe looking back I was one of those boys, but at that time I thought I was lucky to have someone who took such interest in me. He made me feel *special*. He made me feel *loved* and I wasn't lonely for the first time since I'd shifted.

He showed me things, taught me things about myself that would have taken much longer to figure out. Did I get on my knees and suck him off? For sure I did. Did I get nice things from him? You bet I did, but at the time I didn't think of that as him owning me. I just thought he liked me enough to give me gifts and in return, I made him happy, not because of the gifts but because I wanted to bring a smile to his face."

He's looking at my face. His admission is making the hair on my arms stand on end in a way that isn't right. I might be sick - it's hard to hold the gag in. He notices how my stomach faintly heaves and I have to swallow down that bile that wants to spew out. "You had a human man in your mouth?"

"Yes." He's not ashamed, his voice holds no shame.

"You liked it?"

"At first I was leery, I just couldn't do it, because at that time I still wasn't like that. In time I came to a new way of thinking. Not only did I do it, but I enjoyed doing it. I like the feel of it, the taste of it, and guess what?" A sly smirk

now on his face, looking me up and down, "I'm very good at it."

"I could never be like you." My admission causes that smirk to downturn.

"Like what? What's so wrong with me?" His eyes are challenging the truth inside me.

"You know what's wrong with you."

"No, I don't. I used to feel I was wrong in some way but not anymore. I know exactly who I am."

Standing up, his hips are at my eye level, all I see is those swim shorts riding low on hips, exposing more than I should be focused on. His male smell is intruding into my body, clinging to the inside of me. My nose is scrunching up as if it's a disturbing smell, but in all honesty, it's so alluring, making me want to put my nose against his skin and just smell him.

My unnatural perversion, my inner shame.

He's looking down while my body rebels into itself. A shudder is wracking my muscles involuntary. I'm not able to

disguise it. The abomination of sexual desire is tempting me, it's a struggle not to succumb along with my darker needs.

I need Hazel.

"It's alright, Tate, I was once like you too."

His hand is going on my head before he kneels down in front of me, so we're almost eye level. "You think I could ever be like you, Tommie? I won't do that to my family, I won't do that to my pack, and I will never do that to myself. I have no desire to go down on you, I have no desire to let you inside me. I love females. I love how they look, how they smell, I love their softness and taste. I could never swallow down what comes out of you."

He's listening to me patiently, his face not giving anything away, but his eyes hold a depth of sadness to them that is heart breaking to my soul.

"I like females too, nothing wrong with them. I can go both ways." He states this as a truth about him.

"I can't!" Harsh words are coming out in a thickening disgust. His face still so close to mine, he doesn't walk away

just holds himself there as if waiting on what more I might have to say.

"I'm just honest. How do you think it would go if I announced at a pack gathering, 'Hey everyone, Tommie and I are mates, we're going to have a mating celebration.' What do you think they will say? What do you think they will do? How will they react to us dancing together? When we kiss each other? When we mark each other? It would be a disaster for everyone. Our fathers would hate us. Are you ready for your dad to tell you to get out, to never come back to the pack, are you ready for him to say you are dead to him because I'm not ready for that and I will never be ready for that. I love my family more than myself, I could never bring them that kind of shame."

Moments of silence, his hand going through his hair, a nervous habit that I've quickly figured out. "I get it. I understand completely. It's hard for me too, Tate, I just want you to know that, but I will respect you and your wishes. I won't do anything to compromise your family's respect for you or the packs. I only have one question for you - when you take a mate, how will you explain to the pack that she can't hold your mark?"

He doesn't wait for my answer because I have none to give, I haven't figured that one out. I should have thought out the lie I told when I was younger, now it haunts me because I can't claim anyone without everyone knowing I lied. Standing up, turning his back on me with his slow movement forward he disappears into the house.

Giving him some time, I make my way inside. Straightening my back out before my mom's smiling eyes greet mine when I pass by the living room. A group of females are sitting around discussing the next pack event. They all have notebooks open writing down who's going to do what.

She reaches for my hand when I stop by her side. The females are all smiling at me, bowing slightly in respect for my future position. I smile my lies right back to their faces as if I am worthy of the trust they put in me. "Love you, mom." Kissing her head before walking away with words behind me saying, *"Such a good male."*

Walking up the stairs to my room, Tommie's door is closed. Stopping in front of it, I can hear him typing on the keyboard to his computer, the smell of his herb coming from underneath the crack at the bottom of the door. I can hear

him inhaling, his breath holding before he's letting a breath out again. Going into the bathroom, turning on the water, waiting until it's scolding hot.

Once the steam is filling the small space, that's when I step in, skin turning instantly red. It hurts, burns almost, but it doesn't compare to the pain I feel trying to scrub away what's inside me. Somehow, no matter how much I try to clean or scrub, I don't wash away.

As a juvenile, I would spend so much time trying to clean myself right that my arms would be rubbed raw. I'd scrub my flesh so hard while I cried and spit. The water at my feet would be pinking red carrying my blood down the drain, and I thought if I could bleed myself enough, that maybe the inside of me would somehow be replaced with something that was at least half normal.

It never worked.

Chapter 20

Hazel.

Leather-topped stools, maroon velvet curtains, only add to the atmosphere of the fiercely dark room where the only light is from the singular candle on top of the tables. Couples are sitting close together waiting for the show to begin.

He's waiting for me, sitting comfortably in the only high back leather chair in the room, as if he is the only king here. His friends surround him on either side, bottle service all decked out on the small table in front of them - his show to tell others he's a big-baller. Except I know what's inside his pants and he's just all show when his clothes are on.

Trying desperately to over compensate for his
shortcomings.

Mascara is thick because he likes when it runs down my
cheeks.

Lipstick-bold lips give him no smile, but my gaze lingers
all over the man in my own fake show. Making him feel
important, worthy of attention. The women that surround
him and his friends are bought and paid for, his own little
harem of working girls.

It's all about the fantasy for these men - I give them
exactly what they want. After all, it's what's expected.

Expectations are always met.

Chanel black dress, Louis Vuitton heels with that peek
of red, Cartier on my wrist. The facade is real.

Illusions. My out of body experience.

The sway of hips, a slow movement that keeps his eyes
fixated on my waist before they crawl upwards to my chest.
It's covered, not a glimpse of skin, but the dress is very tight

so it leaves everything to the imagination of what's underneath.

With deliberate slowness, I take an empty glass while only putting enough ice cubes to line the bottom of the heavy glass. The lid has a cork and makes a small popping sound when I open it. A tiny vapor of mist hovers above the lip of the bottle before it disappears.

Fresh faces of women holding their champagne flutes, having the bubbly tickle their throats, thinking it's the most expensive thing at the table when in all reality it's this whiskey bottle that probably made the waitress cream herself with a gasp when he ordered it.

Twenty percent tip never looked so good.

Her eyes find mine before looking away with a sly smile. She's good to me, but I am way better to her. Always bringing these men here, having them sit in that chair making them feel like they are all kings except everyone gets a share of that wealth. From the waitress to the bartender to the guy that parked his car. Whatever the owner makes on these big fish bills I get my cut of five percent. Otherwise, I

will take my business somewhere else - to the ones that know how to play my game.

Their expensive cologne stinking up the air, masking all other scents, small fingers clutching the glass he's holding tightly as if afraid he might drop it. He can't hide those eyes that scream.

Desire.

Lust.

Want.

Pouring just enough to cover the ice cubes, I let it sit there for just a minute before the glass edge touches my lips.

The quality of it is smooth, bold, demanding my full attention to its sharp sweetness until it settles into the bottom of my stomach, creating that slow warmth that starts to awaken my senses, notes of butterscotch linger at the back of my throat.

"Hazel, come and sit." Patting his lap.

Doing exactly what he asked, I gracefully move, making his friends understand that I am his good girl.

Showtime.

Sitting on his left thigh, I let the side of my ass rest against his already hardened appendage that resembles a thumb more than what most men have between their legs. Maybe this is why he's so angry at the world, his life, why he never married. He's one of the wealthiest men I have ever met, but the most miserable. That's probably why he has such a powerful drive of anger; he feels cheated, so he takes out his frustrations in life on me.

Raising the glass to his lips, letting him finish the rest of my drink. Letting my Mac bold lips put my mark on his neck, leaving behind my red lipstick smudge.

"I've missed you."

Quivering voice of anticipation glides over my skin. His pulse is increasing as an addict's would thinking of their next fix. It won't be long before his own slow drip starts to wet his underwear.

I've become the addiction that a certain special type of man can't get enough of. The only person to never utter the one word that says *stop, I've had enough*. What they fail to understand is, I can never have enough of what strong arms and a heavy hand can bring.

His friends and women around us stare openly as his hand trails up my bare thigh between my legs that are starting to spread for him. Letting them glimpse a part of me that just doesn't care who enters it. After all, the next few hours are bought and paid for; I'm what he needs, what he longs for.

Providing a service for the under-served. Except I'm not charity, I expect to be *compensated well*.

His eyes screaming his delight that I'm being his good girl, while a singular digit leisurely slides inside me, a soft sigh escapes from my slightly parted lips, pupils dilating from his burning unfulfilled need.

He once showed up at my door - only once he made that mistake. Wanting to talk with me about a partnership. I was too enraged to hear him out, upset he would have someone follow me to my personal residence, gather information on

me. I expect the same sort of secrecy he does. Closing the door on his face, cutting him off from me for six months until his begging became too much to bear. I jacked my rates to triple, and he happily pays with a satisfied smile on his face every time.

What that incident taught me was, I was charging too little for the services I offered. I didn't believe in myself enough to charge what I was worth. I have no problems now, even charging all the other businesses I bring my clients to a five percent cut in what they make off them. Except for the waitresses - I let them keep their twenty percent.

These girls sitting around us, their boss having to pay me five percent for using her company. All of the major agencies wanting me to work for them, laughing in their faces because no one is my pimp but me.

Always, Hazel will look out for Hazel.

Music changing to a soft, sensual feel. The woman on stage seductively walking the length of the area until she puts both hands on the pole, treating it like a lover she's comfortable with.

Everyone's eyes on her, Except his. They're on mine, while he carefully, expertly, handles what he's been waiting this long month for. His other hand is stroking my inner thigh softly, caressing my skin as we both start to enjoy the stage show.

On rare occasions like this, he can be gentle, but most times not so much.

His lips press against my ear whispering the filthiest things I have ever heard, his foreplay game on track with the best because I taught him that.

Heart beating faster, feeling his chest pressed against my back. This is just a little precursor for our real show to begin.

Our table is watching the performers, stripping clothes, leaving nothing to the imagination. The women with us are getting drunker and drunker. Able to handle more than these women, I have finished slightly under half of the premium, I just want a good glow without the numbing that it can bring. I want to have all my senses to feel what's going to happen.

After midnight, the club starts to get capacity full; the real talent starts to take the stage. The girls that hold the big

time names. He calls over the owner whispering in his ear, and I can hear every word because his whispered breath is no trouble for a wolf to hear.

"I want her to go up next," He says, the owner more than happy to take the extra bills out of his hands. "Hazel, give me that special performance I like." He wants to give the impression to all his friends that he has the perfect girl and with the look in their eyes it seems to work.

Walking up on stage the song begins its sorrowful melody. The dance is for the women here showing them that I am the all star to this game, making my point without getting physical. This is my territory, and they are the *trespassers*.

The height of the stage allows new scents to hit my nose, that strong cologne no longer overpowering the rest of the smells in here. Letting my eyes fall to the bar, the *wolf* sits on the leather-topped bar stool with his back to me, eyes watching in the mirror that are now locked on mine.

A nod with the corner of his lip lifting faintly that says, *I found you.*

I hate Tommie.

Flashing my displeasure that he's here, he just turns himself around so he's facing me now. Beer in his hand, he leans back slightly, almost as if getting comfortable to watch the next act.

Shaking my vision away from that male, all my attention falls on the man that has the rights to me for the moment.

Striptease slow, eyes only on his because he's my *benefactor*. This is all for him and his ego that I stroke up. The first time doing this was awkward having everyone's eyes on me, but it was brushed away quickly, replaced by the thought that this stage was built specifically for me and I own it for the few minutes I'm up here.

Unzipping the dress, sliding it down over the rise of my chest, grazing my ribs until it's finally off my hips.

Confident in my skin, of who I am. If I'm going to be a stripper, I am going to be the best stripper that walks this earth. If I'm going to be used for someone's pleasure, then I'll make them understand that there is on greater pleasure but me.

Dancing to his dreams, sliding up and down the length of it, flipping myself around, easily able to hold my body up.

It's a performance in strength. How I can gravitate sideways and up and down on this round 7-inch diameter of straight steel. It's a flexion and extension of limbs that draws intakes of breath from the crowd. My body is able to bend, twist, and contort into very pleasing positions. The bra and underwear stay on; the man doesn't like to show all the goods, he wants the other men to taste that *greenness* of jealousy and envy what he's bringing home tonight.

The song ending has me dressing, the man already standing up and coming closer, he's barely taller than when I am flat footed, but in heels, I feel as if I tower over him.

"We're leaving now." Taking my hand, he leads me forward towards the way out.

Looking at the waitress, pointing to the premium bottle of whiskey, she understands that it goes to my hotel suite. That's why she gets to keep the twenty percent tip to herself. She understands all the hard liquor we don't drink goes back to me.

The town car pulls up with limo tint windows, in the reflection that *wolf* comes up behind us. A monster of a wolf.

Cassius Denver Valentine. Third born from the Alpha line. I've checked him out, done my research.

His mate died during the birth of their twins, with the death he started a non-profit up to save the lives of pups in the same situation he was in. It's one of the few charities I donate to. Cutting them a check once a year from what my ass makes.

I was hoping he would never have found me; I don't want to play his kind of games. I have no interest pretending to be his someone special but I am a professional, and I will give him what he's willing to pay for.

After all, this my business and who am I to turn away clients in need?

When he goes by us, he casts his shadow over the man; his five-four frame is nothing compared to a full-grown wolf, especially one coming from a strong Alpha line.

Cash doesn't say a word as he goes by, no eye contact made, no need for it. He knows I know he's found me and I will see him at seven tomorrow night.

Getting into the car with this man, letting my thigh brush up against his before his arm snakes around, pulling me to straddle his lap.

Pulling away from the club, he's already unzipped, pushing himself inside me, there's no intake of breath with the feeling of it. It's almost thumb like in length and girth. I never lied to him when he asked me about it once. I told him that he needed to work on other talents to please women because what he was born with just doesn't do the job.

He thanked me for the honesty; everyone else always lied to him. Since then he has been developing skills that he didn't even know he possessed, of course, that cost extra for the teaching. I'm no one's practice dummy, nothing free in my world.

Hazel has to look out for Hazel.

Lifting slightly, sliding him into my other hole with a slight grimace on my face that he loves to see. He thinks he's the man now. Nailing into me with a piston action that has a little whimper come out because what he's doing is painful, and he wants me to feel pain when he's inside me.

It's so quick that he releases himself, as spasm after spasm of liquid shoots out of him. He does this before the car makes it to the curb of his hotel.

Fixing my panties straight, while pulling down the corners of my dress, he helps me out of the car, the eagerness to get me inside the suite is evident with the quickness of his steps, the look of anticipation on his face. I swear I even see a light sheen of sweat on his forehead. His breathing picking up as he opens the door for me to walk into the darkened room first while the lock clicks behind us.

Showtime

Walking to the floor to ceiling window, losing my dress along the way, next is the bra, underwear is the last article of clothing coming off before my hands go on the cold glass.

The shoes stay on.

Giving him my back's pristine canvas so he can draw his red lines of rage on.

Breath held in anticipation before the first lash of leather releases my *dopamine of pleasure*.

Euphoria is erupting for the both of us.

He begins to empty his pent-up fury onto me, with lash after lash, swearing to the world, to his God, at his life. Standing there letting my vision blur when the pain is at its highest peak that I catch the faintest glimpse of him in the shadows, watching me. Holding onto that image of him, hoping to get just the faintest smell of my mate, it never comes, but I always hope for it.

Pressing my cheek against the glass while my tears run down my face, the sobs start to escape out as he moans his with every hit. The picture of my mate becoming slightly clearer, it's almost as if I can reach out and touch him but I know better, my hand would just disrupt his image before disappearing from sight.

This man rages and strikes at me until he exhausts himself out, never do I utter the safe word, the word he tries so hard to make me say. If this were a full-grown male wolf this would be a different story, no human man can hurt our skin unless they have silver, their strength is nothing.

Hands-free release racks his body, I have given him what he has been chasing, the rush almost too much for him to stay standing.

All these men are the same - they love looking at my face that's smeared with make-up, untamed hair that's wild now.

I'm a mess.

The black from my mascara cuts its uneven path down my body.

This comes with a price for me, as quickly as I felt full with the pain, now I feel too empty without it. To the point that I'm craving the whip to start back up again.

Once we catch our breath he brings my purse to me, taking the special salve that helps heal these kind of injuries, he rubs it into my back telling me what a good girl I am.

We sit on the floor like this, looking at each other, not saying a word; it was a good session. This has been my week so far, different men, in different spaces and they all have their various reasons for doing this.

He's fully satisfied, while I fix my hair, wiping away the streaks of make-up, he hands me my check, and I walk out the door, promising to schedule in two months from now. After all, to him, I need time to recover from his worst when in reality I will be okay in a few hours.

Turning around, I almost forgot. "Thanks for the stock tip, I did exactly what you said, you were right about the company."

"No problem, Hazel. Glad you took my advice, I don't usually give it out for free, I charge real money for those kinds of tips." He smiles at that because nothing with me is free, even advice on how to improve himself comes with a price. At least he's dating now, before me he was too scared to approach regular women because of how that one girl back in high school treated him, it ruined him for the rest of his life until his inadequacy manifested itself into this self-hatred about his body.

It's an uncomfortable ride back to my suite, the pain, always the price to pay. The driver can't look at me in the eyes, and I don't care as I try to catch his eyes every time he looks in the rear-view mirror.

At three am in the morning, the world looks darker, grayer than at midnight.

Passing by the front desk, my shoes feeling too tight now I almost ask for a piggyback ride up to my room. They would do it if I asked, Vegas is all about the hospitality and how you make that personal connection with your customers.

When the elevator doors go to close, that wolf enters carrying a box. Pressing his floor number, I insert my key card to allow access to the top floor.

"Wolf, I'm tired, I need to go to bed."

"Me too, I've been waiting for you for a long time now."

"Why?"

"I needed to make sure you got this, it's for our date at seven." He hands me the box he's holding, it's light. "I have instructions in there what I want you to do. I expect them to be followed." He keeps looking at my eyes.

"Are you sure about this, Wolf? You might not like what's waiting for you when I open the door up to greet you

at seven. It won't be her standing there smiling, it's going to be me."

"I understand that, *Hazel*. I just want those directions followed. I'm paying for that." The faint ding of the elevator followed by the doors opening has him stepping out.

"Make sure to ask the front desk to let you up. I'll tell them I'm expecting you."

When the elevator closes his face to mine a relief settles over me, he has a disturbing way about him that I just can't pinpoint.

Setting the box on the table, kicking off the shoes that hurt. The dress next to come off, the lingerie is put into the garbage. Never wearing the same set over, after all, I'm not the one buying it - they are - and once the hours are up so is the fantasy they pay for. I get to go back to me.

Something about hotel rooms, the quiet is more pronounced, silence is met with my silence.

Soundless.

Laying my cheeks against the table, eyes wide open, half lying, half sitting, like stone watching the colors of the day start to bleed through the blackness of the night.

Trying so hard to un-focus my eyes, to see my mate. He never comes to me like this, he only appears when I am in pain, doesn't he understand that this pain is *much worse?*

When the alarm disturbs the peace in the room, stone is beginning to come back to life. Arms that have gone numb start to twitch and move while the annoying sound refuses to stop until it's turned off. The stretch of my back, the movement of feet as they shuffle forward to press the button to make the noise go back to silence.

Soaking in the tub, prepping myself for the next appointment. Today's cycle continues over and over again during the day. A break at five because prepping for a wolf is much different to prepping for a man.

Punching the settings into the steam shower, I wait for the mist to fog up the floor to ceiling glass enclosure.

Going back to the box on the table, opening it up, a note of directions sits on top of the plastic air-tight sealed bags that hold clothes.

Hazel,

No other scent on you but hers. See you at seven.

Cash.

Taking the clothes out of the box, but not opening the bag up yet, it's a red dress, some makeup of course, dark blood-red bra and panties. Not my taste but it's all about the fantasy and I will give him what he's paying for.

These poor wolves are all the same. I get referrals from Alphas to help a male wolf try to get over his mate's death. Usually, it's been years before they touch anyone else and the first time is always devastating to them. I think paying for the service somehow cushions the blow for them, it's not about love, it's about getting over the hump to be touched again.

Stepping into the hot steam, letting my pores excrete out all the smells of the past week, the loofah scrubbing skin

raw, turning on the rain shower, washing the dead scents away, only to repeat the process a few more times.

When my hair dries on its own, letting it fall loose without any kind of hair products in it. Doing my makeup until I wear the shades of her. Lipstick is the completion of her mood, it's been used by her, but that's why he's paying me to be used by him. If he wants me to wear used lipstick, well, then Hazel has to wear used lipstick.

We all get used in one way or another, it's just I'm smart enough to be paid for it.

Opening the bags, pillow cases mixed in with the clothes. The scent of a female hits me as if she is standing right beside me. Rubbing her pillow case all over me, making sure to do my hair first, my neck is next, all along my skin until I rub it into my center and crack of my ass.

The dress fits well, simplistic at its best. Floor length, a high slit up the side that exposes thigh.

When the door rings at ten to seven, I answer it with a smile on my face only to see that he ordered room service. Directing them where to put it, a small private space overlooking the city is the perfect spot to eat in. The

architects of the hotel were very smart with the design of this room.

Once they are done with the set-up, it's only a few seconds before the knock comes to the door.

When it's open, this wolf that's standing in front of me doesn't look homeless anymore. His hair tied tight in a low ponytail, beard trimmed right down, looking clean and tight. The suit is perfect for his body type; it lets you understand the physique it holds underneath. Flowers in hand and a small bag in the other.

"You look beautiful." Stepping into my space, kissing me on the cheek before his nose is buried deep into my neck. His body trembles with the assault of her fresh scent.

His lips tremble for just a moment before he rights them straight again. "These are for you." Handing me the arrangement of all different types of flowers, every one of them in place to highlight the one beside it.

Kissing my lips very quickly, can he taste her on them? With the way, he licks those lips of his, he can, eyes dilating.

"You look good, Cash. Please come in." He enters slowly looking all around as if expecting to see something.

All that's here is me, in the illusion of her.

"I hope you don't mind, but I ordered for you?"

"No, I don't mind." Leading him into the small private dining area made for two. The food spread out on the finest china that money can buy. Red wine sitting in the decanter, letting it breathe before being consumed.

Pulling out his phone, asking for the wifi password, he connects to the system as his music plays his songs he wants to be heard.

It's background noise that's not too disturbing.

Going to the chair, he pulls it out for me to sit, tucking me into my spot before taking his.

He can't stop staring, giving him a soft smile letting him know it's okay to stare as long as his time will allow. After that, Hazel goes back to being Hazel, he won't like when that happens.

Pouring me a glass of red, he pours himself one as well.

Steak rare, with delicate baby carrots on the side, a baked potato finishes the main course.

Dessert sits to the side.

Taking his knife, allowing him to put the first bite into his mouth before taking mine. "We never had room service together, I never bought her flowers. This is something that I have always wanted to do for Kennedy."

Lifting the glass of wine taking a few big swallows because it's confession time. They like to tell me what they should have done better when their mates were alive. I'm a jack of all trades; a cock sucker, a whipping post, an illusionist, a psychologist. That's why I demand such high rates for myself - I'm good at what I do.

"Why didn't you?"

"Because I was a stupid, little, weak wolf."

"Were you a juvenile when you met her?"

"No, I was full grown but very stupid." His face looking away into the nighttime skyline where all kind of lights shine out bright.

"Aren't we all sometimes." Saying it between sips of wine.

"I just wanted to have a nice dinner with her; I wanted to show her I could be a *wolf* she felt proud of on her arm. I wanted her to love me *more*."

That first tear drops down onto his face, emotions can't be held back because I bet this is the first time he's admitted his feelings out loud instead of crying them into his pillow. Somehow these males feel safe with me, that I won't tell their secrets to others.

"Sorry." He wipes away the tear that's following the first. Taking a bite of his steak, I can't finish mine. Instead, my first glass of wine becomes empty.

"What happened?" It's good for these wolves to let it out.

"I found her, but she was in love with someone else, someone better than me, stronger than me, someone who gave her everything she needed to reject me. I just wouldn't

take no for her answer. So, I forced my mark on her in a ceremony that meant nothing at that time. That dress you're wearing is something I think she would have worn at a proper mating ceremony in our pack. You look beautiful in it." Watching him take a small sip of wine before putting the glass back down.

"How long where you mated for before she died."

"Not even a year. My mark faded so fast that I don't even really remember what it looked like." His hand touching the spot that holds nothing now.

"Can I kiss you the way I have always wanted to kiss her?"

"You never kissed her?" A little confused because they have pups together.

"Not the way she should have been kissed by me." His head hangs down slightly before it's pulled back up, eyes meeting solemnly.

"Would you like to dance?" He asks so nicely.

"Of course."

Cash gets up putting the cloth napkin on the table, before coming to me, pulling my chair out, taking my hand to help me up. The volume of the music is turned up in the slow beat.

His body movements are easy to follow, leading me into his swaying tune.

"I never danced with her." Another hard confession to utter, while his lips are at my neck, nose pushed into my hair, I bet his eyes are closed.

Are his demons slow dancing with us?

Putting my arms around his neck, melting myself into him. Hands are on my waist, his grip becoming firmer before he pulls back slightly to look into my eyes.

"Can I kiss you?" A pleading voice from a throat that is tight.

"Yes." Breathing out the word.

Tempo slow, his finger glides across my cheek, resting the palm of his hand on the back of my neck, tilting my lips

upwards to his. The kiss is gentle, sweet, not the devouring kind of passion but the one that speaks the *volumes of love*.

It's hidden sorrow that has been buried for so long that it makes those tears come out while kissing someone who isn't his mate.

So, I hold him through his tears, kiss him through his sobs, and sway with him through his pain.

To my horror, my eyes start to glass up, emotions too much, this is why I try so hard never to do wolves. They aren't like men when it comes to this sort of thing. I can take the heavy hand, but the loving touch is painful to bear.

I'm a professional, I have to soldier on.

The slow arch of my back presses my chest into him, lips kissing my jawline, neck, lips becoming more purposeful.

"Tell me what you want, *Kennedy.*" Words I know he's longed to say in the fantasy.

"I want you, Cash."

The zipper of my dress pulls down while the music plays. Hands all over flesh, the dress pools at my feet, lips on my chest.

Tongue tracing my curves.

Hands grasping my thighs as he picks me up, only to wrap them around his hips. Carrying me to the bed because he wants to make love to me, not fuck me standing up.

He's nibbling on my lower lip before his tongue seeks the entrance inside my warm, wet mouth.

Laying me on the bed, he undoes his suit jacket, taking it off, shoes are kicked off. He crawls on top of me, pressing his weight into my body. What's between his legs brings a smile to my face; no pretending with this beast. I'm going to like the feeling of him.

Intertwining limbs, while his body dips into unison with mine over top clothes. Making slow rotations stimulating what's to come.

Suck.

Bite.

Caress.

Fingers are undoing buttons on his shirt, letting my palms now feel a chest that was made to be considered with touch.

Solid.

Strong.

Male.

His shirt comes off, unbuttoning his pants, bringing them down, he's not an underwear male. An intake of breath for what he possesses - lucky wolf.

Hips press solidly into hips, the grind makes me pulse in anticipation.

Nails are turning his back into red lines now. Growls of pleasure vibrating both our bodies.

My bra is next to go while his mouth descends on my female hills. Next is my panties to leave my body, not a stitch of clothes between us. Hands on my thighs, spreading my legs for him while his tongue ventures in.

He's a worker, digging in deep with his tongue and fingers.

Hand in his hair, back arching off the bed, making me explode out. Hovering just above me for a moment, his manhood opens up my womanhood for what he has to offer.

Stretching, filling me to the point of being slightly uncomfortable, I love this feeling.

Head down into my neck where I made sure to put most of her scent. He's inhaling, crying, tears hitting my skin, while his hips are rolling pushing himself in and out of me. Heavy breathing is replacing the crying, body shaking, trembling. A moan from the base of his chest, he's buried as deep as he can be, before a soft whimper comes out and he pulses inside me, filling me up with what he has.

My legs are wrapped around him, hands on his back, just holding him. Until he can move off me.

Looking down at my eyes with tears in his, he whispers *I love you* into the now still air.

Cash clutching my body to him, not wanting to let go. Allowing him the time he needs to pick his head off my

chest. The tears now falling down the side of my body wetting the bedspread.

"I have one request before I leave." Cash looking serious as if he's been thinking about this for a long time.

"What is it?"

"I want you to shave my head."

Smiling to myself because for their pack, that's the first step for him to start his life back up again. "Of course I will, Cassius."

Chapter 21

Tommie.

The tall tree in the front yard looks as if it's being choked by the green vine with blue flowers that only bloom with sunrise or sunset. As if the petals hide from the sun's harsh stare throughout the day, only opening up when the spotlight goes away.

"Bye, Mom."

Standing at the door, waiting for her to do her thing. Looking out the back window watching Tate grilling at the barbecue. He's handing out burgers and hot dogs. Everyone is done in work for the week, coming over for a swim and

some dinner. He's got a smile on his face, talking, enjoying the company he's in.

He looks comfortable as long as I'm *not around*.

He gave the invite out yesterday, spur of the moment. Calling them individually to stop by, bring the family, food provided... everyone got the personal invite except for *me*. I'm just grateful to have a weeks worth of sleep without having to endure Hazel and him going at it, over and over again.

"Have fun, Tommie. When will you be home?" Mom coming over to me to give me a once over.

"I'm not sure yet, maybe on Saturday or we might stay until Sunday, playing it by ear." Not committing a day or time to her. She just worries when I don't show when I'm supposed to.

"Addie's a nice female, Tommie." Her hand is patting my chest, with a look of hopefulness that maybe something might be brewing between the two of *us*.

"She's a friend, Mom." Putting her straight on that line of thought. No need for her to be curving with hopes of the

future for me. Sometimes when we're like this, just the two of us, I want to tell her about me but I just can't ruin her life like that.

The need to scream at the top of my lungs that I am the way I am, and for her to take me in her arms and tell me, "I still love you, Tommie."

"Well, that's how it starts - *as friends.*"

Tate is coming in from outside, grabbing more buns from the counter, his shorts are just on the verge of drying from the late summer air.

Heart racing.

Breathing stills.

Strong legs whose thighs are hidden underneath long shorts. Chest bare, with the sun's heat still attached to it.

"Where are you going?" He's asking a question while gathering the buns.

"The city for the weekend." Eyes, they devour my skin before he pulls them away focusing on anything but me.

"Alone?" Curiosity rattling out in his one-word question.

"No, I'm just on my way to get Addie." Touching my head, the new hair cut feels weird against my fingers. He's watching that hand, it feels warming where his gaze rests on my head.

"Addie?" Her name drips in a harshness that he fails to hide from my mother in the room that stops and looks at him oddly.

"She's never been to the city. I have to pick up some stuff, she said she would go. Problem with that?" Challenging him to say something, *anything*.

"No." A shrug of his shoulders, face not giving away any sign of emotion. His verbal sparseness towards me this whole week is his way of showing he just doesn't care. Neutrality of his sold straight line twists up my gut, causing a stomach ache from deep within.

Exhaling.

Turning.

Walking away.

"Bye, Mom," Saying before the door closes behind me.

Starting up the truck, it comes to life with a deep rumble, vibrating the seat underneath me. Rolling down the windows because the faint smell still lingers inside that stinks of me. Hazel is going to pay for this one.

It's a very short ride to Addie's brother's house, pulling up in the driveway, leaving the truck running. Knocking with a force meant to be heard, her brother opens the door not looking welcoming, yet the doormat says, *Welcome.*

"Hi."

He says nothing back, instead leaning into me. "If you hurt her in any way." Rough quiet meant to intimidate with a threat. He forgot this isn't high school anymore. His threats, his voice, his intimidation means nothing *now*.

"What will you do?" Leaning back into him with my threat.

"Tommie." His mate is coming around the corner until she's standing on his right with an arm around his waist. "Addie's coming up now, you guys have fun. When will you

be back?" It's as if she's a worried mother towards Addie who is just a few years younger than her.

"Not sure yet. I'll leave it up to Addie - if she wants to come home Saturday, we'll be home, but if she's having a good time, then we'll come home Sunday afternoon. Is that alright?"

Somehow this is turning into parents eyeing me up like I'm their daughter's first date. A grumbling growl from her brother exposes a flash of teeth and I'm not appreciating his posturing.

"Hi, Tommie." Addie is coming up from downstairs with a few young pups following behind her. Clinging to the back of her shirt, trying to pull her away from the open door that she's about to step out of.

"Hi, Addie, you ready?" Taking her bags from her hands.

"I'm ready!" A hint of excitement in eyes that have a tiny light in them.

"Don't leave." A young pup who's got a bathing suit on, wraps her body around Addie's leg before her mother pries her away.

"I'll be back soon, alright." Giving the female a little kiss on the forehead. "I'll miss you." Bending down to hug her the rest of the young ones follow their older sister all dressed for a swim, squeezing Addie tight.

She's their *Den Mother* when their mother is away working. The attachment is strong. Letting them have their moment I stand silent, her brother just eyeing me at a side angle while I look him straight in his eyes.

She gives them both hugs goodbye before we are both out the door and driving away along the road that leads to the border of our territory.

"Are you excited?" Giving her thigh a little squeeze, music turning up until the both of us are swaying our heads with the melody.

"I am. I've never stayed in a hotel before, I've never gone into a city."

"Why?"

"Well, my parents never left pack territory. When I met my mate, he didn't want me doing things without him, and he hated the city. So, we always stayed on pack territory. When he-" A swallow of voice before she finds it again. "After, I just didn't want to go anywhere. But now," her head turns in my direction. "I think I'm ready to do different things." A hard blush is creeping on her neck that makes me look away.

"Well, Addie, you're lucky to have me as a *friend* because we are going to do it up proper tonight, I'm going to show you the city, how it should be seen by someone who has never been. Is there anywhere you want to go, anything you want to do?" She hesitates, she wants to say something, but she's refusing to speak her mind. "Addie, just say it."

"I trust you, Tommie. Whatever you want to show me I know I'll like." Regarding me for a quiet moment before a song comes on that sparkles her eyes.

"That's the song I told you about." Her face is wearing a proud smile on it. She loves it when she plays stuff I've never heard of.

"It's a good song, the whole album is great." Loving the fact that someone finally has the same interests as me. She even likes the same books to a certain extent. "Did you start the book I gave you?" While she reaches for my phone, scrolling through my music, I'm cringing slightly with her looking at songs that are personal to me. She plays the next song before the first finishes.

"Did I start the book? It's done, only took two days to read it." Her voice is pitching in excitement as she goes on about the main male character she has fallen in love with. We go on to say our favorite lines out of the book. While she plays me her favorite songs from my phone, singing a few together. I like to listen to her more; her voice has an odd quality to it, old time sound that you don't hear too often.

"We should go out for late night Karaoke, I know a place."

Her face drops in mortification. "I can't sing in front of strangers." Heart accelerating in her chest with an anxiety of doing something she's not comfortable with.

"That's the thing; they're strangers, won't ever see them again. We can do a duet." Giving her thigh another squeeze, her hand rests on mine for a moment before pulling it away.

"Only if you sing with me."

"Of course. *I've got you, babe.*" Singing the last part to her, she rolls her eyes, but the grin is plastered on her mouth that is truly smiling.

Our conversation never stops, both comfortable with the other. Her now playing songs from her phone, new songs that I am falling in love with, she knew I would like them by the way she starts to puff up with pleasure. I want her to play the song again just to listen to the verse, or the lone guitar being manipulated by master fingers.

Making it to the hotel by seven at night, holding the door open so Addie can walk in first. The first thing she does is bounce on one of the beds like she's a little pup. A giddiness has fallen across her face while she checks out the bathroom, drawing the curtains to look at the city skyline that's starting to glow with the sinking sun.

Coming to stand next to her, "Are you ready to have some fun?" Watching her take everything in for the first time

at being away from home. This far up you can see where I went to school at in the distance, where all my *Education* took place.

"Tommie, thank you so much for inviting me with you." Addie's hand on my arm is squeezing my bicep, before letting go.

"No problem, Addie, just happy to have a friend come with me. So, I thought we could get cleaned up, shower, go out for a nice dinner, then meet one of my friends at *The Green House*, it's an upscale club so wear something that's showcasing." Her neck is a creeping blush that's spreading up her face to her ears.

"Tommie, I usually don't wear stuff like that. It's not my style." Her eyes looking out over the office buildings whose lights are starting to shut off as people leave their jobs for the day.

"Addie, I can't wait to see you in it. I know you're going to look amazing." Giving her a little hug of comfort. Her head pulling away from my chest, searching my face for something, but finally pulling herself from out of my grip, tucking her hair behind her ears.

"Sorry, did that make you uncomfortable?" Making appropriate space between us, thinking sometimes I'm a little too free with her.

Forgetting myself.

"No, it's alright." Walking back into my space, she wraps her arms around my waist giving my body a soft squeeze, smelling my shirt.

"We're going to have a fun weekend, let's stay until Sunday. Let's have room service in the morning, shopping in the afternoon and drinks in the evening."

Her eyes are watching my lips move, before looking at my whole face. Hardly anyone just looks at me, she does though, she listens to my words, she knows everything that I like. Somehow this female is turning into a best friend and it's been a long time since I had a real best friend.

"Alright." Her voice pressed into my chest, while I give her a small kiss on the top of her head.

"Good, now go take a shower, I'll take one after you."

Once she's done with her shower, stepping into the bathroom that's steaming with leftover warmth from the water. Taking my shower quickly because the need to smoke one is starting to itch at my skin. Somehow being away from that house makes the need to smoke less but the need is still there.

It's a balance of things that needs to be maintained.

When getting out of the bathroom, she's drying her hair, wrapped up in a towel that showcases her perfect legs.

"You have nice legs." Letting the words fall out of my mouth before looking away. I don't want her to feel as if I'm checking her out. Taking my towel off on my side of the room, she's already claimed her bed with her stuff laying on it. Turning away from her, drying myself off.

"You have a nice ass."

Turning towards her with my full frontal, dropping the towel before pulling on boxers that are brand new. Her eyes completely fall to the ground not commenting on anything else she has just seen, I'm not sure if that's a bad thing or a good thing. Addie's blushing, burnt-cinnamon cheeks, her

embarrassment makes me smile. I love to see her squirm slightly out of her comfort zone.

Once dressed, she's still working on straightening hair that's just been dried completely.

"You look nice, Tommie, I like those pants, they fit you perfectly."

She's giving me a once over while I do up the belt, stretching my muscles out so the material's not so tight. They fit snugly, comfortable, the way suit pants should. The shirt is hugging my body but not in an obscene way. After all, this is how I have been taught to dress; with a tailored fit. The *Professor* always loved the visual of what's underneath, his eyes screaming lust when I opened the door for him to my apartment on our way out for dates that no-one could know we were on. Secrecy at all costs, I understood the importance of it, the need for it.

"Thanks, Addie. I'm going to go down to the bar and wait for you. First I need to go smoke this." Pulling a pre-rolled out of the baggie.

"That reminds me, I brought you something. We have a greenhouse out back, and between the tomato plants, I grow

a plant for my brother. He's not a chronic like you but he enjoys it from time to time, so I brought you some to try. Tell me what you think of it." She's handing me a small bud in a plastic bag that's been double wrapped.

Pungent flavors hit my nose when the seal is broken on the bag. A thick coating of sugary resin sticks to the bud with a loving embrace. This is the most chronic looking bud I have ever laid eyes on, in a sea of green, this is the standout, the one that has no price cap to it. The connoisseur is willing to pay the top rates for this little piece of gold I'm holding.

"You grew this?" Can she read the shock to my face?

"My mate loved the stuff, so I learned how to grow it so that way he wouldn't have to waste our money buying it."

"That was smart of you." Not focusing on her anymore because this plant is calling to me, a little saliva pooling in the back of my throat just picturing what the taste of it might be. Taking my scissors out, cutting just a little out from the bud, delicately, with care not to take more that I need. Not a speck will be wasted. Spinning it up while Addie starts on her make-up.

Putting the baggie along with scissors and paper in my suit jacket.

"I'll be sitting at the bar, don't be too long." Putting the watch on that the *Professor* bought for me.

Once outside, walking to my truck and lighting it up, the first inhale rushing down my throat is everything that I knew it would be.

The flavor profile perfect.

A white cloud is born when exhaling out. The quality is so good that its burning white ash instead of the darker stuff.

Wondrously potent.

Unable to finish even half of this, licking my fingers to put it out. Needing to put the rest back in the bag. Looking down at my feet, one of Hazel's cards is laying there, I pick it up, wiping it off to put in my suit jacket - you never know who might need it.

Baked. That's how I'm feeling while walking into the hotel towards the bar.

I'm not going to be able to drive. Grinning when ordering my drink from the bartender, eyes at half-mast. Sitting around the room are businessmen or couples hunkering in for the night.

Whiskey on their breaths with cheap perfume along their necks.

Part of me wants to call the *Professor* to tell him of my find, but I understand that I'm not his anymore. The dull ache of hurt still hasn't left the pit of my stomach. Sipping on my drink that's been made a double - why not? This has now turned into a no driving night.

Letting the high take me away inside my mind, thoughts always drift back to him and the *education* I received.

The memory of his office comes to the forefront. It was a room, a space that I'd come to associate with good and bad memories. Always walking in and closing the door behind me, his wonderful smile greeting me, him getting off his chair, pinning me against the door. The first kiss, the exhilaration of all crushing passion that followed it.

He would try to turn me around, wanting me to take a more powerful part of his anatomy inside, but always he

met my unbend-able line. So instead I would get down on my knees until the whispered *Thank you, Tommie,* came from his lips while I rose triumphantly from my knees, with a satisfied smile on my face.

For a year, his cream had been solely given to me, I had come to love swallowing it. He would undo my pants then; always a giver himself. His index finger starting to go inside me, a small whimper coming out only to change into a long drawn-out moan when his mouth descended over the head, tongue licking the shaft. Slowly, he would get me ready for him, stretching me, probing me, showing how pleasurable it could be if only I would let him have me.

Tongue tickling pleasure, hips thrusting into his wet mouth before pulling out only for me to bend him over his desk, taking him the way my *Nature* insisted. Fingers digging into his hips, while he held onto the wooden corners of the desk. Pumping myself until spilling everything I had to give, he was unable to hold the streams of me in, overflowing down his inner thighs. Thrusting subsiding with the afterglow that releasing can bring.

Except I'd want to go again, his body was too sore to accommodate my *Nature's* need. A full grown male wolf has

a drive inside them that requires fulfilling. He would shove me away from him, his impatient face, finger pointing accusations at how I get to do him but he can't do me.

It was a happy space for so long, but it was starting to change at the beginning of my last year. Our fighting becoming more and more and it all stemmed from my reluctance of getting ass fucked by him.

I just couldn't cross that line with him.

The first time I saw the fresh-faced eighteen year-old student inside his office, sitting in the chair opposite him, raised the hair along my spine up that something was not right. Smelling for any signs of betrayal - none were there. I couldn't smell anything, so I gave him the benefit of the doubt, what I failed to realize was that the *Professor* was just starting this young man's education, grooming, while mine had been coming quickly to an end.

Nothing more I could learn.

Looking up from my far away thoughts, Addie is standing at the entrance to the bar. She has a small purse clutched in her hands. A nervous look on her face while I take the sight of her in.

Hair straight down her back, a thigh-high split black dress with a neckline that just gives a peek at the soft curves of her chest. The dress is showing off her tanned skin and toned arms. Curves and shape that beg to be explored with the way she is displaying herself.

A thin charm bracelet on her wrist, eyes smokey grey, lips the color of dark coral. This is not the female I'm used to seeing, this is a gift for any male to look upon. Standing up, eyes only for her. Walking straight up to her, around her, looking from head to toe until my mouth pressed against her ear.

"If I was any other wolf besides your friend right now, I would walk you back to the elevator, carry you into our room and not open that door back up till late Sunday afternoon. But I'm your friend, so I will just say this - you look beautiful, Addie." Meaning what I say.

She's having a hard time with the compliment, looking at me all flustered. Taking her hand and leading her to the bar, pulling the chair out so she can sit down first before pushing her comfortably in. The bartender's eyes holding at that peek of rounded breast before asking what she wants to drink.

"Whatever he's having." She's fidgeting with her bracelet. An anxiety causing her to shake in her skin. Taking her hand, giving the top of it as a kiss, just holding it in mine until she settles down enough to hold her glass and take a small sip.

"Can you call us a cab?" Saying it to the bartender as he brings us our second drink. She's loosening up, not so tight.

"So where are we going for dinner?" The straw she was just sucking on leaves her lipstick stains on it.

My mind wondering to the fact if she were to go down on me, I'd be covered in the stains of her mouth. A hand is going to my head because I think the weed is affecting my brain. "Somewhere nice. Hopefully, you'll like it."

"Cab's here." The bartender interrupting the look we're sharing, putting the bill in front of me, I pay it before taking her hand in mine, leading her to our night together.

The restaurant is modern, full of new and exciting dishes. Taking our seat, the men in the room let eyes linger on her thighs. Eyeing them all up as I catch them, they look away quickly. Our tasting menu is coming in waves of

gastric pleasure. Her closed eyed moans making me swell with pride that I could give this to her.

"Do you like it?" Sipping on wine that is not as good as what she makes.

"This is amazing. Thank you, Tommie." Beaming smile, while dessert makes its way to us. Miniature creations of the bigger pastries that are just a sample for people who just can't pick one. The last bit of Creme Brulee held on my spoon she's trying not to eye up.

"Would you like the last bite?" Holding it up to her mouth, she leans in taking what I'm offering her.

By the time we arrive at the club, it's around ten thirty, just in time for a little line to form outside the door. Walking up to the bouncer we exchange handshakes, he's a nice guy that is more gentle giant than a beast. To all these humans he looks like a massive monster of pain if you don't follow the rules. Holding the door open so Addie can walk inside first, the sway of her hips in those heels draws me to her ass that's round and tight and I can't help but look. Music loud enough to vibrate the inside of our chests with shaking rhythm.

"Welcome to *The Greenhouse*." Getting close to her so she can hear the words. Looking into the crowd some wolves are here, eyes reflecting the flashing light. Their nose up in the air while instinct drives us to take a little smell of them. My arm is going around her, bringing her closer against my chest while looking the males in the eyes. Notifying them this territory is off limits.

A hand starts to squeeze my shoulder.

Turning to face the male whose hand is on me the wolf staring back has no smile on his mouth - this male never smiles. Grey-blue eyes hold a hauntingly silent threat to anyone that stares at them for too long.

He never looks away from you, just stares at the inside of you, as if he sees things that you can't.

"Tommie." His voice never rising above the music, but somehow he makes it heard.

Addie stepping into my space, the side of her body pressing against mine. A shiver is running along the spine of her. The large male in front of us standing solidly seems to be stalking us without any movement on his part.

Eyes that give nothing away, a fundamental characteristic that he has such control over.

"Addie, this is Prosper Green, the owner of the club. Prosper, this is my friend Addie."

Chapter 22

Addie.

Expressionless.

"Addie, this is Prosper Green, the owner of the club. Prosper, this is my friend Addie."

The reflection of light blinks away from eyes that hold liquid silver rimmed in a hint of dark blue.

"Hello, Addie." Inflection of tone even, not rising, but meeting my ears strong and easy. Apathetic gaze just a

millisecond long fleets over me before they focus back on Tommie.

"Hi." Trying to make myself heard over the music. It's too late - I don't hold his attention. Pressing myself into Tommie more, his body slightly picking up the beat of the rhythm, I start to sway with his internal natural rhythm. Looking around, the place is packed with sweaty bodies crushed on the dance floor. Rafters packed with strobe lights in every variation of color, flickering bodies and faces in the soft glow of iridescence. It's trance-inducing; watching the movement of the crowd, no one seems to care what they look like just in their own world of dance.

My mate would have never allowed me to come to one of these places.

"Tommie, I have something for you to try." A controlled voice leaving no choice but to follow his back while walking away from us with an animal grace. His movements are fluid, without care. He takes a path right through the dance floor while humans and wolves give him the right of way that he has demanded without the need for any sound from his voice.

Tommie's warm hand clasps mine while pulling me forward to follow this wolf who makes my sixth sense stand to attention indicating something is off. Tommie's looking down with a smile that says, *everything is all good.* That smile does things to me, a constant suggestion that I have to remind myself he has a living mate out there that could come back at any time to claim him, and that mine is waiting for me in the moon.

The music loud, the place smelling like sweat, alcohol, and lust. Bodies are parting as Prosper approaches their space, their sixth senses altering with the close proximity of something prowling near. It's his eyes that they avoid - wolf and human alike. They watch him with sideways glances, the unease of prey needing to flee quickly before the predator decides to run them down.

Opening the door to a room in the back, walking inside, surveillance camera screens showing all the corners and nooks in the club, even the bathrooms are monitored. The wolves in the room turn eyes on us, noses sniffing the air.

"Tommie!" One of the bigger ones getting up from his chair walking over,"How are you?"

"Good, how you doing? How's the mate and pups?"

"Good, everyone doing good, and who is this?" Giving my neck a look for a mark.

"This is my friend Addie. Addie, this is Walter - he's head of security for The Green House and *The Compound*. I worked with him at *The Compound* in my last year of school."

"Addie, it's nice to meet you." He doesn't touch me just nods in my direction.

"Tommie, this way." Prosper opening another door for us to follow him through. He flicks a switch on, bright, almost harsh light in contrast to the last room we just came from, alters my vision for just a flicker of second, but it's enough time to see the shadow of Prosper move without the male actually moving.

Backing slightly up, only to hit Tommie's chest. Looking towards Prosper's shadow, it's falling how it should be, nothing seems unusual. Perhaps my eyes were just playing tricks on me.

"Tell me what you think of this." Handing Tommie a small bud to examine. Prosper seems to be nothing but

business at the moment. Tommie, giving it a smell, touching it, then touching his index and thumb together, it's barely sticking from the resin it holds.

"It looks alright." Tommie smelling it again, but his face says that he's not impressed by it.

"Try it out." Getting a grinder from a desk drawer, opening up the cylinder with sharp teeth to tear through the herb easily, he puts pieces inside it before closing the lid and shredding the contents. He makes quick work of spinning one up before handing it to Tommie who looks impressed at this wolf's skill of the roll.

I should roll some up for Tommie - I always did it for my mate so he wouldn't have to waste his time doing it, after all, he was always *busy*.

Tommie lights it, pulling a big breath in, holding it a long time before it's coughed out slightly in a cloud of white. "It's got some smooth flavor to it. I think this is the best I've tasted from your stock."

"Is it good enough for you to stop buying from that human?"

Tommie has a little smile on his face. "Let's see how high I get then I'll tell you if I'll start to buy from you."

"That's why I've always liked you - you're not a yes male. You just say it the way it is. Why not come back and work for me? You know you have no place in your pack for someone like you." Tommie's hand goes through his hair before looking Prosper in the eyes hard.

"I belong where ever I want to belong, Prosper. I'm no different from you."

"A bit different, wouldn't you say, Tommie?" Prosper's taking the stick out of Tommie's hand, taking his pull from the hand rolled.

How does Prosper think Tommie has no place in the pack?

"Maybe. But now's not the time to discuss this, Addie and I are here to have a good time." Tommie's voice is edging down, his eyes glossing slightly over.

"Alright, no more on that subject. What about this?"

Tommie holds his hand up when Prosper hands him back the stick. "I'm good with that."

Prosper watches. "It's good, isn't it? I'm going to enter it into the Cannabis Cup in Amsterdam this year." His tone is even, without any lift or drop to the quality of sound.

"You won't win because you can't beat this." Tommie's pulling out a baggy from his suit pocket and a business card falls out, a side smile curling that suggests something is amusing him while looking at the picture.

Prosper immediately takes the baggie from Tommie's hands, opening it up, taking it out, smelling it, the resin tacky on his fingers making them stick together.

"Who's selling it?" An *almost* expression on a face that has been stoic this whole time. That's the only rise that could hint at anger, it's quickly put away behind grey-blue eyes.

"No one is selling it, Addie grows it."

Taking the full gaze of him against my skin is unnerving. The feeling of something crawling against my flesh wants me to itch it. Fearful goosebumps prickle skin and not in a good way.

Immediately, Prosper takes a chunk from the bud, cutting it up with scissors he rolls it, smelling the stick before lighting it up. Taking a longer pull, blowing the cloud out to pull it right back in again.

The both of them passing it between each other, back and forth.

Ever. So. Slowly.

Tommie's mouth is getting closer to mine,"Open up".

When my lips part, he blows in his cloud for me to ride high on, by the time the stick is done I'm giggling to myself, with a dry throat that produces an uncomfortable cough.

Prosper sits himself down, so does Tommie, pulling me on to his lap. His nose at the back of my neck, a hand on my thigh while the other hand is on the back of my hand, drawing a circular line on my flesh that is making me feel again.

I have to remember that he has a mate that could come back anytime for him, while mine is looking down from the moon, watching.

"I want that plant, how much?"

My breath catches in a chest that is refusing to breathe.

"I'll give you ten thousand for the plant." Prosper pulling out stacks of green, "Cash."

Tommie starts to laugh, "Prosper, ten large for what she has? Not happening. The way I see it, once you clone it, grow it, harvest it. Win the Cup with it, that ten grand has made you millions. You'd be the number one that everyone else is chasing. You'll be able to name your price and people will pay it. Addie's plant is worth so much more." Tommie's hand inching up on my thigh.

"This is just the first round of negotiations, Tommie. Make your counter." No heavy eyes, Prosper's vision is focused on the business of negotiation.

"Prosper, now is not the time for business, I promised Addie a good time tonight. She's never been to a club, and we intend to have a fun time." He gives my thigh a squeeze, the palm of his hand feels warm on my bare skin.

Again, I have to remind myself that he *has a mate.*

"By all means have your fun, but tomorrow, why not come to *The Compound* for business, say around two? I'll have a car pick you up. Is that alright?"

"Addie, what would you like to do?" When looking into Tommie's eyes, I try to say words, but they stutter turning into a giggle of unintelligible sound that can't be understood, making me feel mortified. Tommie starts laughing, "You're cute when you're high." He gives my nose a quick kiss, for me to kiss the tip of his nose back.

"I thought you didn't play with that kind?" Prosper eyeing Tommie up.

What does he mean, *play with that kind?*

"Lucky for me I like all kinds of kinds. Text me tomorrow, maybe we will meet up with you. Addie, come with me. We need drinks." Tommie stops at the door, reaching into his suit jacket. "Prosper, you might have some use for this female, she's a lot different than what you're used too, remember her rates are negotiable." Tommie hands Prosper the business card, and he can't seem to stop the good-natured laugh that comes out of his chest.

Leading the way out, his six-foot-two frame makes me feel safe in his presence. Nothing can hurt me while I'm with him. Again, I have to remind myself he has a mate when his hand squeezes mine.

Tommie putting money on the bar, "What do you want?" He's close to my ear, his lips almost touching me.

Again, I remind myself that *he's not mine.*

"Something sweet." Turning my head slightly his way, lips brushing against his cheek. He stills, looking at me, before pulling me more into him. Those soft strobe lights pulsing to vibrations of music that has vision singular, trapped into the experience of a light show.

"Here." Handing me a glass that's light pink. Taking a small sip, it's sweet and girly. "It's called The Dirty Flirt." Lifting his glass in the air, my hand rising to our first cheers of the night. Followed by second, third, fourth, and fifth. The shots come next, one after the other in all kinds of flavors and colors.

Wobbly legs standing, the warmth spreading all over my body, or is it because he's standing beside me?

I have a mate....

Looking me in the eyes - no one looks at me the way he does, the way he can. Everyone just pretends that I don't even exist. Tommie makes me feel as if I am alive again, not just putting in time to die.

"Are you ready?"

Nodding my head with a giddy smirk he takes my hand, leading me into the crush of bodies. No one looking at us, all lost in their own little world.

The glimmer in his eyes, that sexy smirk across his lips that I want so bad to kiss, how could his mate ever reject the male in front of me? Does she not realize what she's giving up?

His focus might be hazy right now, but they don't waver from me. Making me feel that I'm the only one important enough to focus on in a packed crowd.

He begins pressing into me, seducing the rhythm of movement, we get lost in the dancing, everything fades away. Our bodies mashing, mingling into the other, rubbing up against hips.

Frantic pulses of music have his hands on my hips, my waist, on either side of my ribs while we roll our bodies into the other. Lost in this moment, my body responding without the intrusion of the logical mind now.

Filthy, wild, raw movement, snake-like back and forth, both our hands touching everywhere.

Sinful sweat is starting to make its way out of my pores with how I'm feeling. Pressing my nose into his chest, he smells of sweet, fresh *sin*.

Internally wanting to cross over that rightful line, but having to keep chanting that he has a living mate. Spine bones are trembling with a deep need, turning me now, my ass grinding into his firmer appendage, rubbing into it more, a groan from him. Big hands on my upper thighs, over the top of my dress that's inching higher and higher up. Fingers are almost on the verge of being inappropriate, resting just under my bra line.

Blood rushing movement.

His breath on my neck, body almost encasing mine while he leans us forwards slightly. He's a male showing me he could take me now if I wanted him to.

Song after song we dance, folding into one another, rocking in perfect harmony, this dominant male leads the whole time, making my drunken wolf want to take a little bite out of him. Just a nip of flesh in our teeth. Turning around, hands around his neck, wishing now he would kiss me, but remembering he has a mate and mine is watching me from the moon. Shame tries to make its way inside but it's pushed out when Tommie whispers in my ear.

"What would you like to do now, Addie?" Hesitation, our bodies flush together, breathing hard we're moving slower now than what the music is pulsing at. "Should we get another drink? Do you want to go back to the room?" He's pulling me even closer to him, his hardness making it completely evident what he's thinking, what he wants to do.

"We could go back to our room if that's what you want?" Saying it almost against his mouth because his head is dipped down, eyes watching my face.

He doesn't let me go, we continue to grind slowly against each other. Our mouths are so close.

"If you weren't my friend, Addie."

Wanting to say back, *if you didn't have a living mate, Tommie,* but I don't say that, instead I allow him to lead me outside to a waiting cab, pretending just for a moment that this is *real*.

Is it so wrong to want to pretend for a night?

When exiting the club, catching Prosper's profile that's leaned against the wall. Eyes flash to mine reflecting the club's light. The atoms of my body screaming to seek shelter from this wolf's vision that leaves me exposed with a coldness settling inside bone.

The cab ride is quick while Tommie tickles my neck with his nose, the cabbie watching in the rear-view mirror.

Making it into our room, his suit jacket is thrown on the bed, his tie is next to go, the belt coming off easily in one sweep. Taking a seat on the stiff chair, his hand going through his hair that he had cut for this trip.

Going into the fridge, "Would you like some?" Pulling out a bottle I had chilling.

"I would." Already he's opening up the glasses that are wrapped in paper. He's also lit a stick, opening the window

up so he can blow the smoke outside, but the smell is potent and lingers in the air.

Pouring him a drink, then my own, he grabs onto my waist, pulling down so I'm straddling his knee. He's taking a drink, finishing it before I even take a sip. The feeling of him between my legs, even if it's just his knee, is consuming my resolve to remember that *he's not mine.*

"Did you have a fun time today, Addie?" A slur of words from his mouth.

"I did." Erratic heartbeat in my chest because his knee is moving side to side, letting me sway with the movement.

"Good." His mouth so close when he said *good.* "You make good wine by the way." Now his hand comes up to my mouth, putting the stick that he didn't finish in it. Inhaling the burning smoke into my lungs it doesn't take long for my eyes to start to look like his - *glazed.*

Wrapping my hand around his neck, tickling the back of his hairline while sipping on the wine, just looking at him, balancing my center against his thick leg. Dress riding up and starting to look more like a shirt, most of my fleshy thighs exposed.

"What are you thinking, Addie?" A gentle nudge of voice.

The weed is making me less scared, less myself, is this why Tommie likes it so much?

"Do you think you can fall in love with someone who isn't your mate?"

"I do." Sounding so sure of himself, so confident that he can love someone else. I can't help but kiss him then with what I feel for him.

A little voice that's chanting inside me, *he has a mate*, but the way he's kissing me back pushes all those thoughts away.

Chapter 23

Tommie.

Spread legs straddling my knee, making me hard, a peak of black, lace underwear. A few of her fingers playing with the edge of my hairline where the neck meets skin. I'm struck by the fact that I'm seeing *us* for the first time as a budding match, not just friends, my family would be *happy* with this pairing.

"What are you thinking, Addie?"

Looking at me quizzically for a moment, she leans herself gently forward before speaking, letting me see the soft rise of her small chest as if inviting me to touch them. "Do you think you can fall in love with someone who isn't your mate?" Her soft, female voice is humming over my skin, the way that only females have a knack for.

"I do." The Professor's face flashing instantly to the forefront. He taught me that I don't need my mate to experience *love*, he educated me in all the ways of love, from the burning consuming passion to the devastation of what happens when love is pulled away.

Her dilated pupils close the distance between us, she presses lips against mine, a kiss so genuine that it tastes of the potential we could become to each other. It's a hard kiss, full of teeth pulling, tongue tasting and moans that fill up the room.

Abruptly she pulls herself away from me and off as she rushes into the bathroom and throws up into the toilet, hard heaves coming out a body that's had way too much of a great time. I didn't think she was that drunk or high, maybe that's why she decided to kiss me like that?

Scooping her hair up in one hand, so she doesn't get any on it, I rub her back as each stomach-emptying convulsion racks her body.

"I'm so embarrassed, you don't have to stay here with me." Her voice is trying to come out between each dry heave that is now consuming her whole body to tense up only to release nothing out. Eyes are watering with the force of her gastric emptying.

"Don't be embarrassed, Addie. Happens to the best of us." Giving her a wet towel now that she presses against her face while I flush the toilet a few times.

She has her back against the wall, sitting on the white tile floor with her eyes closed. Poor thing, riding those rolling waves of nausea that make your mouth water in anticipation of your next heave. We stay like this until she's ready to move. I don't touch her because I know how annoying it is to be touched while you're puking so hard your veins want to burst in your head.

"I'll help you to bed." Walking her towards the bed, pulling the sheets down, taking her dress off and bra. Leaving her in just her underwear.

Mumbling softly *"Thank you,"* to me, eyes are already closed before I pull the covers up to her shoulders.

"Addie, if you have to puke the ice bucket is right here," Placing the bucket beside her head. She nods in understanding but doesn't make a sound.

Remembering the first time I got drunk enough to throw up. The Professor said he'd arranged for something special. He was serving me drink after drink, never letting my cup empty completely before refilling it over and over again. Nothing but the finest weed we were smoking.

The Professor pulling out a blue pill, watching him drink it down with the rest of his bourbon. To this day I still can't stomach the stuff.

"Tommie, do you want to try something new?" The Professor close to my ear, whispering his words into my neck before he placed a light kiss where marks on wolves go. He didn't understand what that did to my soul, but he knew it as a go-to place that made me cum harder.

It's my biggest turn on.

Nodding my head yes, because then his lips were against mine, his hand down my pants, working the length of me up and down. The tip already leaking that clear fluid out in anticipation of his educated skill level. He rubbed it around my head until he brought the pad of his thumb to his mouth, licking it off him. That was a turn on; having him want what I had inside me, someone wanting, almost needing what I had.

Abruptly he stopped when a knock on his door had him smiling ear to ear with a glint in his eye.

When he opened the wooden door, a beautiful girl my age entered. "This is Star, she's going to treat us for a few hours, Tommie." He took her hand and kissed it, before leading her to the bedroom.

Following them, jealousy started to burn my insides. I wasn't sure I liked this Star feature.

I wasn't into sharing something *I love.*

I'm not that way. My heart sinking. *Was I not enough for him now?*

He turned her to face me, her eyes slightly unfocused with the smoke that was still clinging to her body.

The Professor took his slow time with each article of clothing, I'd never at this point in my education ever seen a real woman naked before. He started with her top button, then her second one. The third was next, his hand slipping into the shirt while she gave a light moan out, eyes closing while his fingers played with her nipples through the lace. I found myself unable to pull away from it. I had a feeling he'd asked her to wear this just for the undressing. The following buttons fall slowly, before he pulled her shirt off her shoulders and it fell to the floor.

He stood behind her, watching my eyes as those fingers took each breast out of the bra, "Tommie, have you ever sucked on a woman's breast before?" The Professor asking a question that made my face feel hot.

"No," Saying with a downward face, not wanting to meet this stranger's eyes.

"Really?" The sweet voice of this woman sounded surprised. "Come here," A gentle guiding voice that brought me in-front of her. She took my hand, lifting my fingers to

her nipples and began to instruct me on what made her feel good, while her hips wiggled slightly.

The Professor gave his own lesson plan - having her parade around the room in nothing but her bra and panties.

Looking at me, I could see the gleam in his eyes that said it was going the way he wanted. After all, what the Professor wanted he *almost* always got.

"Tommie has only kissed one girl before, can you believe that?"

The woman looked between the two of us as if were telling stories.

"Is that true, Tommie?" She sounded interested in my story.

"It's true." Feeling that embarrassment again.

"The girl laughed at Tommie." The Professor provided.

Star looked at me with a certain knowing. "Is that why you never kissed another girl again, afraid of being laughed at ? We aren't all like her, Tommie. I'm sure now if you kiss a

girl, she'd have nothing to laugh at." Her voice dropped lower while looking at my lips.

"Tommie, kiss her." The Professor provided the instruction for his something new.

Getting closer to this woman who, when I put my hands around her waist, was curvy - no hardness of muscle, just a fleshy physique that screamed she was all woman and easy to grab onto.

Stepping into her space, leaning myself down, placing my cheek against hers before my mouth slid to the side, letting our mouths meet. It started out as a soft kiss, without tongue. The more we kept going, the more in-depth it became, tongue swiping intrusively into hers. I swear she smiled at the realization that at least I knew what I was doing. Before we knew it, hands and body twisting into each other. When I pulled away from her lips, they were without lipstick, slightly swelled, eyes unfocused as she lent in for a little more.

It hit me then, that I didn't mind kissing *women*.

The Professor stopped our progression by saying, "Tommie, I want to watch you with her." He took a seat on

the chair by the bed; almost like he'd furnished his apartment with this in mind. The couch he liked to be bent over, the bed small enough that you had to be pressed against one another all night along. The table solid enough to hold a body on top of it without breaking. His counter-top the perfect level for someone to drill into another person. I don't think he picked out everything with the idea it was him that was going to be bent over and regularly used like I had been doing to him.

"Why don't you do that little show I like, show her why I love you so much." The keywords that he knew would make me smile - *I love you so much.*

Not paying attention to the word *why* in front of love.

He'd tipped his glass to his lips, draining the soft amber liquid while his eyes screamed out lust. He watched from a comfortable spot, legs spread and the bulge in his pants that then looked just average to me, and not the monster I thought it was in my first year of school.

With liquid courage, I began to undress in front of a woman for the first time. She watched me with curiosity, looking between the Professor and me, until my shirt came

off. I held all her attention - I'd finally made the transition from juvenile to an adult male, and my body showed it off in every detail. The Professor always yelling at me not to work out - that he didn't like all the muscles that were now a permanent part of my body. But he did love what grew between my legs.

Star's eyes started to shine when the zipper of my pants pulled down. Button undone, belt coming off with one hand. Pants falling to the floor, stepping out of them, leaving me in just a pair of tight boxers. An intake of breath from her, a little lick of her lips as if it might be more fun than she thought. The palm of her hand feeling me over the top of the last remaining article of clothing I had on. A little hum from her chest when she bent down to kiss the tip of me that stuck out of the waistband. Her tongue sliding across the exposed surface, tasting me with a low murmur of sound that hummed against my shaft.

She went down on her knees, extracting the piece of equipment that she seemed fascinated by. Her lips giving it a simple kiss, before her mouth opened good and wide, only able to take the head inside. Tongue licked where the head met shaft in an up and down motion. My inner thighs shaking slightly with how she made me feel, hips starting to

move with my hands on the back of her head. Going just a little deeper, making her eyes water, trying to touch the back of her throat.

It was the first time I had ever had a woman do this to me, and I was surprised at how good she made it feel. I'd thought that I wouldn't enjoy a woman doing that to me but I was proved wrong by skillful lips.

"I don't want him to go yet." The Professor's voice made her stop.

She stood and took my hand, leading me towards the bed. The Professor standing up and getting closer to the bed, taking his clothes off before standing behind me while I looked down at the girl on her knees. He had me in his hand, working my hardness while Star was on the floor, sucking one of my balls into her mouth, her finger starting to rim around my hole.

I was the center of their attention.

Almost to the point of no return before he stilled his rhythm, but she didn't stop what her tongue was doing to my balls. His body pressed flushed behind me. A growl almost escaped out of my chest with being so close, but he

denied me what my body wanted. Demanded. This was the hardest part for me - not being able to be fully myself in front of him, holding my *Nature* back, my secret from him that under no circumstances could be revealed.

"I want you to be inside her while I'm inside you. How good would that feel?" He said this while sucking the flesh of my neck into his mouth, his hand picking up the pace. She watched him please me, while she started to touch herself, I could smell how turned on they both were.

He pressed his cock against my ass, trying to make me comfortable with what he was hell bent on doing. The tip of him trying to press into my tight opening, trying to get inside me while she concentrated all her attention on my hard cock. Both of her hands tugging and pulling around me, tongue licking the sensitive underside of my shaft. My eyes wanted to roll into the back of my head.

He was right there, slowly trying to gain entrance, except I was way too tight.

"I can't." My voice sounding out my *sorry*.

"Get out." His voice sounding out his fury, with a push of his hands on my back, I almost tripped over Star on the floor.

"Are you serious?" Sounding shocked at how his reaction to me was so violent. He looked at me with thin eyes that are made his face look like all the love for me was gone.

"Get dressed and get out." Picking my clothes off the floor and throwing them at me.

"Can we talk about this?" Holding my clothes in my hands, the hurt in my voice evident.

"No, I'm sick of this, Tommie. I plan something special for us, and you ruin it." He looked at me with disgust. No longer the loving eyes, but eyes that screamed out my failure to be able to please him.

For a shifting second, I contemplate letting him do it, get it over with but I just *couldn't*.

The wolf inside me would allow no man to enter inside us, to dominate us. It just goes against the fabric of *Nature*. A human male would never be able to dominate a *male wolf.*

Dressing quickly, leaving his house, only to go to my apartment, thinking drinking a bottle of whiskey was a good idea to drown my sorrow at what I couldn't do. Once it was finished, I threw up so bad I had to sleep on the bathroom floor that night. It's not long after that night that he officially broke up our secret affair. Calling me up to meet him at the coffee shop we had our first date at, I thought he was going to apologize to me, say how sorry he was for acting that way. Instead, I had to face my final year of education, without him.

I was kicked out of his program, no longer teachable.

Looking at Addie passed out, making sure she's on her side in case she pukes some more, so she won't choke on it. I get into my own bed, closing my eyes and letting the drinks and pot rock my own body slowly to sleep.

The sound of the shower running opens my eyes back up that I thought I'd just closed - it was a dreamless sleep. The water stops, and it's at least ten minutes before Addie comes out fully dressed for the day with a towel wrapped around her wet hair.

"Good morning, Beautiful." Saying this so I can see her blush and not be embarrassed at what happened last night.

"Good morning, Tommie. About last night, sorry, I didn't think I was that drunk."

"No that's okay, I've been there before and a part of me thinks I'll be there again." Giving her a smile, so she doesn't have to feel bad. Getting out of bed, her eyes go over my body before looking away out the window, taking her towel off, she starts to brush her hair out. "I'm going to take a shower, you want room service or do you want to go to a restaurant?" Acting as if everything is fine and we didn't kiss, and it's not weird right now.

"Tommie, I'm sorry for kissing you last night. I wasn't thinking clearly. Let's pretend that never happened."

"Pretend it never happened? Is that what you want?" I can see her face in the reflection of the glass, eyes are closed tight, lips a thin line. She nods her head, *yes*.

"I think that I just got carried away with everything, and it felt good to have someone paying attention to me, but you have a mate out there and what happens if she comes for you?"

"Addie, if I fall in love with someone, I will *love* them. My mate will understand this. Besides my mate won't come around. That line will never be crossed. They are in their territory, and I'm in mine, it's a hopeless situation. I just hope that when I do find someone, they understand that they could never hold my mark. That we could never be fully bonded like real mates. Could you fall in love with someone again if you couldn't bear his mark?" Saying this as if testing her lines.

"Tommie, I never want to be marked again. I had a true mate, that spot is only for him. I could never let another male mark it. He would just have to love me enough to understand." She's holding her breath in this moment, looking at me as if trying to decide something. She's stopped brushing her hair, waiting for me to say something.

"Addie, would you like to date me? We could take things slow, no pressure. We could just see how things go?"

"We could go slow, no pressure." She mirrors my words, in her voice that sounds so hesitant.

"You have a mate out there, Tommie."

"I do have a mate." Stating the fact out that we both know, it's just she doesn't know the real truth. Would she like me if she knew that about me? No matter who I will be with, part of me can never come over the line that I try to hide from.

"I'm not sure. I'm scared." Big eyes with a face that holds her leeriness of what a future with me holds.

"We just keep being what we are, best friends." It's true, we've grown into the best of friends now.

"You think I'm your best friend?"

"Yes, Addie. I consider you my best friend." That brings a smile to her face.

"I'm going to take a shower then let's go out, grab some breakfast. I'll show you around the city after. See no pressure, just best friends hanging out." Walking up to her, placing a kiss on her forehead before turning around to get ready for the day.

She's ready by the time I get out, drying my hair with the towel, dressing quickly while she tries not to watch. She's afraid to look but I can help her with that *fear*.

It's a short drive to the restaurant that was the Professor's favorite spot. He liked all the finer things in life, and he made me appreciate the same things.

Once inside, the place holds a few empty tables that we are seated at. Addie is ordering waffles that are piled high with fresh cut fruit and whip cream. I get the big man's breakfast which has Addie smiling down at her menu when I order it.

"Would you like to see where I lived while I was here, it's not that far?"

"Sure." She says in between bites of her food.

Looking out the window, I see the Professor coming inside holding the door open for his new student. He doesn't see me right away; all his attention is focused on the boy coming inside. He's the same guy that I saw in his office at the beginning of my final year. Raising my nose inhaling, I can tell that his education is proceeding at a very fast rate.

"Are you alright, Tommie?" A concern is etched in a caring voice.

"I'm fine." Taking a bite of toast while watching him now search for a table. How many boys does he take here? How many does he use just to throw away in search of his next victim?

His eyes find mine, a little misstep before he composes himself. Eyes are looking at Addie before back to me. He has no choice but to go past my table to reach the one behind us. Sitting straighter the closer he gets.

"Tommie, how are you?" He puts his hand out for me to shake, which I don't. Instead, I just look at him without a smile. He's looking towards Addie as if he wants to be introduced. I make no introduction.

"I'm alright." No curvature of sound, it's all monotone.

"I thought you moved back home?" His words are coming out slowly. His eyes are darting back and forth between Addie and me.

He looks smaller than I remember, his hair graying more at the sides.

"I did, but we're just visiting for the weekend." Keeping my voice as even as I can. It's hard to stare at the face of

someone I loved for a long time knowing that I was just a sick fantasy to him. What I want to do is warn the boy with him, warn him to run as far as he can because in the end he will just be thrown away like me.

"It's nice seeing you again, Tommie."

"You too." Dismissing him when my eyes fall back to my plate putting another bite of food in my mouth.

When he walks away from the table, Addie leans in. "Who was that?"

"No one, just some Professor I took some classes from." I don't look at her face when I say this, just concentrating on finishing my big man's plate in front of me.

Paying the bill, not giving him another look, I leave the restaurant hand in hand with Addie.

The day is filled with showing her where I used to live, the campus of the school I went to. She looks on my life away from the pack. We go to the mall shopping for a few hours, watching her try on clothes, telling her what looks good, what doesn't. dinner is nothing fancy just a great

burger place that we had to wait ten minutes in line for before a table opened up.

By the time we make it back to the hotel, the sun is starting to set. Our hands are full of bags with all the new things we bought. Going to my phone on the table that I'd forgotten this morning, a text from Prosper is the only thing that's waiting for me to read. It's asking, *where are we?*

Shooting him a quick text back, *sorry forgot, just getting this now.*

Addie pulling out two shirts from her new purchases, "Which one, Tommie?"

"I like the black one." Pointing towards the low-cut shirt that makes her chest look great. She goes into the bathroom to get changed.

Sitting at the table, opening the window up, I realize that this is the first time in a long time - I haven't smoked one all day long. I haven't felt the need for it, the necessity for it.

When Addie comes out fully dressed in the outfit that she's going to wear tonight for karaoke, I realize that with

her, I don't need that stuff to help me feel right, she makes me feel *good* without the need to have something fade me out.

Chapter 24

Tommie.

Apparently, we might have had just a little too much to
drink as we make our way up to the Karaoke stage, Addie
accidentally knocking over a stool on our way up. The both
of us laughing into the microphones before the song begins.

Addie's eyes shine under the spotlight of the main stage.
Her hand on my waist as she begins to sing the chorus of the
song it took her a half hour to decide on. At first, she refused

to even think about standing on stage to sing. It was more than an hour of listening to all the people going up and off stage to change her mind. Some repeat offenders going for a second or third time and I wanted to yell out, "*No second turns!*" instead we did more shots. On occasion, I would go to the bathroom just to take a few quick puffs of Addie's million dollar weed.

When the song started, Addie was standing slightly behind me, looking at the screen, letting me sing the first few bars of *Desperado.* Her nose touching the sleeve of my shirt, inhaling. Did I feel the finest brush of lips against my bicep? Looking down at her quickly, she's pulled her face away from my arm. Our eyes connect, giving her a broad smile. Putting my arm around her shoulder, angling my mouth close to her ear, "You gonna sing with me?" The words barely a whisper so the mic doesn't catch the sound of words not meant to be heard.

Addie pulls in a breath, lifting the mic to her mouth. She exhales the words in a voice my ears appreciate. Not needing the screen to read the phrase, she closes her eyes in a long blink while the words tumble out, a shine to her eyes, a quiver of sound that's meaningful. This song holds a depth for her that only certain tunes can hold for individuals.

Quiet, the crowd listening instead of talking to one another. They're paying attention to Addie who's singing with a soul. The music swaying her body from side to side as if she wrote and lived the words herself. The ending has both our voices hitting the others and Addie no longer holds that rippling anxiety that she had at the beginning of the song.

We bow to each other, her posture much lower than mine. Turning to the crowd of humans, Addie bows, forgetting herself momentarily that she is a wolf and this is a sea of human flesh that can be eaten.

Taking her hand, walking back to our table that is now occupied, our full drinks pushed into the middle, as if we'd left for the night. Pulling a chair out, letting Addie sit down, pushing her comfortably back into our spot. The two guys looking at us oddly, "We were here first, those are our drinks." Taking my seat now, handing the drink to Addie who's taking a sip watching with keen eyes.

"We didn't know this table was taken." The one guy with awkward looking freckles telling me this, he makes no move to leave. He does take a long moment to regard Addie. His

eyes going to her small chest that's been boosted up by a bra that's worth the money she paid for it.

"Well, it is." Taking my own drink, finishing it before showing the empty glass to the waitress who nods knowingly that we need a few more. Making myself comfortable, letting them understand we're not moving.

The wolf ascending, flashing eyes to Addie, he's going to take care of the situation without words. Within Addie, her own wolf watching mine, not taking sharp eyes off of us. Her bottom lip pulling into her mouth, do I see a flash of pointed teeth hidden in there?

The waitress bringing us another round, paying for them. The guys trying to hold ground while I angle my chair towards the one closest to me. Turning to him, with a look that says *get the fuck out of my space*. There are no words, just a look that says I'm going to fight for this space and you're not going to win. They both pick up their drinks, mumbling an apology while leaving. Addie's not saying a word, just staring in contemplation.

"Why the song, Addie?" Curious about why she chose that song from the hundreds on the list.

Contemplation leaving her eyes, "It was my mate's favorite song. He loved that song." The edge of her voice holding a melancholy edge to it. Their time together so short it doesn't even count as a blink of the eye. There seems to be a fight within her, looking towards me, before looking down at her now clasped hands. All the fun we were having together leaving her suddenly, as if something striking a cord inside, stiffening up her back. "I need to go to the bathroom." Addie getting up suddenly, wobbling towards the bathroom, her voice sounding now as if she might cry.

"Are you alright, Addie?"

"I'm fine." She says while her back is to me, walking slowly towards the bathroom.

Sitting back, enjoying the song that's a popular one, some tables even humming along with the singer. Eyes falling on the one who's running the Karaoke booth - she's still the same one who was running it when Carson and I came here, that was the last time I'd been to this place.

The stepping edge of memory at my peripheral, looking back about the first male wolf I ever kissed. Carson and I sitting together. We'd just finished a workout, showered and

shaved. He made it a point to shave his head with clippers in the mirror, while I used my own on my body. I liked the feeling of being trimmed tight everywhere.

On occasion, I would catch Carson eyeing me up, he would look away quickly. The both of us pretending he wasn't just staring at me. It was better that way. His friend Jake left almost the same time the Professor kicked me out of his program. The both of us loitering around after our workouts, not really saying anything to each other, just deep in our own purgatory of feelings.

Asking him once, "Where's your *friend?*" They weren't mates, that much I found out about them. Carson said that one day he woke up and all of Jake's stuff was gone including all his bedding, it's as if they didn't share a room together anymore. No note, no goodbye, nothing.

Carson looked worse than me, it showed with his workouts, there was a dragging of his character, feet shuffling along barely picking up off the ground. He would always look up when the door opened to the gym, hope in his eyes that his *friend* would be walking in the door. That never happened, and after two months of doing that he

stopped looking up when that door opened as if something settled inside him, his *friend* would not be coming back.

It took two months for a decision on my part to be made, I could drop out of school with only a year left, my tail curled between my legs because I couldn't get over a breakup. Or I could finish and go back to the pack with a something that could be useful and meaningful. Not too many wolves get an education beyond high school.

Our workouts together evolving, becoming more aggressive. On more than one occasion while on top of him, pinning him to the mat, I'd become hard, pressed up tight against his ass, his back arched, pushing the crack of his ass into me more. He never said a word at those times, when I rolled off him, laying on my stomach so he wouldn't see what was happening. I'd hold my place while he would turn on his stomach, breathing hard. He'd look at me in those times, but I refused to acknowledge him - as far as he was concerned I loved pussy. He wasn't wrong, I did love pussy as much as I loved cock.

When the Professor pulled his love from me, I dived into the opposite sex willingly. They're softer, rounder, and so gloriously wet. No need for lubrication when they're truly

turned on. So I began my education in the womanly body. Carson observing my flirting with them. He held back, not going to house parties with me, making an excuse that he had to study. Always women, I was with. Never a female wolf, those were too few to come by at college and usually they had protection around them. I found I really loved the taste of women as much as I loved the taste of men. The only thing with women was most couldn't accommodate what I had, telling me not so deep when I forgot the *Nature* inside me.

I had to hold back with them in fear of really hurting them. The Professor's ass was stretched out from me, but these women were too shallow to accommodated the full thrust of a male wolf. On occasion, I did find some that could take everything I had even on hands and knees. Grabbing those few by the hips, fingers pressing firmly into the flesh, delivering the both of us to completion. They would look over their shoulders at me, dreamily while I'm trying desperately to hide my teeth from them.

I could never truly let myself completely go until *Carson Daytona Valentine.*

Our training sessions were becoming so intense they would leave the both of us bruised and bleeding. Carson had a great firm ass, not like the Professor's that was losing its tone with age. Carson's back stretched in dips of musculature, my hand feeling those muscles through his shirt in the disguise of holding him down on the mat. After all, he still thought I preferred females - that it was my preference of choice. I would notice his hand would go against my bare thighs when my shorts rode up my legs as we grappled with one another. His nose pressing against the middle of my back as his full body weight would lean on me. He'd become hard at those times, I could feel it through the light material of his shorts. I'd flip him on his stomach, getting on top of him. Making my body rub into him on purpose, causing his lower half to grind into the mat. A low moan from him that he would try to cover up with a cough.

I'd catch him looking at me more and more. His hands touching with the excuse of fighting but there was a difference in them. Fingers would linger over my chest before claws would hook into flesh to throw me down on the mat. He'd straddle me, his fist coming down only for me to turn my head. Looking between his legs, he'd be so hard that his bulge would strain the material between his legs to the point of obscenity.

He caught me looking once, his face flushed mumbling, *"Sorry."*

That's what he'd say, getting off, walking away embarrassed that I'd acknowledged his dilemma.

"It's alright, happens to the best of us." Trying to ease the awkwardness that was starting between the two of us.

I still pursued the opposite sex because I wasn't ready to admit to Carson that I could curve his way.

Our last year of studies taking a toll on the both of us. More assignments, more expectations. We would team up together for the group projects, and we sat side by side, no lines separating improvised territories.

He came to my apartment, we'd just finished the last project for our first-semester class. A project on starting up a small business, we eventually got the highest mark in the class. We'd just finished smoking one, my beer empty. Carson getting up, "You know what that looks like?" Carson saying to me.

Looking at him strangely, "What?"

He gave me a sly smile, "Another." Taking the empty bottle of beer from my hands.

While he went to the fridge, I turned up the surround sound. He had just shorts on because the start of spring was nearing and it was already warm. I wasn't wearing a shirt, and carnivorous eyes greedily eyed me up all night. When I'd catch, him he'd just look away with his head down but the back of his neck reddening. A few more beers had my mouth loosening up.

"Does your family or pack know about you?" Asking Carson the question that had been plaguing me.

"No, they don't." Carson's face falling, a heaviness resting on those shoulders.

"What would they do if they found out?" I knew my answer - I would be kicked out of the pack instantly. That deviancy is not tolerated.

"I'm not sure." A flash of fear on his face as the words leave his mouth. His pack must be the same as mine.

"What about you?" Carson asking a question that I wasn't prepared for.

"What do you mean, what about me?" My tone straightening out quickly, no curvature of sound.

"Does your family know that you like males?"

"What? I don't like males." Acting confused.

"It's alright, Tommie, I've smelled you in the Professor. You like males just as much as me."

Now it's confession time. "My parents don't know either. I would be kicked out instantly. They don't tolerate that." Silence between us, but when Carson got up for more beer he then sat close to me, our thighs touching. Lighting a joint we share it between the two of us until nothing is left. Hazy eyes, fuzzy brain.

Carson's lips part when I look at him, his hand clasped by the other wrist covering his lap. His breathing increasing, he wasn't looking away, and neither was I. Leaning in towards the other we kissed.

That was the first time I kissed a male wolf, his lips soft yet firm. His tongue testing the open space between my mouth, a glide along my bottom lip.

Carson's wandering hand traveling the range of my chest down my abdomen, stopping where the band of my shorts meet flesh. It hovered over there while our kiss started to deepen, my mouth consuming his. Teeth scraping against the tender skin of his neck, he whimpered out loud before the both of us tumbled off the couch, grinding against one another on the floor. My body weight lent in on his, pushing him into the floor boards while his legs spread for me to place myself between.

Fingers gripping onto my ass with a low moan from his throat had me all over his neck, sucking in the flesh. His hips rolling into mine, rubbing our swollen, hard cocks against the other. My chest heaving because Carson could take my teeth and I could take his against my skin. Nails ripping into my hips, my back that made me shudder from the pleasure he brought me.

The excitement of the situation causing me to kiss harder than normal. It didn't matter because his lips could take it.

Carson hooked his leg around mine, rolling me over on my back. His hand feeling the length of me through my shorts. Up and down was his motion. His tongue teasing my

nipple before going to the other. That hand continuing to harness me in a grip that understood how males like to get pleased.

Raising at times in his hand, pushing myself more into him. The both of us making characteristic sounds more animal than man.

My fingers sliding to the edge of his shorts, feeling him. His head going back with a groan in the air, when he turned eyes back on me, they were darkening with lust. Before long the both of us were naked.

His length sliding up and down in my hand, hips pulling up and back, while we continued to kiss non-stop. It was then he pulled his mouth from me, to kiss my neck, to kiss my chest, traveling downward to nip and suck the skin of my torso. Spreading my legs, getting comfortable because I understood where those lips would be wrapping around. Leaking slightly for him, as that tongue licked away the clear fluid with a murmur that he liked what I had.

His tongue running along the ridge of the engorged vein of my shaft up and down, the tip of his tongue gliding, flicking over it. Sucking it into his mouth at times while his

other hand had my balls gripped firmly. Opening his mouth wider, he was able to take me all in, loosening the hinges of his jaw with a clicking sound. That was the first time I had ever been deep-throated completely since my transition from juvenile to an adult male.

Pushing into him, he gladly took it all. Every thrust, that free hand never taking the pressure off my balls, while his other hand pumped me up and down with his mouth. His saliva acting as a wet pussy. Growls of my excitement and his could be heard even above the music. It wasn't long until I gave him the tap, letting him understand I was about to go. He stayed down, working me harder, faster, that tongue teasing my hole. My heartbeat in my ears, closing my eyes, jaw tight on a hiss of breath. Lifting my hips up, he descended further, balls pulling up tight as I spasmed into the back of his throat.

Once done, he licked me completely off, nothing of me wasted.

Carson crawled up my body as I grabbed the back of his head and kissed him, tasting myself on his tongue. I'm not sure how long we stayed like that - enjoying each other -

before it was my turn to roll him on his back. It wasn't only about receiving pleasure, but giving it too.

A whimper from his throat when I wrapped him up in a wet embrace, sucking, teasing, pulling him. His girth filling my mouth completely up. Saliva coming out when he began to thrust himself without caution into me. My hand on his balls before they started to rim around the edge of his asshole. His legs spreading, welcoming the invitation to have something inside him. Inch by inch my finger going inside. His hips taking on a pace that was more furious, needful. Not once did I let him out of my mouth, consuming him on the most intense level that I became hard again. His sound pouring out of him with harsh grunts and loud groans. His hand tapping on my head, but just like him, I enjoyed the taste, the texture of what was about to go down my throat.

His hands in my hair, with one powerful upward stroke he began to gush out. Swallowing him down, licking him off, before the both of our breaths finally went back to normal. We remained naked, exploring each other's bodies completely, again and again.

Into the night we satisfied each other's needs, until passing out in my bed. It was the first time a male wolf slept with me over night. His body littered with my bites and slash marks and mine looking exactly the same as his.

In the morning, before he left his phone rang. He put his finger to his lips before mouthing it was his family.

"What happened?" He listened, "You're kidding right?" A moment of pausing, before asking more questions. "I'm coming, I'm not missing that." He turned off his phone putting it in his pocket.

"Is everything alright?" Looking at Carson because he wasn't looking solid at that moment.

"It was my brother, Crane. My older brother Cash is going to get his ass kicked by my oldest brother Clayton. I need to go home to see this." Carson looked for his keys that he'd stashed near the door.

"Have fun." Saying it to him before he left, I wasn't sure whether to kiss him goodbye or what.

"Tommie, you feel like going to my pack for the weekend?" Carson putting the invite out. I had nothing

going on. Tate was supposed to go away that weekend, but I'd heard he'd canceled his plans with Hazel. So I wouldn't be going back home for a visit.

"Sure why not?" Nothing else to do but sit alone, and I would have only been missing one class that day anyway.

My memory clearing, looking around the bar, Addie hasn't come back from the bathroom. Standing up going to see if she's alright, asking the women coming out if she's in there. Their heads shaking 'no' with their answer. Not believing them, looking for myself, only to find Addie really isn't in there.

Looking to see if she's ordering drinks, she's not at the bar, looking all around, a panic gripping into the bottom of my stomach that she's not inside the bar.

Chapter 25

Tate.

Tommie's room.

Opening the door, his scent clinging to the walls, the floor, the bed. A discarded shirt lying crumpled in the corner has me bending down to pick it up. Bringing it to my nose, inhaling deeply.

Without anyone around to witness this, I let my muscles relax from the constant ache they hold from their disguise. Suppressing my bodily instincts towards my mate.

This room represents my fight. Battles won, battles lost. Memories of me standing outside his closed door, talking

myself into not opening the door - to not go inside. It was a battle of wills, especially when I knew he'd just left from visiting for a long weekend. I'd make sure to come home late Sunday night, knowing that my parents and his parents would be out doing something because Tommie's mother would be heartbroken that he'd left again for another few months till the next holiday weekend came around. Tommie's presence beginning to feel like a tourist coming for a weekend with a few belongings packed, only to take everything back with him like he'd never been there.

Those Sunday nights when I would make my way up the stairs, an involuntary tremble would rush through me, the fresh scent of him lingering, sticking to the walls the further upstairs I got. His door would be closed and I would tell myself every time, *don't go into his room, just walk past it.*

In the beginning, I listened to myself. The first year he was away was easy, simple actually. His door stayed closed, I'd just walk past it on those Sunday nights as if it was any other door inside the house. Tommie's visits started to stretch out after the first year, he didn't come home as much, so when he did the scent of him was that much more toxic to my nervous system.

A deep repulsion within me to not go inside the room, a burning compulsion saying just one time, go inside.

Curious.

A sensation rocking within, momentarily holding me still before my hand involuntary opened that closed door.

Stepping inside the room, eyes darting around, chest heaving, just breathing him in. The sensations taking over, elevating me to a new level that I didn't want to step on. The nervousness, the temptation, the wrongness all sinking in deep.

I remember looking at the floor, a forgotten shirt discarded was a piece of treasure that I quickly picked up, holding it to my chest as if it was *gold*.

A perverse arousal heating, rolling deep inside, I hadn't wanted the reaction but I couldn't control it, I was unable to harness it back inside me.

My hand already undoing the button of my jeans, bringing the zipper down quickly. Walking to the bathroom, turning the shower on just in case someone came home. The need to keep it a secret always at the forefront. Putting the

material of that shirt to my nose, gagging, smelling, gagging while fucking myself with my hand. Up and down, faster and faster, sucking on the fabric that held his scent. Eyes rolling back in my head, back against the wall, knees bent while thighs shuddered, quivered. My balls so heavy, as if I hadn't spent all weekend cumming into Hazel.

Trying desperately to picture a female, *any female,* that I was kissing instead of kissing Tommie's shirt, pretending it's Hazel. A whimper coming out, balls tightening, pulling up with one last firm stroke while I groan out into his shirt, pumping streams of fluid onto the tile floor, wishing it was Tommie's ass I was filling up. Once that extreme desire passed, being quickly replaced with how wrong that just was - the guilt setting in - I told myself I don't like males, *I'm not like that,* repeating it constantly while cleaning my cum off the tile with Tommie's shirt only to put it in the shower with me. Not only did I have to scrub that shirt clean, but I tried desperately to clean the inside of myself up.

Calling Hazel over that night, trying to hide the shake of my voice. I was a wreck when she came into my room. I cried in her arms, she never understood why, never asked, she just held me, kissed me, we fucked. I felt better because I

liked females, that was just a fluke accident. I'd had a weak moment that wouldn't happen again.

The next day I was able to walk by Tommie's room without the need to go inside, except when he visited again a few months later that rush consumed me, only more powerful this time.

Nirvana has a way of making you do things you just don't want to admit to yourself you want to do. While carefully closing his door, making my way to the bathroom, this time I came over and over again, unable to stop the build up of frustration that needed to be let out. Pumping it all over the tile floor, one session after another until I was completely empty and once again stepped into that shower to scrub his shirt clean and try to wash the wrongness of my soul away.

"What are you doing?"

My mother's voice slamming through my memories, back stiffening up, not letting her see my face, trying to hide the shirt with my body. "I was just looking for something." Remaining facing the room and not her.

"You don't belong in here." Her voice a caustic hiss of sound against my skin. "Stay out and away from his room, Tate." Each word expressed solely for me to understand that this was not acceptable to her.

Her footsteps sound heavy against the wooden steps as she goes down the stairs. Dropping the shirt, walking out, closing the door behind me. My muscles already starting to flex outwardly to hold my skin in its place, straight and solid.

Walking into my room, all these years Tommie never once entered my room. I've always wondered how he could do that. How he could just come home, stay the weekend, then leave without having any of the curiosity about me that I hold for him. I would subtly question Hazel if she saw him, asking jokingly if he's still a runt. Her eyes would get big, and she'd pull her bottom lip in, *"He's starting to grow."* A look on her face as if to say she's thinking about everything that's growing on that male's body.

Back then, up until he came home for good, I still thought of Tommie as the runt that was constantly picked on, he'd win math awards then get his ass kicked for winning them. Constantly harassed, teased and tormented

to a degree where most would just drop out of school. The pack of male juveniles were merciless once I'd distanced myself from him. His eyes would find mine on occasion, but I'd look away, walk away, leave him to fend for himself.

He'd have to walk into the house after school and face his father's eyes, they'd hold a disappointment in them - no father wanted to have a weak male. No father wanted to see that it's their son that gets picked on constantly. Tommie would get better at defending himself in time, but when that time came he was packing up and leaving for University.

We never even said bye to each other. I think the night before he went away, Hazel and I fucked all night long, over and over again. My goodbye present to him, making sure that he understood that I didn't care he was going away, hoping in a way he wouldn't come back because we could never be together.

It's late when I hear Tommie's footsteps make their way up the stairs. The floor vibrating with his body weight. Stepping out of my bedroom, Tommie has his bags in his hand, opening up the door. He doesn't bother looking at me, but when the current of air hits my nose, all I smell is Addie

all over him, like a second layer of skin, clinging and holding onto something that is mine.

"Why are you so late?" Not wanting to ask the question but I am beyond curious of his weekend away with Addie.

Tommie looks at me, not a word said, he just closes the door behind him, while I stay in the hallway with the scent of him and Addie drifting on the current of air.

Willing myself to turn around, just turn around, walk back into my room. Screaming the sound in my head, but unable to follow through with good advice. I take the step towards his door, pausing uncomfortably for a minute before heading forward, desperately convincing myself not to go into his room, not to open that door.

It's Tommie who comes out of his room, heading into the washroom, his shirt off, pants off, just a pair of tight boxer's stretched across his thighs. His thick, round ass hidden behind the material, but you can still see the rise of the top of it. An overwhelming desire to put my hand just above the top of it.

Walking into the bathroom, blocking the door, he looks at me as if I just lost my mind.

"What are you doing, Tate?" Tommie regards me, turning the water on for his shower. The scent of that female all over his body vilifies my impure intentions towards him.

Two steps are all it takes to push him into the water, wetting the both of us. "I don't like the way you smell." Thinking his hands are going to push me away, instead they pull me into him.

His lips going to my ear, "You don't like my smell?" Warm breath all over my neck, his hand slipping on the side of my shirt that's soaking wet now in the water. "What's wrong with my smell?" That hand of his moving under my shirt, up along the left side of my ribs to my chest, feeling me, grabbing me, all the way up to my neck. He's got me by the throat which my Nature does not appreciate. His mouth filling up with water only to let it fall out from the space between his lips.

His other hand pulling my shirt up and off and I'm not fighting when his fingers tighten against the side of my neck, bringing my face towards his.

Lingering seconds, nothing happening.

"I'll smell the way I want to smell, Tate." His eyes challenging me to do something, anything. For his part, he's standing taller, straighter, impressively male.

He starts with my shoulder, teeth nip flesh, a tongue going over the marks. Canines scrape over my collarbone, while that tongue effortlessly tastes skin. His mouth careful not to pull too rough - no marks will be left by him.

His other hand now on my back, running the length of it, squeezing the material of my wet pants. I let him do this; I let him pull me closer so I can feel how hard he is against me. This is so wrong on so many levels but the perversion of it can't be fought against. It's too good to stop.

A basic necessity this is turning into, I've fantasized about this exact scenario.

Tortuous.

Tommie's lips drag up my neck now, against my pulse, licking, flicking his tongue behind my ear before his lip captures it and pulls it into his mouth. It's hard to continue to maintain my standing position as a low toned sigh drops out and down the drain with the rush of water coming out of the shower.

A cheek pressed against my cheek, he holds his position solidly against me now. I know this is wrong, I know this shouldn't be happening but...

"I'm going to kiss you, Tate." Those words are spoken low, his hand going to my lower back while the other hand holds my throat in his firm, meaty grip.

It's a harsh breath that's huffed out when I feel that cheek start to move, his lips getting closer, a gasp when they touch mine.

Eager.

Willing.

Curious.

Primal trembles coursing through, my hips grinding into his. He's squeezing the flesh of my ass in his hand, the other hand never leaving my throat.

The palm of my hand on his bare chest, feeling the pounding of his heart beat. An amplified sound from deep within Tommie's throat groans out, only loud enough for me to hear.

Tongue tasting, feeling one another without the need to stop, curious hands roaming all over Tommie. Making sure to stay away from his cock. I'm alright with kissing, I'm fine with this.

That hand still has me by the throat, Tommie's other hand undoing the button of my pants, zipper pulling down, his hand reaching inside and that's when I lose it.

The loud moan is captured by his mouth.

"Shhh." Tommie's low word presses my sound back into me.

He now has my back pressed against the shower wall, his hand inside my pants, mouth on my mouth. His long strokes, working me, pleasing me, that hand feeling so good, it's hard to swallow. It's hard to think of anything else except the sensation of this.

This is an onslaught of touch, my hips now participating with his hand's movement. He's down my shaft, while I quietly moan out, then he's at the head of my cock rubbing around it before he strokes that grip downwards again to the base, only for my hips roll away so that hand goes right back up to the top. Thighs shaking, breathing rougher, it's hard to

get enough air in with the way his hand is slowly constricting the air I'm taking in.

A hand on his shoulder, Tommie's eyes blacken, his canines are down and poking into his gums, pressing my mouth to his, kissing him while his hand fucks my cock. It's not long before I rise up slightly, the pull on my balls tightening before I cum hard, long, and it's actually so horrifyingly perfect that I fail to take in enough air and become dizzy enough that Tommie has to hold me up slightly until I can recover.

Tommie steps away and out of his wet boxers. My eyes glued to his appendage that is extending past his belly button. He's the biggest male I have ever seen, even in those porn movies that I told myself to stop watching when I was younger, I have never seen something like him before.

"I can't, Tommie." The magic is now gone.

"I understand, Tate." Tommie turns himself away from his visual, starting to lather himself up with soap, while I step out of the shower.

I'm not like this, I can't be like this, I don't want to be like this. Hitting my head on the way out of the bathroom,

desperately making it to my room, to call Hazel over. She more than willingly comes, she was rattled when I picked her up from the airport, not herself. All she said is, "I hate Tommie." There was a viciousness in her words that doesn't suit her character, she might be a lot of things but she is not the vicious type.

We aren't quiet throughout the night. Lots of sounds that never have to be kept secret. Getting up early because there's a meeting at the offices today, Tommie has something that he's presenting to the board, my father wanting me there.

When I get to the kitchen, only Tommie is there, eating a bowl of cereal with his head down, looking at the real estate section in the newspaper. He's all by himself, quiet, the only sound is him chewing. Lifting up his head, his eyes look puffy, a trace of redness seeping into the white. His lips are turned down faintly but the hurt can't be hidden on his face.

Chapter 26

Tommie.

Moving slower, there was no sleeping for me last night. Tate put on a show of impeccable magnitude which made me realize I needed to get out of this house, even out of this pack.

Opening the fridge, looking at the white Styrofoam container, lifting the lid up expecting to see writing on the inside of it. Remembering the first time Carson did that to me - when he left my apartment in the early morning for a class he couldn't miss. Going to the fridge, looking forward to the leftovers I was about to tear into. When I lifted the

container up it was light, opening the lid, all of it was gone. The only thing that was there was writing on the inside of the lid.

Tommie,

Guess I owe you dinner, I'm picking you up at 7.

Carson.

Right at 7, he was there at my door. That was our very first official date, we'd been sucking each other's cocks for a while, but that was the first time we went out. It wasn't for lack of trying on Carson's part, I just felt weird out in public with him. He didn't keep his hands to himself. Even when I tagged along to his birth pack, where I'd thought he would be discrete - more so than usual but still not my kind of discreet.

It was as if he subconsciously wanted to be caught and outed.

He'd brush against me, place the palm of his hand on my back, just above the rise of my ass. He'd lean into me, press his chest against me and speak low in my ear. Males

just didn't do that to other males without a sideways glance towards them.

When I'd entered their pack house, his mother was there to welcome me. The palm of Carson's hand was against my back as he made our introductions. She gave me a look, then to Carson, but said nothing as Carson introduced me as *a friend from school*. I think when he said he was bringing a friend home they thought it could be a female.

A younger male then ran in breathless, "He's almost here." He looked just like Carson except younger, his hair buzzed cut, just the same.

"Crane, this is my friend Tommie from school. Tommie, this is number 5 Crane."

His brother gave him a look. "You just got home, Carson, and you're already starting up on me?"

Crane tried to hit Carson who smacked his hand away before they pulled each other in a quick hug, Carson rubbed Crane's head in a friendly way. It reminded me of the way Tate used to rub my head before we shifted, he was always rubbing my head or smacking my back, before I'd try to smack him back only for us to end up wrestling around.

When Tate would pin me down with his body, he'd look at me strangely before getting off, not helping me up.

"Let's go watch Cash get his ass handed to him." Crane already out the door.

"Just leave your bags here, Tommie, we'll take them to my room after."

"About your room - we moved you and Crane to the basement, Kennedy needed a room, and so did Cash." The Luna talking to Carson who didn't seem to care that he'd lost his room to someone else.

A female walked slowly by with her head and shoulders bowed down. I couldn't see her eyes because her curly hair acted like a curtain, covering her features. She looked sickly to me.

"Let's go," Crane yelled from outside next to a truck he was standing beside.

"Are you going, Mom?" Carson asked his mother the question.

"No, I'm staying with Kennedy."

Carson's eyes fell on the female that was sitting by herself at the kitchen table. She was just sitting there with her head bowed, looking at her hands that were covered with specks of paint.

'Hi, Kennedy." Carson called out to the female who looked up, and had eyes that I swore resembled Hazel's somehow. Except Hazel's eyes didn't hold what stared back at me. They looked faded out, the shine burnt out of them.

No smile of greeting back from her, just a, "Hello, Carson."

Walking out the door, looking back through the screen, Luna Grace had her arms around Kennedy, who had her head on the shoulder of the Luna.

Getting into the truck, Crane was driving, Carson in the middle and I got the window. It was obvious when Carson pressed his thigh against mine, it was obvious when he had his arm brush against mine. Crane just talked excitedly on how long his brother Cash would last against his oldest brother, not saying his name, just calling him number 1.

A bet is made between brothers.

Jumping out in time, a large group had gathered. A car pulled up, a male whose head was shaved jumped out of the driver's side door, and at first, I thought it must be number 1. But then a male got out of the passenger side, his hair long enough to curl at the ends. When he started his walk forward, I understood *that* was Carson's oldest brother; a first born.

"Close your mouth, Tommie," Carson whispered in my ear, his body so close to mine.

"That's your brother?"

"Yes, that's Clayton, but he likes to be called Dallas."

"Why?"

"Long story." Carson's hand was on the side of my hip before pulling away. The doors to the building open and all I could do was take a step back into Carson's body. "That's my father." The breath I was holding released. I'd never seen a male like that before. "Close your mouth, Tommie. That's my Dad."

"Damn." That's all I could say before number one went to a female with a blanket on her shoulder, her hair clumped

in blood, a blue sling holding an arm in place. Her eyes were white, completely white, with just a hint of light blue to them. They almost matched number 1 who approached her. I swear it was only them at that moment, snowflakes falling, the pack clapping. He picked her up, kissing her to the point of uncomfortable. Carson pressed against my back, the crowd pressing in on us. I felt his breath on my neck, a soft touch to my shoulder, did his lips press into my back for a moment?

They talked within themselves, before he put her down, tucking the blankets around her shoulder.

"Cash." That sound is heard loud and clear. A male came out, standing there almost bracing himself.

"I knew what I was doing." That must be the brother whose ass was going to get handed to him.

"Then I'm going to give you the same chance you gave her. I expect a perfect effort from you, Cash." There was no time for that male to answer him back, it was a rush. A sprint from number one, his thigh muscles making his feet dig into the ground, propelling solid muscles to crash against the other male. No one speaking, just observing,

watching number one handle a brother who had no hope of winning the fight.

Number 1 took his arm and broke it with a sickening crack, and I'd thought, *they are brothers, I couldn't even imagine what they would do against someone that wasn't their brother.* The brother that got his arm broken continued to fight until the big fist rose and plummeted down on a face that crumbled under the power of the hit. Knocked out cold, he made it all look too easy.

Getting off the ground, number one squared his shoulders, pointing a finger towards Carson's father.

"I blame you too." Everyone held their breaths, the breathing of the entire pack ceased.

Carson had his hand on my hip again. "Number one's going to get fucked up." Carson's thumb underneath my shirt, rubbing into my bare flesh. When I looked back at him, he was watching his father and brother as if he didn't have his hand on me.

"If you come at me, I expect a perfect effort, Son. Do you understand what you will be doing?"

Number 1 looking at his father, I wanted to scream, *run, save yourself*. But I'd had a feeling the Alpha could have chased his ass down, easily.

"Let's go, it's over." Carson pulled me away from the crowd, walking away into the woods on a path that still had snow on it. Much colder up there than where schools at. It was a long walk, while Carson pointed out things like where the trail would lead, and which trail would get you to a lake that was just beginning to thaw out.

When no more sound was heard Carson grabbed my shirt, pulling me to him. Pushing him away, "Someone could see us."

"I don't care." His words barely came out before his lips were on mine.

If he didn't care, why should I? No-one could trace me, I was just Tommie there.

When we heard some footsteps, he did pull away, fixing himself inside his pants. I did the same - thinking he wasn't so keen in getting caught with his hands down a male's pants.

Taking our time getting back to his home, we went down stairs to his new room. It held all his stuff, but not up on the walls, just laying on the floor for him to organize. He left me down in his bedroom when he went to his family dinner. Apparently, they had not had a solid family dinner for a while with everyone at home. I decided to stay back because I would have felt funny up there.

When he came back down, he got on the bed with me because I took a nap. "We have some time if you want to take a shower?" Carson wanted to start up what had gotten started from our walk in the woods.

"Your parents?"

"They won't come down here." Carson coming closer, my hand on his belt buckle, pulling it off.

"What happens if someone comes?" Kissing his neck, a button came undone, zipper pulled down.

A moan from Carson when I started to handle him. His tongue teasing my ear, pulling it into his mouth. His hand underneath my shirt, feeling my chest, making me hard, again.

He didn't care if he was caught to a certain degree, willing to take risks, unlike the Professor, where secrecy had to be maintained at all times.

Shaking those memories away, I put the container back, grabbing the milk. It's cereal for breakfast. Sitting down, looking at the houses for sale in the area, contemplating what it would be like to leave for good.

Each footstep is heard down those steps that he takes one at a time. He has no rush in his walk. When looking up at Tate, sleep still hangs heavy in his eyes. He's tired, and it shows. After all, he was up with her all night long.

"Tommie, how are you?" Hazel says coming down the stairs behind Tate.

"You owe me a window, Hazel." Shoving the last spoonful of cereal in my mouth. Getting up, putting the dish in the sink.

"I do, how?"

Her expression is saying she has no idea what I'm talking about, but the shrewdness in her eyes tells me she understands exactly why she owes me a new window.

"When you gave my shit back to me, you locked my keys in the truck. I had to break the window."

"I never knew your keys were in your ignition, who leaves their keys in the ignition of their truck? Sorry about that, Tommie, I was in a rush to leave for the airport and I know how I hate to forget my crap. I thought you would be happy that I gave yours back to you." Hazel has a sweet smile displayed across sinister lips.

"That was thoughtful of you, Hazel. Unfortunately, I had to break my window to get in, and I suspect you did that on purpose on the hottest day of the year." Direct eye contact with Hazel is alarming; she just doesn't care how she looks at wolves.

"Tommie, not me. Who leaves their keys in the ignition? I know I don't. This is a lesson to learn from - not to leave shit where it doesn't belong."

"You still owe me for the window, Hazel, and I will leave my shit where ever I want." Putting on my suit jacket, making sure the collar is straight in the mirror.

"I could work that money off, Tommie." Hazel coming closer and her breath smells of my mates cum. Her finger circling around the top button of my suit pants.

"Hazel, as I said, I've already had a taste of what you're offering, nothing special. You're not worth me pulling down my zipper let alone my pants." Grabbing my keys on the way out.

"I like you, Tommie." I can't tell if Hazel is joking or serious with the way she's regarding me.

"What's this?" Tate holding up the section of the paper I was just looking at.

"I'm looking for my own place. I like my sleep at night." It's hard to keep my tone straight. It wants to arch upwards into his face.

"Good idea, Tommie."

Closing my eyes with the words Tate just spoke. Part of me wanted him to say or do something, *anything*. He's smiling now, nodding his head that this is a good idea, while I smile back; all show.

"I have to go." Saying it quickly, brushing by them.

"We'll see you there, Tommie."

That stiffens my back up before turning around from the words Hazel just spoke. "Why would you guys be going?"

"My father wanted me to sit on your presentation."

"Why is Hazel going?" Saying it as tone deaf as possible.

"She always sits with me at these presentations." Tate's stating this fact out which I'm not liking.

"It's almost as if she's your soon to be Luna." Looking at Hazel, back towards Tate.

Hazel starts to laugh uncontrollably, "Tommie you say the funniest things." She keeps laughing, but there's no real laughter held in the sound.

Tate is silent, Hazel looking at him sideways, and I walk out the door with my stomach turning sour.

It's not too long before my truck pulls up to Addie who is walking on the side of the road with a tea cup in her hand.

Rolling the window down, "Hi Addie." Trying to make myself look calm.

"Hi, Tommie."

Stopping at the side of the road for her to come to the window. "Are you feeling better, Addie?" Looking at her still puffy eyes.

"I'm better." Her head hangs down slightly before looking back up at me. "Are you mad at me?" Her voice holding the quiet uncertainty of our last conversation on the way back home.

"Addie, I'm not mad. I understand you have a mate you want to honor. I respect your decision, and I would never make you do anything you don't want to do. I just thought it would be nice to be friends, that's all."

Addie's eyes tear up. "I can't be friends with you anymore, Tommie, you're no good for me. You have a living mate out there. If she was to come back to you, where would that leave me? Plus I have a mate waiting for me in the Moon." Addie shakes her head sadly.

"Addie, I promise you that I won't touch you at all. I just want a friend. Is it so wrong to want a friend?"

"I can't just be your friend. It's just best for the both of us to part ways."

"That's what you want, Addie?" Trying to look into my friend's eyes that won't meet mine.

"It's what I need, Tommie." Her tea is done, the cup hangs limply in her hand.

"Alright." Giving her a promise of an answer, so she doesn't have to worry about me going back on my word. "I'm still going to get you the best deal for your plant, Addie. Prosper's willing to pay big money for that plant." Remembering our last conversation with Prosper Green.

I was looking through the Karaoke bar for Addie who disappeared. When I went outside, Prosper had her sitting on the curb of the road waiting for me to come out.

"Tommie, you should take care of your female better, you never know what could come and snatch her away." Prosper regarded me before standing up, bringing Addie with him.

"Tommie, his shadow moves." Addie swaying back and forth drunk. She just couldn't handle her smoke and drinks at the same time. She looked a shade of light green.

"We have some business to discuss; I expect negotiations to begin at the end of the week, Tommie." Prosper walked away not looking back.

The cab back to the hotel was quiet, but when we got into the hotel room, Addie's truth spilled out of her drunken mouth, her thoughts about me. How I have a living mate and that she can't even be my friend anymore, it's not good for her, not good for me to pretend we could ever have any future together.

The ride home was too quiet, too constricting in the cab of the truck. No amount of music could hide the sadness between us.

"Tommie, it's alright, I'll just give him the plant if he wants it that bad."

"No. You have to think of your future. You don't have a job; you never went to school after high school. This could at least get you your own house. Plus with the wine, I think you could become very successful. You just have to believe you can do this." Trying hard to convince her that she has natural skills that if harnessed correctly she could provide for herself instead of living with her brother.

"I've gotta go, Tommie, let me know how it turns out alright. I'll see you at dinner tonight. The Luna called me this morning and said two wolves are coming over for a meet and greet. An Alpha is looking for a potential mate for his sister, but she knows that he has no mate either, so she thought Hazel, and I should be there as well. I hate going to these things, it's degrading." Addie's features on her face start to turn down.

"Then don't go, Addie."

"I can't do that, the Luna insists. You can't say no to her." She looks beaten.

"Well I'll see you at dinner then, I have to go." Addie turns away from the truck and strolls back in the direction of her brother's house.

Parking, walking slowly into the board room, some of the council is already there, I still have ten minutes to set things up. I've been putting the finishing touches on it all night. Looking the spread sheets over.

The Alpha and my father walk in, followed behind by Tate and Hazel. Once everyone is seated, they start to look over the proposal I wrote up for the pack.

Some start to laugh at it, throwing it on the table before finishing it. Tate reading through it along with the Alpha before anyone says a word. Hazel plugging numbers into her phone, writing down stats, probably checking my math.

"Let's begin. Questions?" Sitting near the end of the Table because that's my spot for now.

"Are you serious, you want the pack to get into making wine?"

"I'm serious, there's a market out there that's lacking quality fruit wine. We market it as organic, sustainable, with energy and water conservation in mind. We have so much land that we could set a section out for the crops and not even miss out on the space. We build the winery, employ our pack members. Run tasting events, supply restaurants, this is a niche that can be developed into something great."

"The energy costs to run this kind of operation?" A senior member of the pack asking an important question.

"We make it all wind and solar, the energy we don't use, sell it back to the city at a discounted rate." Taking a glance at my Dad, he's reading through the proposal with his glasses on.

"Start up cost is a lot of money, Tommie. I'm not sure that we can put our pack members money into something that isn't more secure."

"We have the skill to do most of the work ourselves. We have all the skill needed to plant, maintain, build and execute this plan. We only need to out-source the material, everything else we can do ourselves. This is an investment in the pack, in the future of the pack. Just think about this. We

have an opportunity of starting something great, Addie's wine is very good. I have connections in the city that can get her wine on the top restaurants' wine list. We promote it, go to all the festivals, all the competitions." Trying to sound confident but my Dad won't look at my eyes, and I understand that he's not on board with my idea.

"It's a lot of money to put out; the pack members have worked hard for their money not to be blown on a maybe like this. We need a solid investment, not something that might work out or might not. It's too risky for me." Another board member throws the proposal in the middle of the table along with a few others, not even listening to anything more I have to say.

"It's too risky, Tommie, I'm going to have to pass." My dad puts my hard work on the table on top of the other dismissed piles.

Everyone after that places their papers on the pile, completely shutting me down.

"It was a good idea, Tommie, but for right now in these uncertain times, we need to concentrate on the safe investment for our pack. Tate, what do you think?" The

Alpha turning to his son who looks up from the last page of my proposal.

"It won't work, too risky." Tate shuts the folder up and places it on the table. Hazel sets hers on her lap and doesn't say a word.

"Thank you for your time everyone," The Alpha stands dismissing everyone who eagerly leaves.

My father won't look at me, it feels the same way when I came home from high school after getting my ass kicked again, the disappointment is felt hard on my skin.

When everyone leaves, gathering up the papers, throwing them in the garbage, it's hard to concentrate on anything else throughout the day. The time even seems to be mocking me, ticking slowly at an irritating rate.

It's a long drive back to the house, windows down, my hand against the wind.

A car that I don't recognize is parked in my spot....Always someone is taking my place in this house.

I'm a little late for the meet and greet that's waiting for me inside.

Coming through the front door, it seems no one is inside, they are all outside in the setting sun. A big male with a shaved head is sitting in one of the patio chairs talking with the Luna. A small female is beside him, her shoulders hunching forward until the male puts his hand on her back and she straightens herself up. Watching them for a few minutes before Tate and Hazel come inside, just getting home from where ever they were all day.

"What's going on?" Tate asking but not looking at me.

"A meet and greet." Pointing my head to the backyard.

"This is bullshit! Why didn't you tell me this?" Hazel backing up, giving a Tate an accusing look.

"I didn't know." Tate is flinging words back at her the same way she just said them.

Addie coming to the front door, opening it up. "Hi," She brought a few bottles of her wine.

"Finally everyone is here." The Luna coming in from outside, ushering us outside through the back door.

When making it through the door, the big male stands up along with the female. "Hi, my name's Clayton, this is my sister Kimberly." He starts the introduction before the Luna could get the words out.

"This is Tate, Addie, Hazel, and Tommie." The Alpha pointing to all of us.

"Your eyes." The male named Clayton immediately goes to Hazel, in a rush of sound.

Addie backs away, putting the bottles of wine on the table, to go towards the pool with her back turned to everyone, her shoulders slump down. She doesn't stand a chance when Hazel is around. The male pays no attention to Addie, all his sight is consumed by Hazel who starts to back-pedal away from hands that want to touch her hair.

"Don't, Clayton." The female called Kimberly grabs his hand into hers.

Clayton looks shaken, his breathing coming out a lot harsher than normal. "I apologize, I didn't mean to scare

you. It's just you look like someone-" His voice cracks while looking away towards the pool. He blows out a deep breath, as if trying to get rid of every emotion he's holding onto.

"Who's that again?" The question pointed to Addie, who stands by herself away from the group, shoulders turned in, head bowed, looking into the water of the pool.

"That's Addie." The Luna speaking lower towards a male who is having a very hard time pulling himself together. "Addie, come here."

She does exactly what she's told to do. No smile on her face, just going through the motions of a meet and greet.

"Clayton, this is Addie."

She puts her hand out towards him. He shakes her hand quickly, letting go of the contact immediately, but he looks right into her for a moment that is not comfortable for Addie.

"Please everyone come sit down." The Luna is in charge of this gathering. The Alpha's eyes on Tate and Kimberly.

Kimberly is looking right at me with a blush on her face. Taking a seat away from her, letting the Luna have her sit right next to Tate. It's as if she is trying so hard to set up her son with any female that is available to be claimed.

Once everyone is settled in their chairs, Hazel immediately goes to the wine; I don't think she likes this surprise the Luna sprung on her.

"Clayton, why don't you tell us a little about yourselves." The Luna sipping on some ice tea.

"This is my sister Kimberly, I'm Clayton. My pack is further East of here just a few hours away actually. I'll be perfectly honest with everyone. My pack has gone through some transitioning, which is my fault." He looks towards his sister momentarily before speaking some more.

"We have been visiting members of other packs looking for a potential partner for my sister. Her mate passed away."

"How did he die?" Hazel drinking cup after cup of wine, I'm surprised she's just not tipping the bottle down her throat.

"Jake committed suicide two years ago." Kimberly's words are spoken without any emotion.

Silence.

A click in my mind, I wonder if this is the same Jake that was with Carson at school.

"Sorry for your loss," Addie speaks out to Kimberly quietly.

"I was also telling the Luna that I'm looking for a Beta for the pack, we are without a strong Beta." Clayton's words directed at me, while the Luna's cunning eyes hold mine as if to say, she set this all up.

Chapter 27

Tate.

Tommie's eyes hold my mothers before he looks away to bring his hand through his hair in that uncomfortable way he has about him.

My mother smiles at Clayton, then at me, before putting a piece of apple pie in her mouth.

"We don't have any Betas for your pack." Tommie's mother is quick, and her point is etched into a voice that is sharp.

She's looking at her best friend *oddly*.

"Well, I just thought that Tommie would like a *chance* at an excellent opportunity. We have plenty of good Betas to pick from. Tommie just doesn't fit in anymore with the pack. He never fit in since his shift. Sometimes it's good for males to go somewhere else if they just don't fit the mold of what's expected of them." My mother's voice makes both Tommie and his mother sit back in their chairs. Addie stops eating, and Hazel puts the glass of wine down.

"Tommie is a good Beta, he would be an asset to this pack." His mother's voice is shaking, and I'm not sure if it's from rage or if she understands what my mom is trying to say. "He fits in this pack, this is his pack." Tommie's mom now visibly upset, his father going to her side, rubbing her shoulder.

My father stands up and stands with my mother.

When my mom opens her mouth to speak, I can tell this is going to be hard for Tommie. "This isn't his pack anymore, he hasn't fit in for a long time, and I'm just looking out for his best interests. He would be happier somewhere else. We love Tommie. Unfortunately, for

our pack, he has become an outcast. He just isn't socially accepted. Maybe in another pack, Tommie would live a life that will make him happy. Here, I'm not sure if he would be able to find that happiness. We can tell in Tommie's eyes that he's floundering, that he's in a state of just going through life instead of living it. This could be an opportunity to venture out, live a fuller, more meaningful life that I know he deserves."

Tommie's trying to swallow down a lump that has formed in the middle of his throat. He's refusing to look at anyone at the table, just down at his lap.

It's exactly how he always looked after we shifted, forced to attend the rare family dinners together. Having to sit side by side. We would push our chairs away from the other, but I could feel him. The heat of his body soaking into my side, I'd have to try and hide the way my cock would stand at attention underneath the table. My thigh muscles jumping and shifting, the tension so heavy in my balls that it was hard to get up from my spot without a groan of discomfort.

Those times I would learn how to have a self-imposed noose around my neck that I would tighten in my mind - the longer we had to be in each other's space, the longer I would have to go without actually breathing. I had to figure out a way to curb the tremble, to put a restraint on my body's natural response to my mate. At times I would win over my soul, other times, not so much, that's when Hazel was needed.

Tommie wouldn't have any trouble leaving the table, he was quick, never sticking around for dessert, making excuses that he had to study. That's all he did; he had no friends, the only things were his books. The odd time that his door was open, I'd pass by it. He loved reading on his stomach, with no shirt on. My legs would hold themselves in the spot, just staring at him. He would feel it, the way the muscles would tense up, his hand going on his head. He'd stop reading, without looking at me, he would ask if I *needed something*.

His voice would startle me, rarely did I hear him speak back then. He was content to stay quiet, in the background. Hovering on the edge of pack life, not wanting to interact too much with the wolves our age.

He was leery, looking over his shoulder constantly for an attack from the group that somehow could sniff out that he was different. They never knew why they felt he was different, they just knew some way deep inside their *Nature,* that he wasn't like them.

Deep down, I was afraid that they would be able to sniff me out, to pinpoint how different I was from them. In the shower, I would try to scrub away the *different,* try to clean myself of myself. Wishing that part of me would wash away down the drain.

How do you clean yourself away?

"Tate." Mom's voice makes my eyes focus on the conversation at the table, instead of everything that's in my head.

"What?" Only now do I see everyone's eyes on me, even Tommie's eyes are on me. That heat spreading, except now I have almost control of my body's functions.

Suppression once mastered is a powerful thing.

"What are your thoughts? After all, Tommie would be your Beta, do you think this could be an excellent opportunity for Tommie?" The table is waiting for an answer.

Interlocking my hands with each other, the index finger rubs against a knuckle.

Swallowing.

Breathing.

Speaking.

Tommie waiting for an answer, his eyes don't leave mine, which I find odd because he never looks at me *now*.

"This could be the opportunity Tommie needs in his life to become more than what we can offer him here. He seems to be floundering, not knowing what direction he's going in. He's been away for four years, I was hoping when he came back he would interact, become more involved within the pack. He's not, he still keeps to himself, he barely has any friends. Even at

work, he just seems to have such different ideas that go against what's good internally for the pack."

"You don't think I'm good for this pack? That I don't fit in?" Tommie's voice is rising, his chair scrapes against the wood floor as he pulls away from the table. His shoulders are back, head straight, nothing is curved about him. It's me that wants to curve down, but I don't. Instead, I stand rigidly against the tone of his voice.

"I think that you would be better somewhere else. Start fresh, somewhere that you could be yourself." The last words are hard to get out of my mouth without a downward drop of my voice. If only I had an opportunity to be myself. Looking towards my family, my mother and father standing side by side, it would all be gone if I was to be myself.

Tommie's hand goes over his head, fingers through his hair. He looks uncomfortable, his neck reddening, face flushing. The muscles of his jaw clenching, I'm surprised teeth aren't heard

breaking. "This is my pack." Tommie's voice is losing its strength.

"It hasn't been your pack for a long time, you know this. Deep down you can feel it. Sometimes wolves need to let go and move on. Find a different territory to make a fresh start." The voice of my mother seems so loving towards Tommie, almost as if she sympathizes with him and his situation.

Tommie's mother starts to cry; her tears aren't hidden. Clayton and his sister looking on at private business without saying a word. They stopped eating their food a while ago, refusing dessert. Hazel's stunned which says a lot. Addie doesn't know what to do with her hands; they keep fidgeting with themselves as she looks at Tommie.

"You think I should leave?" Tommie's directly asking me a question that I have no choice but to answer in front of everyone.

"I think you should, there isn't anything here for you." That self-imposed noose, tightening, constricting

all of my breathing. Tommie's eyes are looking towards Clayton with contemplation.

"Tommie, we'll give you a chance. You take a chance on the pack, we take a chance on you. We've learned to give everyone a solid opportunity." His sister puts a hand on Clayton's shoulder. They look at each other with nodding heads.

"We've taken in a few wolves that don't fit into other packs like *normal*. You might like what you see. Come next weekend for a visit, I'll show you where you'll live. It's a little place on the water, I don't need to be there anymore, it's not okay for me to keep living there. It's time to give it to someone else that needs a place to stay." Clayton looks away briefly, swallowing before continuing. "We aren't the biggest pack, we aren't the strongest, heck we might be the poorest, but I think you might like the community that we're trying to become." Clayton says this while Tommie's hand goes through his hair again, he holds his blink for longer than normal. When he opens them back up, a shine coats the outside of them, another blink, and it's cleared away.

"I'll come for a visit, check things out." Tommie's voice is monotone. He neither seems happy with this nor upset, just speaking everyday words. His mother starts to cry, but she says nothing for him to stay and neither does his father. It's as if they know this might be the best thing for their only child. To move away and start fresh in a pack that will accept whatever difference he has that has made him such an outcast to the wolves that he grew up with. His father seems to stand a little smaller, but he still holds his mate in his arms.

Tommie looks at his parents, then out the window before standing up from his spot and leaving the table. A thought comes over me - this might have been that last Sunday meal shared with him at the table. We might never share another meal at a table ever again. When Clayton gets up to follow Tommie outside, I can't help but grab this Alpha by the shirt, trying to pull him into me. It's a move I wasn't prepared for; he steps into my space instead of me pulling him into mine.

He stands up entirely. "Don't touch me." His voice loses everything that was just projected at the table, and the silence extends outwards as if waiting for something to happen.

Green eyes the color of pine icing up, becoming much colder than anything I have ever faced before.

"I just wanted to say, if he does decide to come to your pack, treat him well, he's been through a lot and he deserves good things to happen to him." That noose so tight that the words come out constricted, the edge to sound trying to hurtle towards a crack in my voice. A display of emotion that should not be coming out of my mouth. I want to follow Tommie but I don't, instead I let Clayton go outside, running to catch up to Tommie. They stop in the middle of the driveway facing each other, talking. Both males have their hands in their pockets, natural stances.

Not looking at anyone, retreating to my room. Hazel gets up to follow me, but I just can't have her around. "Hazel, not tonight." She doesn't even try to follow me.

Getting into the shower, the water once again is scalding my skin. It's as if I'm young again; trying my hardest to wipe away my own skin. The water falling on my face brings the tears that refuse to stop down the drain. Muffled sounds carried away with the rushing water. Once I'm finished, the self-imposed noose circles around my neck, tightening so it's almost to the point of strangulation.

When the morning comes, Tommie's truck is gone which is odd because he doesn't leave for work for another hour. Tommie's mother is outside looking at the pool, drinking her coffee. Somehow she looks older to me today as if overnight she's aged.

My mother greets me with a quick brush of a cheek.

"How are you feeling this morning?" She asks the question while handing me a plate of breakfast.

"Good." That strangling feeling suffocates everything else out.

"Where's Tommie?"

"Tommie said he had to do something in the city. He won't be back for a few days. He said he needed to do some business with someone. He also gave his resignation to your father. He quit his job today." She says this quickly almost joyfully as if she's not talking about Tommie.

Swallowing down breakfast, holding the food down. It's all I can do not to throw it back up. But I hold it down until it has no choice but to settle. Hazel walks in without knocking. My mother bristles and Hazel welcomes it.

"Tate, I have a favor to ask you?"

"What, Hazel?"

"Do you mind driving me to the airport on Thursday."

"No problem."

"You should think of staying out there, Hazel. It would be good for you to get away, just like Tommie." My mom's voice makes Hazel's face cringe. She doesn't like my mother.

Hazel doesn't say anything, just takes some food off my plate and eats it in an exaggerated show for my mom to walk away from.

"Are you alright?" Hazel comes to sit on my lap.

"I'm all right, Hazel."

"Why did you say that Tommie should go?"

"He doesn't fit in here."

"He fits in?" Hazel licks her lips.

"Hazel, stop. It's better that he just goes somewhere else."

"Why? This is his pack. Why don't you like him, Tate? He's a good male that can fit in, but it's you who doesn't allow him to fit in. As soon as you guys shifted, you stopped being friends. You allowed him to get picked on. What happened between you guys. Everyone says it's me, that Tommie hates you because he was in love with me when we were

younger, but we know that's bullshit. So what are the problems between you two?"

"Hazel, nothing. We have no problems between us."

"Then why don't you like him?"

"It's between him and me, Hazel. Stop asking questions." I want to scream at her that he's my mate, tell someone, anyone, but instead I ask her to come for a run with me, which she does.

Tommie's door to his bedroom is closed when I get back. The temptation is there to slip inside, let my nose press against his pillow but I don't. Instead, I just walk past it.

Tuesday comes, and the temptation to open his door is real now, every time I pass it, my feet refuse to move, and I'm stuck looking at the closed door.

Wednesday my hand goes on the door knob, but I don't open it. Instead, I just put my head against the door, letting the noose around my neck squeeze until

my tongue feels thick and I gag my secretion out because I can't swallow anything down.

On Thursday after dropping Hazel for her late night flight out, parking the car at her house and getting out, Tommie drives by in his truck, he pulls into the driveway and gets out.

"Where's Hazel?" He asks looking around.

"She's in Vegas for the weekend, something came up she needed to go there."

Tommie steps closer to me.

"You're leaving aren't you?" I don't know how I know, but I do, my gut tells me, he's going to take Clayton's offer.

"Tell me to stay." Tommie's voice is dangerous.

"I can't do that." My voice matches his, too dangerous for him to stay, our secret will be exposed.

"If I go, I go. I'm not coming back." Tommie's voice holds a believable edge.

I believe him.

"It would be best if you didn't come back."

His body falters to the side as if he's going to tip over, but he doesn't. "I need something from you first. Is Hazel's house open?" Tommie's voice is getting further away as he starts towards her house.

"It should be, why?" He doesn't answer my question. He just opens her front door letting the screen door shut behind him.

When I follow him inside, he's on one end of the couch, lighting up a hand rolled.

"This is Addie's stuff, here." He hands me the joint, I take it from him, inhaling, holding, blowing the smoke out.

Tommie takes another puff in, he's holding it in his lungs, I've never wanted to be that smoke so bad in my

life. His t-shirt is tight across his biceps, while it stretches slightly over his chest. He hands me back the joint, it's passed between the both of us until Tommie pops the rest of it and swallows it down.

Both of our eyes half opened. This weed sinks me into the couch, heavy, relaxed, a small laugh comes out that I never knew was there just under the surface to come out.

"It's good," Tommie says talking about the weed.

"Best I ever had."

"I just sold the plant to this wolf I know from the city, Addie's life is about to change." Tommie smiles with those lips that curve upwards displaying a flash of teeth. His tongue comes out to wet those lips of his, and my cock starts to strain against the material of my pants.

It's hard to restrain myself and not to adjust in front of him. Tommie doesn't care, he grabs himself, adjusting to a more comfortable placement.

There is no music playing, nothing except our breathing. We're alone, within the darkening house.

"Tell me to stay." Tommie's looking at me now.

"I can't, Tommie. I can't."

"Then we can leave, we can get jobs somewhere. Just you and me." Tommie holds a crack to his voice.

"I'm not leaving."

He gets up from his spot, making me press my back against the couch. He kneels in front of me, between my legs. His hands on my upper thighs, gripping them firmly to pull me into his hips.

Eyes are darkening, locking together.

Hands on his shoulders, around his neck, feeling the back of his hairline. It's without a thought to touch his shoulders, his chest. His hands are spreading my legs more, to reach around, grabbing my ass in both his hands. A moan from him is unsettling, I don't want

another male moaning about me, but at the same time, he's Tommie, and not just any other male.

It's uncomfortable but fuck, it's too much to fight against my rising moan when his hand starts to rub me through my pants.

The noose is not there, with Tommie this close I can breathe without fear of discovery.

"I'm not like this." Saying the words into the hollow of his neck.

"I know." His voice is spoken low in my ear. A kiss just behind it, while his tongue gently swipes at my earlobe before sucking it into his mouth.

I don't take my hands off him, and his hand just keeps rubbing me, feeling me, pumping me up and down through my pants.

"We need to stop." Trying to sound as if I mean it but my body refuses to leave the place I'm in.

"Just one time, Tate." His fingers unbutton, zip down, to release me from the confines of material. "Close your eyes." Tommie's soft words breathe out while he's got my cock in his hand, slowly going from tip to base. His thumb is spreading the drop of clear fluid that's starting ooze out from the tip. He brings his thumb to his tongue and licks it off without gagging. I almost stop this, but something inside me just can't. My ass muscles start to contract when Tommie takes me into his mouth. His throat relaxing enough to fit the whole cock inside.

He lets it stay there, it's me who shifts my hips to start to pump myself in and out of that tight wet space. Nothing that I have ever had can compare to what's happening right now. Tommie holds me from the base, pumping his fist up and down as his head bobs. A slurping sound is starting the faster he starts to go. My fingers in his hair, hips raising, stomach pulling in.

Wanting, needing to close my eyes from the sight of this, but I can't stop staring. When Tommie pulls away from me, his mouth and chin

are damp from his spit. He gives the tip a lick before his pants come off.

He continues to stroke me in such a grip that I think I'm doing it myself. I've never had anyone do it better than what I can do myself but Tommie, he's got me beat.

"I can't touch your cock, Tommie." The thought brings a gag up, but at the same time, want has my mouth watering to just taste it. Just the head, lick over his hole, taste that drop of fluid that just fell on Hazel's floor.

"I know, Tate, I don't want you to suck my cock or touch it. I want you to fuck me. I need for you to be my first." His mouth is getting closer to mine before he consumes it.

He nips my lip, sucking on the bottom lip. Our tongues meeting and happily feeling the other.

A moan from the both of us at the same time comes out for the other to swallow down. Tommie takes my

everything off of me, nothing but naked flesh for his eyes to take in, and they take me all in.

Tommie pulls me off the couch, so I lay on him, our hips grinding into each other, the sensitive underside of our shafts rubbing together. Tommie gripping the both of them, pumping them as one big cock.

The sensation almost to the point I need to cum.

Tommie still kissing me, his hand fucking my cock, his cock together. This is wrong, but I can't stop it, I can't do anything but see this through, just once.

So I kiss him back the way he's kissing me.

His shirt is ripped off by claws that have pierced out of my skin, red lines mark his chest where I can't stop from putting my lines on him.

Something is taking control from the inside.

Instinctual, moving me forward to take my mate as a male should, except he's also a male.

It's a quick move that has Tommie on his stomach, pressing his ass into my weeping cock that wants to cum. Lifting his hips into mine, lining up with his pink, tight asshole I try to push myself in and a moan from Tommie comes out.

"Fuck me."

That's all it takes, inch by inch I push into him until all of me is inside all of him. A groan of discomfort from Tommie comes out. When I look at the side of his face, he's crying with his head down.

Chapter 28

Tommie.

Zipper sliding up.

No words exchanged.

Tate stumbles out of Hazel's house as if he's having a hard time standing, needing the walls for support. His legs are shaking the way mine are. I don't move for a few minutes, catching my breath.

Grabbing the tissue box that's on the side table, taking several tissues out wiping my eyes first, trying to gain some control of myself.

It feels as if I can't breathe right anymore, *deep breaths*.

When I reach behind and wipe my ass,
blood and semen mix soaking through the
thin paper.

Getting up, my turn to hold onto the wall while
going to the bathroom, turning on the shower, letting
the water warm up. Looking at myself in the mirror,
the tears just can't stop. I want them to stop, I will
them to stop, but they don't.

"You're going to be alright, Tommie." Saying it
out loud while looking at my eyes, trying so hard
to make me, *believe me.*

Feeling my head, the hair soft between my fingers.
If I'm going to do this, then I need to do this right.
Looking into the drawers, finding a pair of clippers.
Plugging it in, the buzz vibrates my hand, so at least
they are shaking from a mechanical vibration instead
of what my soul is doing. Starting down the center, the
hair is cut close to my head. Turning my head so I get
the sides, hoping I got all the back evenly once done.

When I look at myself, it's still me, and I'm alright with that.

Stepping into the shower, letting everything just sink down the drain.

Lathering soap, washing every inch of skin, wiping Tate's scent off of me. Lifting my balls up, giving them a small squeeze, they're heavy and ache. Tate never touched me, keeping his word. He just kept his nails dug into my hips, never moving from that spot, his balls did slap against mine as each of his thrusts became more and more violent. He did exactly what I asked him to; he fucked me, nothing more than that. In a way, I never expected anything more than that.

While he groaned and gagged, I cried, and a part of me wishes I didn't. I didn't want that to be the last image he had of me. I wanted something different for our first time together. Instead, I took what he could give me.

It hurt, I knew it would hurt, he wasn't gentle, not loving. He fucked me as if he blamed me for everything. He fucked me without restraint, the blood

leaking down my balls to splatter against his thighs, It didn't deter him, he just kept pounding inside me. I took my pain, and I took his pain, until he unloaded himself deep inside me. His tears sliding down his face to come down mine. He threw up beside my hand when he came, he couldn't stop vomiting, and I couldn't stop crying. Once done, he just got himself dressed and left, without turning around to look at me. I wish he would have looked back, he didn't and I won't either.

Drying off, lighting candles, opening the windows, trying to get the scent of *our love* out of Hazel's house - it needs to be cleaned away. The small drops of blood on the carpet are challenging, but Hazel has a wealth of cleaning supplies in her house. She has everything you can think of below her kitchen sink. Taking a good look around, everything is meticulously clean as if she spends all her time cleaning everything inside here.

The bathroom is the last to be cleaned, my hair in the sink cleaned away, even the Clippers get a good cleaning. Nothing in my eyes out of place when I close

Hazel's door shut. I'm sure she will understand something went down inside here.

Some things just can't be cleaned away.

The drive back is quiet. The house is dark when entering it, I can hear the shower upstairs, but that's it, nothing else stirs. Walking into my room, closing the door for the last time it hits me - this will be the last time I will have to close my door shut.

Taking out a few bags, packing because I won't be coming back here. This place is not my place anymore; I just don't belong. Sparking one up, inhaling the thick vapor into lungs that are craving something to expand them instead of the feeling as if they are being crushed from within.

Looking around this room, deciding what to take, nothing of importance here. There is nothing that I even want to keep for memory's sake. Deciding to take only my laptop, clothes, my guitar and the watch the *Professor* gave me. Even the books that got me through my juvenile years stay behind.

Satisfied with everything I'm taking, making sure that I haven't overlooked anything, the shower finally turns off. Light footsteps in the hallway before Tate's door is quietly closed shut.

The last to be packed is the idea for a winery, Addie gave me her great grandmother's recipe for her fruit wines. She gave it to me without charge, even though I wanted to pay her she said she has enough money now, she doesn't need any more.

Prosper wasn't very happy with the deal, but then again he's never happy about anything except for that plant Addie sold him. She's going to spend some time at The Green House for the start-up of production, Prosper's only term that he would not concede to. Addie was agreeable with this; he will pick her up within the week and return her the same way she left.

In the morning, getting up early, it's a six-hour drive North East towards this pack that I'm going to

take a chance on. Tate's not here to see me off - maybe he thinks I'll be back.

Mom made breakfast, and she's crying too hard to even eat, she's holding her stomach and I know she knows this isn't a visit to see if I'm going to like the pack, she understands this is my departure. It's a struggle to swallow down the food she made me, bite by bite I eat my last meal at this table. The Luna and Alpha are not around, it's just my parents and me.

They sit on either side of me, hands on my back. Mom's cheek now and then brushes against mine. Nothing is said for me to stay, nothing is said at all, everything seems to be swept under the rug.

"Tommie, be safe. Call us when you get there. Just know, your father and I love you, no matter what. We love you, and we want you to do well in life. You won't do well here, you won't be able to be who you are meant to be here." My mother's voice is low in my ear when she hugs me goodbye. She seems smaller when I hug her, I can feel the bones of her. Has she lost weight?

"Tommie." Dad hugging me but that's it. Nothing else from the man that I love as my father.

Picking my bags up by the door, putting the straps over my shoulder, walking out to my truck, Addie's there leaning against the driver side door. Two brown paper bags in her hands.

"Tommie, were you going to leave without saying goodbye?" She's been crying; her eyes are bloodshot and swollen.

"I thought we already said our goodbyes." pulling her into a hug before throwing my bags into the back of the truck.

"You're not coming back are you?" She's looking at me now.

Hardly anyone sees me.

"I'm not coming back." The gasp is hard to hide, the feeling of a set of eyes on the side of my face makes blood flush the surface of the skin.

Tate's somewhere, watching in the background.

"You're still going to come for a visit
right? Once I get settled in, you promised."
Holding her to her words.

"Nothing can keep me away, you're my best friend,
Tommie."

"You're mine too, Addie." Wrapping her up in
my arms, chin rests on her head. She's inhaling my
shirt, while I inhale her freshly shampooed hair.
Pulling away. "I need a few weeks to get settled, I'll
call you." Giving her forehead a kiss. She raises up on
tiptoes touching our lips very gently, quickly, and
smiles with a blush on her face when she steps away.

"I made you lunch, and the other bag, it's full of
something you might enjoy for a few weeks." She
doesn't need to tell me what's in one of the bags; I can
smell that top quality coming out of it. Addie had two
strains - one she sold to Prosper Green and then she
had the mother of all plants that she kept to herself.
Her creation that we thought best not to give away.

"Thanks, Addie."

"You're welcome, Tommie. I'll see you in a few weeks." She gives a little wave, a smile and turns to walk away.

Tate's eyes are still on me. Looking for where he is I don't see him, hidden away somewhere, so I raise my hand up and wave goodbye before getting in my truck. Pulling out of the driveway, swallowing down that hard feeling, I don't cry, but I do need to take several deep breaths in and out.

The windows down, music up, I keep telling myself this is alright, *I'll be alright.*

Pulling up to a small home on the lake, it's more of a cottage than a home. It's minimal, with nothing grand about it. This is different. Usually, the main house displays the wealth and pomp of the pack. Parking beside that tricked out minivan I saw at my old pack, the windows are down, and when I look inside, there are empty juice box containers all over the floor and four car seats.

"Tommie," Turning my head to face the voice. Clayton's coming out of the house, an inviting smile on his face. "Find the place alright?"

"I did, it's not a bad drive." Reaching in the back seat, pulling out my bags.

"This won't be your house, I live here. I'll show where you're going to be staying, it's just across the lake." He points towards a smaller cottage, that's barely visible through the bushes that line the lake edge almost blocking out the view from here. "We were just going to have some dinner." Clayton holds the door open for me to walk into. Once inside, it's got a good feel to it, open concept living room and kitchen all in the same room. "Tommie, this is Caleb."

He's almost as big as Clayton, his hair is tied back in a bun, slight shadow of a beard on his face gives him an almost feral look. Looking at his neck, he holds no mate mark.

"Caleb, Tommie." Clayton makes the introductions.

"You want a beer?" Caleb is going to the fridge, pulling out three, I don't want to refuse.

"Sure." He gives one to Clayton first, then me, he opens his and takes a quick sip.

"You're my brother's friend aren't you?" In that look I know he knows about me. I don't know how I know, but I can tell by the way he looks at me.

"Carson and me are friends, we went to school together."

Caleb takes another sip of beer. "How good of friends were you with my *little* brother?"

"I never fucked him."

Caleb's beer comes out his nose, and he can't breathe. Clayton spits out his beer. I'm not going to lie anymore.

"Is that going to be a problem, Clayton?" Waiting for him to tell me to leave, feeling myself edge towards the door.

"What, that you didn't fuck his little brother? No. I have no problem with that." Clayton starts to laugh to himself. "To each their own, it's not my place to judge, I have no place judging others."

"I'm just glad you didn't fuck him, now I don't have to kick your ass." Caleb is wiping his nose with the bottom of his shirt, a glimpse of his hip. "This is all taken," Caleb's hand gestures to his whole body, while Clayton just shakes his head.

"So are you alright with this?" Asking Clayton.

"Okay with what? That you like males? Makes no difference to me. I need a good Beta, I heard about you through your Luna. She said you graduated top in your class, that you're very smart but just didn't fit the ideals of the pack. She told me you were gay, I already knew this before you told me. It doesn't make a difference to me."

"She told you I was gay?" How did she know? If she knew then she must have known about Tate and that means she wanted me out, and this means that I need to stay away forever. She could have just outed me but then she would have been outing her son. This way everything is kept quiet, behind closed doors. He lives his life, I live mine.

"She did." Clayton says it like it's no big deal.

Caleb starts to set the table for three as if he's been doing this for a long time.

"Are you guys together?" The both of them laugh at my question, but I'm serious.

"He only wishes he could be my wifey right, Caleb?" Clayton pats him on the ass with a squeeze.

"You have issues, Clayton, serious issues," Caleb says while he ties a baby blue apron around his waist. A number two has been bedazzled in Ruby red fake gems.

"I don't get it, how can you not like females?"
Caleb has a serious question he's asking me.

"Oh, I believe in equal opportunity, I love both."
Saying this out loud, it feels as if a weight has been
lifted off my shoulders and I can actually breathe again.

Chapter 29

Tate.

Tommie's hand waves *goodbye*.

Burning his face in my mind, deep down I understand he will not be coming back.

This is our ending.

Addie seems unable to move. She just watches and waves as the truck pulls away, the tires kicking up dust in its wake. Even when the truck is out of sight she still doesn't move, the both of us are immobile in our spots.

She begins to cry, and so do I.

There's a cold shiver that races across skin that feels as if it is fevered. The more time that passes by, the less I am convinced to move. They say when a mate dies, a part of you dies too, I don't agree with that; a part of you can die while they still live.

I'm in no rush to get back home, no rush to walk up those stairs to pass his now vacant room, no rush to even *breathe*.

The tree holds up my weight, looking at the big limb that stretches across instead of reaching up to the sky. A few nails are embedded deep in the bark above my head. Tommie and I would climb this tree, play in it for hours. We even tried to make our own tree-house where when we were eight and dreamed to live in it forever, *together*.

Best friends with childhood dreams.

We'd look at the sky through the leaves, smiling. Hiding out from everyone until my mother started to call us in for dinner. We would come in with our tool belts buckled to our waists, pretending we were professional builders. Hammer hanging on the sides, nails in the pouches, my mother would ask what we'd been up to all day.

Tommie's reply to her was, *"We were building our house."* Tommie's voice had held the soft innocence of a child.

My mother's face had scowled, *"Males don't live together forever, they have female mates that they will live with."*

The next day we never went back to our tree-house. Over the years the boards fell down, the wind tore the roof off. Until just the nails remained buried into the bark.

Climbing this tree, smelling the bark, nothing of our youth remains. It's way past midnight when I'm able to hold my head up again. Yet, I can't go home, so I stay in the tree remembering us, him. But I'm not like that, I can't be like that, except I was made like that. The moon is out - big, bold, hanging huge in the sky.

By the time I do decide to open the door to the house, my mother is there waiting for me in the fading shadows of the day. There is no hiding my face, I can't hide from yesterday or today.

She pretends that she can't see me right now. Her makeup is done perfectly as if she's the most perfect Luna to have ever lived.

"Where have you been?" Her voice scowls.

"I've been out."

"Well go get dressed, we have guests. A female who is, in my opinion, the perfect match for you."

"I told you I'm not taking a mate." My foot on the steps leading up the stairs before my mother grabs the back of my neck, pulling me back to face her teeth.

"I'm telling you that it's time to take a mate, Tate. You are an Alpha of a pack that requires an heir from you. You're getting older, the pack expects a mate. This female is the perfect candidate for *you*. Unfortunately, she will not be able to hold your mark. Her mate still lives, unlike yours."

"If her mate lives then why is she not mated to him?"

"She has an affliction for females, don't worry, she's been reconditioned in the way of the Moon. Her mate has been shipped over-seas to be bred, and she is being shipped here. Think of this as a test, Tate. The Moon is testing you, she's testing your beliefs in what's *right*. Take the female, over time I'm sure you will come to love her the way mates love each other. Think of this as the start of an excellent

partnership. With time and pups, you will grow to love her. Trust me on this." Her point is sharp, cutting deep into the skin. This is the way it will be.

Walking away when I hear my father enter the house through the back door. A slight pause at Tommie's door before entering the bathroom. Not stepping into the water until its scolding, a hard scrub of skin, the flesh red and hot.

Mechanical movements, getting dressed, making sure I look the way I should. Voices are rising from the open windows, they are sitting outside in the backyard.

Company is here.

Coming down the stairs, suitcases are beside the front door. Not too many, three in all.

Taking a look outside through the glass. A large male is sitting with his back to the window. A female is sitting across from him, she's looking in the window, but it doesn't seem as if she sees anything.

A blank expression on her face, vacant eyes. She does appear to have a hard time breathing, like the way I'm starting to feel now. Her hands are under the table, back

straight. Her hair is cut short to her head - like the way I wear my hair. Her lips are red, full with a flush of heat to her cheeks.

Putting my hands in my pockets because the tremor can't be hidden. This is a serious meet and greet, or else luggage would not have accompanied her.

My mother's eyes find mine.

"Tate, come out and meet our guests." I can tell in her voice how happy she is.

Walking outside, the pitcher of ice tea is underneath the canopy of the umbrella that is casting shade on all the wolves around the table.

The female's eyes find mine, a profound sense of hopelessness reflects back at me. Does she see mine reflecting back at her?

Big breath.

This is my new beginning.

Smile, stand straighter, smile

"This is my son, Tate. Tate, this is Frank and his daughter Wynn."

My eyes find the males first. Putting out my hand, shaking it hard, firm, all male. He shakes mine the same way.

"Tate, it's nice to meet you."

Smiling to him, my voice just can't say that I'm happy to see them. When Wynn stands up to greet me, her jaw is shaking, and a single tear rolls down her cheek, everyone pretends not to see it, even me.

"It's nice to meet you, Wynn."

She can't say anything back; she's too concerned about breathing right. All she does is nod her head, a sound does come out, but it's like a muffled sob.

This isn't right.

Taking my seat next to her, she slightly angles away from me.

My mother pours me a cup of tea, gulping it down until it's finished I still feel the dryness of my throat. It's thick and sticky when I try to swallow my spit. Looking at Wynn, she's looking away from me - her eyes are on the treeline. Her body is shifting in the seat, she looks to be in great pain at times.

This is who my mother thinks could make the best possible mate for me, and the next Luna of the pack?

"We've just made it official, Tate. Wynn will be staying with us. The ceremony will be held next weekend."

My father says nothing, letting my mother run the show.

"Don't you think that we should get to know one another first, see if we are even compatible?" Trying hard to backtrack out of this real-life horror movie.

"This is a match that will make both our packs prosper from the union. It's time, Tate, to start acting like the next Alpha. I know she can't take the place of your *dead* mate, no female can, but with time, we are positive that this will all work out."

Another tear leaks down Wynn's cheek, she wipes it away with a napkin. Her plate of food is untouched, yet I can smell the sweetness to her that all females hold when coming into their heat.

"Dad." Her voice quakes when she says that word.

"Wynn, we talked about this. You're lucky you're getting this kind of opportunity. You should be thanking the Moon for your good fortune and not crying on things that will not change. Stop it, you need to start acting like a Luna and not feel sorry for yourself."

Her head hangs down with the napkin to her eyes while she silently sobs, her shoulders shaking.

My mother goes over to her, putting her arms around the crying female. "It's been a long trip for you, I understand this is all frightening, but I'm here to help you through it." Her cheek and Wynn's cheek nudge each other. My mother's hand on her back, trying to soothe the female who's falling within herself.

"Wynn, stop, you're embarrassing yourself, our pack and me." Her father stops eating, focusing on his daughter. She does settle down, *barely*. Her father gets up, "I'm trying

to save your soul, Wynn, and this is the thanks I get." A hard fist comes down shaking the table and the food that's on it.

Wynn instantly stops, silent tears coming down without a voice to them.

And I thought I had it hard.

"I'll show you where you'll be sleeping before the ceremony. It's going to be alright, Wynn. You'll come to love it here." My mother walks Wynn away, her father doesn't even say goodbye to his daughter.

He gets up, looking at me carefully. "Be good to her." With those words, he leaves his daughter with us.

Looking at my father, he takes a breath out. "This is the for the best." That's what he says before walking away, leaving the table full of food but no one around to eat it.

Sitting there for a few minutes before even I leave the bountiful table. Walking up the stairs, Tommie's door is open, a suitcase sits on his bed, while two are on his desk. It looks as if most of his room has been stripped bare, nothing of him remains, even the sheets have been taken off the bed. The mattress looks new, never been used. Wynn is just

sitting on the edge of the bare mattress holding onto the edges with fingers that are straining white in a grip that halts the flow of blood to her fingertips.

Her eyes hold the color of pale amber.

"If you need anything just let me know, I'm in the next room."

She makes no response back, so I close the door to Tommie's room.

It's not long after that my door bangs open.

"You!" Hazel's voice is shaking in a restrained rage.

"Hazel, what's going on? I thought you would be away until Sunday. What's wrong?" Her eyes are burning into mine.

"I came home early. I called you to come pick me up, but your mother answered your phone." Looking on my desk, my phone is gone.

"She told me you were busy and to find my own ride home. Can you imagine what I came home to find?" Her

voice is rising, just like her body. She's starting to pant, holding her chest. I thought I would have time to clean her house this weekend.

My throat tightening, threatening to choke away my life.

"How could you do that to him?"

I've never seen Hazel like this, holding her stomach as if her guts are twisting themselves up.

"All those years of Tommie listening to us, then when he came back-" her hand goes over her mouth, while her face crumbles. "How could you use me like that?" The sound tears through a throat that's having a hard time now making any sound.

"Hazel, let me explain." Trying to hold her shoulders.

"No, don't you touch me. You knew I didn't do that with wolves who have mates, you knew that! It was my only rule. How could you? How could you do that to Tommie? Everything makes sense now, why you guys stopped being friends, why he went away." She's trembling and so am I, her mind putting together everything. "Why didn't you trust me and tell me he was your mate?" A hard slap to my face

by her open palm hand. "You lied to everyone about your mate dying. You're sick, Tate. You could have moved away, you could have started a new life somewhere else with him. Why didn't you just follow him to school or-"

Grabbing Hazel by the arms, picking her off the ground. "I'm not like that, Hazel." Shaking her hard. "I am not like that!" Again a hard shake to her that almost snaps her neck, I need to release her or else I might hurt her.

"But you are, you're only lying to yourself. You can't possibly say you're not. He's your living mate, how could you do this? No wonder Tommie hated me. I couldn't figure it out, now it all makes perfect sense." She's holding her lower stomach again. Deep pain etched in furrowed brows. "I need to go find, Tommie. I have to apologize to him. I didn't know. Tate, I never want to see you again. I might be a lot of things, but I'm no mate-stealer."

Hazel runs out of my room, watching her out the door, Tommie's door opens.

Wynn's looking at me, *differently*.

Now she knows my secret.

At the same time, we both close our doors. Going into the top drawer, pulling out the silver knife, placing it on the desk, taking a few breaths of encouragement. Gripping it by the handle, placing it against the soft part of my wrist, the door opens.

Wynn's standing there.

"If you do that, you'll never meet him in the moon." She talks as if she's been exactly where I am right now.

Epilogue

Tommie.

Three places set at the table.

Caleb places a steaming casserole dish in the middle of the table with one serving spoon in it.

"Tommie, sit down we were just going to *eat.*" Clayton gives Caleb a swift glance.

Both males sit down with their elbows on the table, as if claiming a personal territory around their plates. Their bodies become puffed out, breathing getting

heavier. When I sit down, eyes flash wolf encased in skin and bore into mine.

"Let's eat."

Clayton's voice causes a feeding frenzy that I have never seen before, growls tumble from male chests. Hands fighting for every last piece of what's inside that dish. While their plates are heaped full, mine remains empty. I'm not sure what I just witnessed, but I know somehow I failed some kind of test.

Caleb puts a forkful of food in his mouth, chewing greedily as if he hasn't eaten in days.

"Tommie, it's alright. I couldn't eat at first either, not until I went away and learned how to eat again. Once you're settled into the pack, I'm going to have you go and live with the *wild* wolves of the Valentine pack, up north, high in their mountain range. You'll learn to become a wolf again. When you come back, you will always take your share." Clayton hasn't taken anything yet off his plate. Instead, he scrapes some of

his food off, putting it on my plate. It's not a big piece, just enough for a few bites.

Caleb does not share with me, but he gives me a smile that has his teeth quickly flashing outward, before his next bite.

"So I'm going to go live with a pack of *wild* wolves?" Saying it a little shocked, I never expected something like this.

"Problems with that?" Clayton asks between a bite of his food.

"No, I just never lived in *wild* form before."

"Good, it's a great opportunity that the Valentine Pack is allowing for some of the members of our pack. They don't do this for everyone, you're very lucky, just like I was. You won't be going for a few weeks, I want you to get to know the area, the members first. I want to make sure that you want to stay first before we start your training."

"How long will I be gone?"

"Until you can eat." Both males at the table say at the same time.

Clayton's hand stretches out, punching Caleb in the arm. "Got you." Another mouth of food placed in his mouth, while Caleb holds his arm.

"That hurt. You need to stop being so rough with me." Caleb sounds as if he's in pain. I'm really confused by this male whose wearing his hair in a bun, with messy strands falling out. He's nothing that I have ever been exposed to. Looking at Clayton's head, it's been buzzed cut, short on a number two setting on the trimmers. I like a number one setting - it's a cleaner shave.

Once their plates are cleaned Caleb gets up, walking into the hall. "Tommie, I cooked, you got dish duty." He opens the door to the bathroom and shuts it.

Clearing the table, starting the water for dishes, this is not what I expected.

"Caleb, you better not be shitting again," Clayton yells out while I clear the dishes from the table.

"You know what hot sauce does to me, I can't help it." The words are just barely heard from behind the door, it sounds as if he's destroying the toilet bowl.

Clayton shakes his head while getting up to dry the dishes and put away. "Tommie, it's good to have you. I hope you stay and make this your home. If you don't, I'll help you find the best possible place for you."

"Thanks for the opportunity."

Caleb comes out with a guilty grin. "I would give it a minute before going in there, it was like spray paint coming out." He pulls out his phone. "Look." He's captured what he released into the toilet bowl. Clayton refuses to look.

Who is this wolf?

"Put it away, I don't want to see it. I've seen enough of your crap."

"You're one to talk, I got the latest pic you sent me, I demand a different angle."

Clayton smiles but says nothing back.

"Ready? I'll take you to your new house. In the morning, I'll come and bring you around to meet everyone." Caleb beats me to the door, walking out first.

Clear skies, with a few white clouds.

The drive snakes around the edge of the lake until we pull into the driveway of my new home, it's right on the water. Caleb and Clayton are already walking to the back, while I grab my bags and guitar from the back of the truck.

First impressions - it's weathered yet solid. Needs some fixes but nothing that requires immediate changing.

Stepping inside, the smell of cedar smoke still seems alive inside of the cottage by the lake. Looking around, it's open concept, functional. There is an underlying smell of Clayton in this home as if he's been living here for a while now.

Caleb perches himself down on the couch, looking at the screen of his phone, typing something that has him smiling to himself before he sets the phone down on the coffee table, screen facing up.

He's acting as if he's very comfortable within the space of this house.

Clayton hasn't come inside yet, staying on the back porch by a colorful hammock that's swinging in the fresh wind. He's looking at the water, where a small island with white tip waves is washing on its rocky borders.

I could get used to living Lakeside.

There's a full garden in bloom at the side of the house, it's the most uncomplicated but unique garden I

have ever seen before. I think Addie will appreciate this when she comes for a visit in a few weeks.

When Clayton turns to face me, he's got a neutral face without too many outward emotions. "Tommie, what do you think?" He sounds as if he cares about my answer.

"It's good, I've never lived Lakeside before." Anything is better than my bedroom right next to Tates. Anything is better than staying up all night listening to your mate fuck someone else. "Clayton, I have a question."

"Ask." He's going inside the house.

"What do you prefer me to call you? Alpha Clayton, Clayton, Sir? I haven't met too many Alpha's before except Caleb's father." Looking at Caleb, I give him a wink, just for fun. He can dish it, let's see if he can take some teasing.

"Did you just wink at me, while talking about my father?" He's shaking his head, "My mom would kick your ass if she was here."

"Your mom's hot too."

Caleb's mouth opens, he's looking as if he can't take the thought of his parents being hot. "Listen, Tommie," Caleb rises up, "Parents, brothers, are off limits. We don't go there." There's a seriousness about the way he's speaking of his family.

"Noted." Starting to plant my feet firmly in the doorway because he takes a step towards me.

Clayton stands in the middle.

"We aren't very strict here, call me what feels comfortable to you. Most just call me Clay or Clayton. I'm trying something different, no need for formalities, most know I'm in charge, if they don't, I *show them.*" Those last two words he speaks out have a harsh roughness to them. The way he can change the tone of his voice is compelling enough for me to practice that later tonight.

The phone starts to chirp out and Clayton looks down at the table. Clayton's hand reaches it before Caleb can swipe it from him. Caleb stretches himself up but the Alpha raises his hand, so Caleb has to jump to try and take it. Clayton's chest makes contact with Caleb's which forces him to take a step back from the Alpha's space.

Caleb is looking at the Alpha, who now is just staring at the screen while the phone keeps chirping. His finger is touching it, all of his concentration is on the picture that I get a glimpse of. It's that moon blessed wolf Rya. She's holding a small male and a newborn pup smiling into the camera.

Caleb quickly grabs the phone back. "Stop finger-fucking my brother's mate."

'I wasn't fingering her." His voice is becoming uneven.

"What's this called?" Caleb's finger rubs into the screen showing Clayton exactly what he'd just accused him of doing.

"I was just looking at her." The way Clayton says *her* sounds as if it's coming out as a chest pain.

"Clayton, you have some big issues, you know I love you, but you need to get over this. You had a chance, you ruined it."

"I know." There seems to be a defeat to the exhale of words out.

"Tommie, you play?" Clayton is looking at the guitar case that's leaning against the wall.

"I play, do you?"

"I do, next time I have a fire you'll have to bring your guitar, we have some good singers, they just can't play."

"Sounds good."

"I stocked the fridge and cupboards. You have my number, call if you need something. I'll come get you in the morning, show you around."

"I'll be ready in the morning."

"Good." Both Caleb and Clayton go to the back door, Caleb tries to slide out before Clayton, but he shifts his hip pushing Caleb out of the way as a trace of laughter sounds from his throat.

Looking through the fridge, it's full of food, homemade dinners in glass containers. They each hold notes that welcome me into the pack, with names I don't recognize at the bottom.

Damn, he's even got several varieties of beers from the regular to the crafts stocked on the bottom shelf. Looking into the freezer, he's got the whiskey and vodka chilling that have a fine film of ice crystals clinging to the outside of the bottles.

Cracking a beer, it's a craft that I've never seen before

Opening the lid off one of the dishes, putting it into the microwave, figuring the buttons out. It's a quick heat and eat. Taking the beer outside, sitting on the hammock, it's a quiet sway back and forth. The tip

of my toe is just touching the wooden deck. The late afternoon sun on my chest, the gentle rhythm has me wanting to melt into the fabric that's suspended by strings.

Within no time the beer is done and I'm bringing out the guitar. Within a few songs played a female comes from around the corner holding a dish in her hand. She's the same female that was with Clayton at my old pack house.

"Hi, Tommie." She looks unsettled, fingers gripping hard into the dish she brought. Eyes are darting from my face, to the water, back to her feet. The hem of her red skirt ruffles in the breeze, giving glimpses of her mid-thigh before it flutters back down.

"Hi, Kimberly right?"

She frowns to herself. "You remembered my name."

Listening closer to her voice there is the finest of
a nervous stutter to it. She seems surprised I
remembered her name. "Why wouldn't I?"

"Most don't." A drop in sound tells me that she's used to
not being remembered. "I brought you something as a
welcome to the pack." Standing up, she's short, shorter than
Addie. Stretching out her hand, she offers me her gift.

"Thanks."

"No problem." An awkward hesitation on her
part, her mouth moves, but no sound comes out. She
starts to tear up and I have no idea what's going on.

"Are you alright?"

She shakes her head no. "You went to school with Jake,
did you know him well?" Now she's searching my face for
something, looking for something.

"I went to school with him, we trained together
for just a short time before he just left."

"Did you fuck him, or did he fuck you?"
There's a desperation, almost an unhinged edge
to her sound.

"No, do you want a beer?" Turning from her, going inside, placing the food container in the fridge, getting two beers out. Cracking the first, handing it to her, before cracking mine open.

"Sorry, I just want some answers, I don't know too many wolves that knew him at school. I just want to understand why."

"Why what?"

She's starting to tear up, looking at the lake. "Why he just couldn't love me the way I wanted him to love me. I tried to be perfect for him, I tried everything, and even with the bond it wasn't enough for him to stay with me. He just left, not even a note for our Max. One minute he kissed him goodbye the next we were burying him." A single tear drips down from her cheek onto the patio table that she just took a seat at.

Palpation of a heart as trembling hands lift the beer for a small sip, her face scrunches - not a beer lover.

"Kimberly, I only knew Jake slightly. He seemed like an alright male. We never knew he had a mate. He never told any one of us."

"I know, Carson explained. I used to hate Carson, but it's not his fault because he didn't know. We've talked about this, I've gotten past the fact he fucked him more than me. I just don't understand why. Why would the Moon partner us up if he didn't like females?" She is starting to hit a nerve inside me, something fresh that hasn't been closed or even begun to heal.

"I'm not sure, maybe he would have realized in time he liked females just as much as he like males." Not able to answer her the way she wants or needs to be answered.

"Maybe." Her voice is just above the winds. "Sorry, Tommie. My brother told me not to bother you right away. I just couldn't help myself, I thought you might have known him better. You could have told me stories about him."

Looking at her, the stories I could tell are not what she would want to hear. "Sorry, Kimberly."

"Just call me Kim," She hands me the beer back. "I'm sorry this tastes like crap." Giving me a quick laugh, "No matter how many times I try to like it I can't." She stands, "See you around, Tommie." And as fast as she came, she's gone.

After the third beer out on the deck, I've decided that I should unpack. Walking into the bathroom, there are fresh towels and washcloths. Everything is stocked with soap, body wash, shampoo. Someone thought of everything.

The next few days are busy, Clayton is taking me to meet every member of the smallest pack I have ever seen. Most are young adult wolves, barely out of their juvenile shift. They are all very different, from different places. Not too many original pack members left, and I think this is a heavy weight that Clayton carries around him. He seems to be always weighted down in his mind. He's not the most talkative either, which suits me fine because I don't feel like talking. My nights are better being able to sleep without hearing my mate fuck someone else. At the same time, I'm lonely.

I miss Addie.

When Clayton drives me back to the house, Hazel's car is in the driveway, she's not in it.

Clayton gets out because he wants to hear the proposal about the fruit wines. The major employer in the area shut down the parts plant - just one reason for the desertion of the previous pack wolves; no jobs, no food, means you have to move to where the money is.

Hazel rounds the corner and Clayton has a stumble before he regroups himself straight. His eyes don't leave hers.

"Tommie." She flings herself at me. "I didn't know. I had no idea." Hysterical sounds from a female that needs me to hold her up. This isn't the Hazel I have ever seen before; this is someone suffocating on their breath. She presses her cheek into the ridge just below my sternum. I can feel the shaking pulse of her body. "All those years, all those years, I never knew. He never told me!" Tumbling words out of a breaking up voice.

Putting my hands on her head, letting my fingers run down her hair. "It's alright, Hazel. I knew you didn't know. It's not your fault." Trying to stay calm, because this wolf is having a breakdown right here in the driveway.

It's when I see Addie come from behind the house, red face, swollen eyes, a long braid is thrown over her shoulder that I'm getting confused as to why both of them are here. "Addie, what are you doing here?"

"Hazel told me. I had to come and see you." She is standing off to the side while Hazel keeps mumbling her apologies to me. Clayton's looking between the two females staring back and forth between them.

"Let's go inside." Untangling Hazel from me. She's not wearing any makeup, and I realize how young she looks without it, how unblemished she is. "Addie, you're supposed to be with Prosper at The Green House."

"I told him he just has to wait for a week or two, my friend needs me."

Her hand goes out, and I grab onto it as we walk to the back porch. There are suitcases by the door - someone thinks they will be staying here for a while. Opening the door, letting everyone inside. Both Addie and Hazel grab suitcases. Clayton steps inside as well. He's in for a story.

"Drinks? I need a drink." Everyone raises their hands except Clayton.

"Water." The Alpha says.

"Stop looking at my eyes, Wolf. I'm not her." Hazel's sharp words hit him sideways. He looks away from her, but he sits down on the end of the couch with the water I just handed him. His eyes on Addie who gives him a polite, tight-lip smile.

Pouring the females vodka and juice, I take a beer.

Hazel downs hers, and decides to start chewing the ice, Addie takes small sips. My beer is getting nursed down slowly because my insides feel tight.

"Why didn't you tell me, Tommie?" Addie's the first to speak.

"I couldn't, I was ashamed, I was afraid that you would stop being my friend, I needed you as my friend, it was all I had." A hard rush of air out of my burning throat.

"You could have told me, it doesn't change anything. I wish you would have told me. I could have helped."

"How could you have helped? If I would have come out the whole pack would have turned against me. I would have been forced out, my parents would have been humiliated. Tate would be thrown out. I think this way is better for me, for Tate. It's hard, I won't lie." A big breath, clearing of my throat. "I'm going to be alright. When I moved away for University, I realized that I could be happy without a mate. That I can love someone who isn't my mate. It might not be a perfect life, but I plan on making it the best life I can have."

Both females are wiping their eyes.

"Tommie, if I would have known I would never have been with Tate, I want you to know that. I don't do that to wolves. I'm not a mate-stealer." Hazel's voice is a tortuous bending of her sound. "I feel so dirty, Tommie. I don't feel dirty ever, but just thinking of all the times we were together while you had to listen to that, I can't even imagine what you went through." Her focus is solely on my eyes as if trying to seek an absolution of the past.

"Hazel, it's alright."

"Are you sure?"

"Yes, Hazel, I'm sure."

It's as if a hard wind just blew up and took the anguish, the tension she had surrounding her, away. "It just makes sense. I understand why you didn't want seconds - it wasn't me, it was him. You like this ass." The side of her mouth curves up, in a slick smile.

"Hazel, don't flatter yourself. I've had better, and you need to work on that ass." Taking a sip of beer and giving her a wink.

"I call bullshit on that. I've never had problems with this rose gold, *ever*. Now my ass, it looks good shaking from behind, no one wants something that doesn't have a little meat on it." The Hazel I know has just shown up. "Is it alright if I make another?" Hazel holds her glass up.

"Sure, anyone else?"

Addie still has most of her drink, Clayton holds his empty glass of water up, "I'll take another water, do you mind putting some ice in it?" He asks Hazel as she grabs the glass from his hands. She doesn't say anything to the male who can't pull his eyes from hers.

"Next round is yours." Hazel says as she chews on the last of her ice cube.

"Can I ask why you have so much luggage?" Asking Addie and Hazel.

"I've decided to stay with you for a while, I can't go back there. I'm going to sell the house, and why not move here?"

"Hazel, I only have one bedroom."

"Tommie, I have no problems with you taking the couch, no problems at all." She's looking at me while pouring the vodka in a glass that's filled heavy with ice. She just splashes a touch of juice before turning on the tap and getting Clayton a glass of water. He might have three ice cubes in his glass that are quickly melting.

"Hazel..."

"Tommie, look, I can't stay there. I just can't anymore. It's not good for me. Maybe if I start somewhere fresh, I might be able-" She holds her voice momentarily. Blows out a breath. "If you can leave your mate, why can't I? I've always wanted to leave that pack, I just couldn't because he's buried there. But since the Luna kicked me out,

I've got nowhere to stay." Hazel is looking with big eyes, fluttering long lashes that don't work on me.

"I have an empty house if you want to stay? We have lots of room in the pack for you." Clayton sits his glass on the wood stove. "You too, Addie." Clayton turns to Addie whose been quiet in the background. Clayton is looking at her long braid, then at her face. He is just staring at her, like the way he was staring at Hazel. He has some problems with keeping his eyes to himself. I'll need to talk to him about it; he could come off as creepy to them.

"Hazel talked me into staying for a while, to get the business off the ground."

"Business?" Looking at Addie confused.

"The fruit wine business. I was doing some research - your pack holds a lot of land. This could be something that unites this pack properly. A business everyone is involved in and profits from." Hazel is talking in a business-forward voice. No nonsense.

"We aren't the richest pack, what's the start up cost?" Clayton is listening to her and not looking at her eyes.

"That's alright, I've got the money covered, I'll take my cut off the top until I'm paid back properly with interest." Hazel drinks down her vodka as if it's water, raises her glass to Clayton who gets up and makes her another one. "Tommie has a proposal, I have the paper." She takes my papers out from her purse. Handing it to Clayton while she takes her drinks. He's looking it over, slowly, until a smile spreads across his face.

"I guess we need to cheer - to the fruit wine business." Clayton raises his glass, followed by Hazel, Addie, then myself.

"Cheers." Everyone says at once.

Sipping my beer, looking around. The wolves are all wearing smiles, and I realize, I am too.

I'm excited about this new beginning. It might not be perfect, I might not walk with my mate in this

life, but at the end of the day, I have to do what makes me happy.

I'm alright walking within my curves.

The End.

If you enjoyed this novel, please think of leaving a review!

Every one helps.

Thanks for following the journey, keep tuned for new releases and follow the author on Amazon to ensure you're notified.

Coming soon -

Clayton.

The Girl Who Stole My World.